"You
Mr. Ballenger."

Meg's voice rose in anger. "I want nothing from you or the Ballenger family. There's no need for lawyers or papers or intimidation tactics."

Nick very deliberately matched his tone to hers. "It wasn't my intention to intimidate you, Ms. Linley. If you'll just hear me out—"

"Then quit dancing around and tell me what you want."

"Very well." Nick placed a contract folder on the table and extracted a tiny black box from his jacket pocket. He flipped open the lid, glancing at the contents before turning the box toward Meg.

"What's this? A bribe to get rid of me?" she asked, staring at the most beautiful diamond ring she'd ever seen. And the biggest.

"No. It's not a bribe, it's a proposal. If you are, indeed, pregnant, and this child is, indeed, a Ballenger, it will be raised as such."

"Just what, *indeed*, are you suggesting?"

"An alliance. For the good of David's child." He took the ring from its box and held it out to her. "We're getting married, Ms. Linley. Temporarily."

Dear Reader,

I've always wanted to write a "marriage of convenience" story, and I think I've finally come up with one worthy of being a Superromance novel. I hope you'll enjoy reading about Meg and Nick, a couple brought together by "his brother's baby." They manage to turn tragedy into triumph, and along the way discover that keeping secrets might not be the best way to keep a marriage together.

This book also gave me a chance to use a little more of my Charleston research—no, not the dance, the city (the one in South Carolina). I visited there several years ago in spring and fell in love. The azaleas were a riot of color, the wisteria hung like heavy clusters of grapes, and the citizens had graciously thrown open their doors for the annual historic homes tour. Charleston is a wonderful place. Don't be surprised if I set another book there someday.

So here it is. I'm letting go, turning *His Brother's Baby* over to you. If you like it and feel an urge to tell me so, my ego can be reached at P.O. Box 14, Dexter, MO 63841. I'm not a speedy correspondent, but if you include a stamped, self-addressed envelope, I'll write and say thanks.

Enjoy!

Connie Bennett.

HIS BROTHER'S BABY
BABY
Connie Bennett

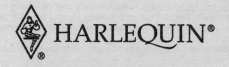

HARLEQUIN®

TORONTO • NEW YORK • LONDON
AMSTERDAM • PARIS • SYDNEY • HAMBURG
STOCKHOLM • ATHENS • TOKYO • MILAN • MADRID
PRAGUE • WARSAW • BUDAPEST • AUCKLAND

This book is dedicated with affection and gratitude
to my editor, Zilla Soriano,
for her unflagging patience and support.

ISBN 0-373-70796-7

HIS BROTHER'S BABY

Printed in U.S.A.

HIS BROTHER'S
BABY

PROLOGUE

MEG LINLEY SHIFTED nervously as she studied the black clouds pressing down on the Airtropolis terminal. Forks of lightning periodically illuminated the runways as Singapore's distinctive brand of thunderstorm turned the early-evening sky to midnight, and Sumatra winds lashed torrents of rain onto the window, obstructing Meg's already-limited view and adding to her growing agitation.

David's plane was late. Earlier this afternoon he had called from Bangkok and asked her to pick him up at six-thirty. It was seven now, and the Sumatra didn't show any signs of abating. While Meg waited anxiously in the terminal, the Ballenger Pharmaceuticals jet was circling somewhere overhead, waiting for a break in the storm.

After six and a half years in Singapore, Meg had grown accustomed to the year-round heat, suffocating humidity and the almost daily rain showers, but the violent thunderstorms that rumbled through April and May still rattled her. She would have been a nervous wreck this afternoon even if David's plane hadn't been up there.

The percussion of another thunderclap made the huge terminal window vibrate, and Meg instinctively backed away from the glass. Her reflected image, that of a petite young woman with almond-shaped eyes and upswept blond hair, receded from view, as well. Behind her, the shrill, electronic jingle of a cellular phone drew her attention, and she returned to the row of chairs where she'd left her briefcase.

She took the slim handset from the outer pocket and flipped it open. "Hello?"

"Meg? It's Fletch. Has David landed yet?" The voice sounded as though it was coming from halfway around the world instead of twelve miles away in the Singapore business district. Static garbled the line, and Meg put two fingers to her ear to blot out the sounds of the storm and the busy airport terminal.

"Fletch? I can barely hear you. We've got a terrible connection."

The man on the other end of the line raised his voice. "I know. This storm is wreaking havoc with the cellulars. I can't raise the jet at all," Fletcher Matson told her. "Has David landed yet?"

"No. Is somethin' wrong at the office?" Concern brought out stronger traces of the southern Missouri dialect Meg hadn't quite eradicated from her speech.

She barely heard her friend's groan, but she could imagine the grimace on his thin, angular face when he told her, "I'll say. Nick's on the warpath again. I've been on the phone with him for an hour, and the fax machine is about to go into terminal meltdown."

Meg glanced at her watch, calculating the time differential with the ease of someone who had been doing it by rote for years. "Fletch, it's six in the morning in Charleston."

"Well, you know Nick. He never sleeps. He spent the whole night going over the projections David faxed him from Bangkok and he's fit to be tied. Big Ballenger wants to speak to Little Ballenger the second David's plane lands.''

Meg bit back a curse for the dictatorial monarch who ruled the multinational Ballenger Pharmaceuticals. While older brother Nick was safely ensconced in his palatial Charleston, South Carolina, home enjoying all the pleasures the United States of America had to offer, his younger brother, David, had been exiled to the Far East, far away from family and friends.

''Does he need to come back to the office or can he call from the apartment?'' she asked Fletcher.

''He'd better come to the office,'' Fletch replied regretfully. ''I'm really sorry, Meg. When you left here earlier, I got the impression you were planning a special welcome home tonight.''

Special? That didn't begin to cover the homecoming she had planned. She had news for David that was going to change both their lives. It had been everything she could do these last few weeks to keep from blurting it out on the telephone, but she'd kept her silence because she wanted to see David's face when she told him that he was about to become a father.

Part of her was certain he'd be happy about the pregnancy; he'd been flirting with the subject of marriage for months. But part of Meg was still a country girl from the Ozarks who'd grown up in a shack, living on food stamps and wearing faded hand-me-downs from the snooty town girls who attended the Charity Baptist Church. *That* Meg Linley knew she wasn't good enough for a wealthy southern aristocrat like David Ballenger, and she needed to look into his eyes when she told him about the baby so that she could be sure he was as thrilled as she was.

Now, thanks to Nick, she was going to have to postpone David's homecoming celebration. "Don't apologize," she said to Fletch, one of the few people at the company who knew about her relationship with David. "It's not *your* fault."

Even over the staticky phone there was no mistaking who she blamed, and Fletch chuckled. "Shall I tell Nick you think he's a cold-blooded bastard who deserves to have a stake driven through his heart?"

"Don't you dare. He's been putting pressure on David to get rid of me since the day you two created the personnel counselor position and hired me to fill it. If Nick knew how much I dislike him, he'd fire me himself—with an honest-to-God firing squad."

"You're probably right," Fletch agreed. "Tell you what. I'll keep your opinion of Nick to myself if you'll get David down here ASAP."

"All right," Meg said reluctantly. "I'll give him the message the minute he lands."

Apparently her answer didn't satisfy Fletch. "And point him toward the office?"

Meg shook her head in disgust. "Fletch, you know as well as I do that when Nick says 'Jump,' David asks, 'How high?' Otherwise, he wouldn't have taken this trip. Hell, he wouldn't even be here in Singapore! Of course he'll come directly to the office."

There was a moment of staticky silence as Fletcher digested her tone. She was known around the office as The Peacemaker—a soft-spoken mediator who could usually see both sides of an argument. She was rarely even mildly irritable, and she certainly didn't cuss. "Meg, are you all right?"

Meg realized how out of character her comment sounded and she took a deep breath that put a lid on the antagonism toward Nick Ballenger that had been building steadily in her since she started dating the dictator's younger brother a year ago. She knew how unhappy David was, and she couldn't wait for the day that David finally stood up to his brother. She was praying that her news would be the catalyst for a showdown that was long overdue. David would want to raise his child back home, near his family.

"Meg?" Fletch prompted when she didn't answer right away. "Are you still there?"

"I'm here and I'm fine, Fletch. This storm just has me rattled, that's all."

"Are you sure?"

"I'm certain," she replied definitively. "I'll deliver your message and I'll even try to do it with a smile."

"Okay. See you in a few minutes."

The line went dead and Meg slid the phone back into her briefcase, mentally cursing Nick Ballenger with a vehemence that would have alarmed Fletcher. David had been traveling for nearly a month, troubleshooting problems at the new facilities of Ballenger East in Thailand and conducting the tricky negotiations that would expand the company's operations into Vietnam.

Officially, both of those countries were eager to attract multinationals like Ballenger Pharmaceuticals, International, but making that expansion a reality was more than a logistical nightmare. It also meant dealing with crippling bureaucracy, an unstable currency and rampant corruption.

Meg had spoken with David at least once a day during his absence and she knew what a toll this trip had taken on him. Every time they talked he sounded more exhausted and depressed than the time before. Nick had been in constant contact with David, too, so he had to know what kind of shape his brother was in, but could he allow David one night to rest and regroup?

Of course not. Nick was too greedy and self-centered to recognize anyone's needs but his own. He was determined to expand Ballenger's operations and double the company's profits no matter what it cost in human terms.

It infuriated Meg that David blindly followed his brother's orders no matter how unfair or arbitrary they were, but David believed in things like duty and family loyalty. He seemed to worship the ground his older brother walked on, and no matter what Nick ordered him to do, David did it without complaint.

Meg had a hard time understanding that kind of blind devotion. She had been raised in a world where family loyalty amounted to nothing more than keeping the family secrets.

In that sense, at least, Meg was as devoted to her family as David was to his. She had a lot of secrets. Some that she hadn't even found the courage to share with David yet. That was about to change, though. It had to. She had to tell David everything before she told him she was two months pregnant. If the truth about her sordid past was on the table and David could still talk about marriage, still give her that sweet, wicked grin and tell her he loved her, then she'd tell him about their child.

It sounded so simple, but it wasn't. Just the thought of telling him the truth terrified her. She trusted David Ballenger more than any man she'd ever known, but handing her secrets over to him would take more than trust. It would take blind faith. Meg had spent most of the last month convincing herself that she was ready to take that step with David. She had everything planned, her confidence was bolstered, her speeches were all re-hearsed.

And now everything was ruined. Nick would think nothing of keeping David at the Singapore office for hours. By the time they completed their business, David would be too exhausted for any kind of a welcome home. Meg would have to wait. She'd have to build her courage all over again, find just the perfect moment.

Damn him!

When a middle-aged Caucasian businessman sat down in the chair next to Meg's briefcase, she tried to shelve her irritation with Nick. The businessman shot her a non-committal half smile to prove that he was harmless, but Meg nonetheless picked up her briefcase and slipped the strap over her shoulder as she resumed her vigil at the window.

The Sumatra had abated. Rain was no longer coming down in sheets and the sky had lightened. It was now the color of dusk instead of midnight, and Meg directed her gaze at the misty gray clouds that had been black and ominous a few minutes ago. She was even able to see in the distance a huge Boeing 747-400 of the Singapore Airlines fleet gliding into its landing pattern over the Johore Strait to the north of the airport.

She looked to the southeast and a reserved but hopeful smile lit her face when a small Learjet broke through the clouds. She squinted, searching for the distinctive electric-blue stripe that bisected the fuselage of the Ballenger East jet, and as it grew larger and closer, her smile blossomed. It was David's plane. He was back, finally. Safe and sound. No matter that he had to go straight to the office or that it would be hours before she could be alone with him. He was here and he'd be in her arms soon.

Meg fought the silly urge to wave at the plane as it descended. Her polite manners and veneer of sophistication had been acquired in adulthood, not drilled into her from childhood, and occasionally she forgot her sense of decorum; but not today. Today, she stood like the proper lady she had taught herself to be as David's jet angled toward the runway, seeming to pick up speed as it grew closer.

And then it happened—almost too fast for Meg to see, let alone comprehend. One second, the jet was two hundred feet above the runway on a perfectly angled descent. A second later, it dropped straight down, as though it had been slapped out of the sky by the hand of an invisible giant. Nose down, it hit the concrete runway with a jolt that Meg felt in every part of her body. A blast of flames spewed out of the explosion that shook every window in the Airtropolis terminal.

Screams of shock and panic reverberated inside the terminal, but none of them came from Meg. She was too stunned to move, to think, to even feel. Instead, she stood frozen, staring at the billows of black smoke and orange flames that engulfed the jet. From somewhere far away, a Klaxon sounded, calling the airport's emergency equipment to the scene, but deep in Meg's cold, quiet heart she knew the rescue effort would be an exercise in futility.

Nothing could survive the inferno on the runway—not the pilot; not Marian Wychevski, David's fiercely loyal secretary; not Lien Chu, the representative of the Singaporean government who'd been helping David through the minefield of expansion outside of orderly Singapore; not David Ballenger himself, the youngest member of a small but powerful family that traced its roots back to the founding fathers of South Carolina.

They were all dead or dying.

And so was Meg's heart. The only flutter of life left untouched was the tiny soul of David's child that she carried inside her.

CHAPTER ONE

IT WAS A PERFECT spring day in Charleston, the kind David used to tell Meg was his favorite. The humidity was low, the breeze was warm and the sky was a cloudless blue. Azaleas of every imaginable color blossomed in profusion, and the breeze was scented with the fragrance of wisteria that hung in enormous clusters on the wrought-iron fence encircling the cemetery.

Meg studied the wisteria. Opposite her, at the other end of David's silver casket, a minister was mouthing words that were meant to be comforting, but she couldn't hear them. She didn't need comfort, she needed David. Since she couldn't have him, the next best thing was the numbness she'd been clinging to since the crash two weeks ago. If she listened too closely to the minister, he might say something to penetrate that protective veil, and Meg wasn't ready for that.

So she looked at the wisteria.

It was beautiful. Stretching unbroken down a segment of fence at least thirty feet long, the huge lavender clusters cascaded over the wrought-iron spires like a bubbling waterfall. She'd never seen anything like it, though the blooms did remind her of the lilac bushes that had grown along the dirt lane from her house to the school-bus stop on Sugar Creek Road back home. The only time Meg hadn't dreaded walking down that road in the morning and back up again in the afternoon was when the lilacs were in bloom. She would stop and smell them, touch them, bury her face in a handful of the fragrant blossoms, but she would never pick them, not after that first time when she was six, when she'd torn off a home-made bouquet and put it in a jelly jar full of water. She'd been so proud of the improvised centerpiece on the kitchen table. Until her father came home.

Meg glanced away from the fence. Maybe looking at the wisteria hadn't been such a good idea, after all. She was only barely handling the present; this wasn't the time to delve into the past. She searched for something else to focus on, something that wouldn't create images of lilacs, jelly jars and broken glass.

Her gaze lit on David's silver casket. Definitely not an improvement.

He would have preferred wood, she thought. Cherry or oak...something warm and burnished, not cold and untouchable like this metal box with expensive gold trim. She thought of David inside and suddenly found her vision blurred. Her throat ached from fighting the desperate need to cry. She looked away from the coffin.

I shouldn't have come, she thought as she wiped at the tears. It had been so important to her that she be here to say goodbye, but she wasn't ready yet. She couldn't let him go. It hurt too much. She should have waited and come later, when she could be alone, when there would have been no one to question who she was and why she was in so much pain.

But she was here now, an anonymous face on the fringes of the crowd. The family, friends and a handful of dignitaries—city officials, politicians and business ty-coons—were off to the right of the coffin, fanned out behind David's grandmother, Eleanor.

Nan, he'd called her. She was in the center of the

enclave looking like the exquisitely elegant aristocrat that she was. Tall, slender. Silver hair swirled back into a chignon, a corsage of white roses on the lapel of her black Chanel suit and a choker of pearls at her throat... Head up, features composed, betraying nothing.

Although she didn't seem to be focused on the minister, either, Meg noted.

Was she looking at the wisteria, too?

Meg dismissed the thought and went back to studying the woman who had raised David after the death of his parents in a boating accident when he was nine. He had adored her. He'd always said she had the kind of beauty that age couldn't touch, and now Meg understood what that meant. Even on a day like today, Eleanor Tate Ballenger radiated beauty and grace. She wore her bereavement well, standing erect at the graveside, and though her arm was linked with that of the man beside her, she was leaning on him only lightly, if at all.

The man beside her. Nick Ballenger. Six years older than his brother... Tall, lean, aristocratic... A younger, unquestionably masculine version of Eleanor. All in black today...black suit, black hair, black sunglasses, black heart.

Some of the women in the Singapore office claimed that he was almost too handsome to look at, but Meg didn't agree. He had strong, classic features, but Meg knew from the one time she'd met him that his dark blue eyes were as cold as David's silver coffin.

She hated him. She was trying not to, but the rage was there and couldn't be controlled. She'd done enough bereavement counseling to know the danger of transferring her grief anger onto Nick, but this was more than that. If it weren't for Nick, David would be alive. It was that simple, and she had no plans to forgive him for causing David's death.

More tears threatened, and Meg dug her fingernails into the palm of her hand. She tried to find someplace else to look, someplace distracting, but this was a cemetery and everything—except the wisteria—reeked of death. She finally located a spot over the minister's right shoulder. She stared at the contours of a stone cherub, and before she realized it, the service was over. The minister had stopped speaking and the crowd began to stir as Nick and Eleanor stepped toward the preacher.

Good. She could escape now.

I'll come back soon, David.

She wasn't sure if she said the words out loud or in her head, but it didn't matter. David couldn't hear her either way. She wouldn't be able to pretend otherwise for much longer.

As the mourners around her drifted off, some to offer their final condolences to the family, some toward the bottom of the hill where a queue of limousines lined the narrow blacktop road behind the hearse, Meg turned toward the crest of the hill. Her rental car was parked near the wrought-iron gates of the entrance because she hadn't known what the proper etiquette was for a graveside service. She'd never attended a society funeral before, and she hadn't wanted to disrupt this one.

She wouldn't mind the walk back to her car—it was an old cemetery with a lot of history, just like the rest of Charleston. She'd try to remember what David had told her about this section on the outskirts of the city.... It was an effort to think, but she tried to focus as she walked. Some of the few surviving plantation houses were near here, as she recalled. David had always wanted to show her Middleton Gardens. Maybe she could tour it, if not today, then tomorrow. She had a vague, half-formed plan to stay in Charleston for a few days to see some of David's favorite places. She wanted to picture him in the city he had loved so much.

And then she would come back here and try to say goodbye.

"Meg? *Megan?*"

She recognized the voice and stopped. Everything seemed to be moving in slow motion as she turned to Fletcher Matson. "Hello, Fletch." She held one hand out to him and he took it. "It was a beautiful service, wasn't it?"

David's best friend squeezed her hand. His voice was ragged with emotion when he told her, "I've never found anything beautiful about funerals, Meg. This was no exception."

Tears swam in Meg's eyes, but she struggled for something that resembled a smile. "Is that a polite way of telling the Ballenger personnel counselor not to waste her time on platitudes?"

"No, that's one friend telling another to stop pretending. Why weren't you with the family, Meg? I tried to reach you at the hotel this morning, and I looked for you again before the service began. You should have been with David's family and friends."

More tears threatened and Meg stiffened her jaw against them. "It doesn't matter where I was standing, Fletch."

"Yes, it does," he insisted, visibly fighting his own emotions. "David would have wanted you to have the comfort of the other people who loved him. He wouldn't have wanted you to be alone."

"But I am alone," she murmured. She'd meant to sound matter-of-fact about it, but the words magnified the empty ache in her heart and the tears finally caught up with her. A sob she couldn't choke back shook her, and she didn't protest when Fletcher put his arms around her. He rocked gently as she cried, letting his own grief mingle with hers to comfort them both.

But the moment didn't last long. Embarrassed by her weakness, Meg pulled herself together quickly and stepped away. "Sorry. Self-pity is very unbecoming."

Fletch maintained a hold on her hand. "Will you stop that, please. You've spent most of the last two weeks holding everyone else together—eventually, you're going to have to let yourself grieve, Meg. You shouldn't have to do it alone."

She squeezed his hand in gratitude for his praise, but she knew she didn't deserve it. He was the one who'd been holding people together, her most especially. He and his wife, Mei Ling, had stayed at Meg's side during that first hellish night after the crash, seeing her through the awful hours when the pain was so bad she hadn't known how she would survive.

He'd helped her organize a memorial service in Singapore for the benefit of the employees who couldn't make it back to the States for this one. And when Nick decided he couldn't be bothered with making the trip to Singapore to collect what was left of his brother's body, Fletch had handled the red tape that secured the release of David's remains. He'd even made it possible for Meg to fly with him on the Ballenger jet that had transported the body to Charleston yesterday.

She couldn't have made it through the last week without him, and she didn't want to think about having to say goodbye when he returned to Ballenger East.

"I'm fine, Fletch, really. I want you to stop worrying about me."

"I can't." He managed a smile for her. "If I don't take good care of you, David will send Marley's ghost back to haunt me, chains and all."

Meg grinned as she brushed away the moisture on her cheeks. "Heaven forfend. Well, if you're determined to take care of me, why don't you walk me to my car. It's just over the hill."

"All right. Then you can follow me to Ballenger Hall," he said as they started moving.

Meg snorted in a distinctly undignified manner. "Now why on earth would I want to do that?"

"Because Eleanor invited you."

She stopped, stunned. As far as she knew, David had never told his family anything about her. "Me?"

"Yes, you," he replied. "I told Eleanor about the memorial service you organized, and she wants to thank you."

Meg stood there for an indecisive moment. David had told her so much about Ballenger Hall that she could have found it in her sleep. She knew the style of the house, the layout of the rooms, the colors of the carpets, the name of the architect who'd designed it in 1782.... She knew when it had been remodeled to bring the kitchen indoors and split the largest ballroom in Charleston into a grand dining hall and an elegant music conservatory. She knew how much land it sat on—one and a half acres—a nearly unheard-of extravagance in the crowded historic district. She knew how much David had loved that house, how much he'd wanted to return there to live, how much he'd wanted her to see it. How much *she* wanted to see it.

But she shook her head as she began moving again. "No, sorry. I can't. Please convey my regrets and my condolences, but I can't go to the Hall."

"Why not?"

She looked straight ahead as her grief began receding, overpowered by a hatred that didn't allow room for anything else. "Will Nick be there?" she asked.

"Of course. It's his home. He and Eleanor are having a few people over—the mayor, family... When Nick saw you at the service, he asked me to make certain you were invited to the wake."

"He recognized me?" That was a surprise. They'd only met that one time, shortly after David had hired her; he'd grilled her for twenty minutes on her nursing background, her counseling experience at the American Clinic in Singapore, and why on earth Ballenger East needed the services of an overpaid, underqualified pseudopsychologist. He'd made his opinion of her perfectly clear, and now he was requesting a command performance? "Well, you can tell Nick Ballenger to go straight to hell."

Fletch frowned. "Meg! I know you don't like Nick, but—"

"Don't like him? I loathe him. David would be alive if it weren't for Nick. If you put me in the same room with him, I'll tell him that to his face! Is that what you want?"

Fletch was clearly distressed. "No, of course not. But you can't blame Nick for what happened."

"Oh yeah? Watch me."

"Meg! This is not what David would have wanted," he argued. "He loved you, and he loved Nick. He would have wanted you and Eleanor and Nick to take comfort from each other."

She laughed bitterly. "I'm gonna take comfort from the man who killed him? I don't think so."

Fletch grabbed Meg's arm and pulled her to a halt.

They had passed over the crest of the hill, and David's grave site was no longer in view. They had the cemetery to themselves, but Fletch still kept his voice low. "I want you to stop this right now, Meg. Blaming Nick isn't going to bring David back, and it's not going to make it any easier for you to accept what's happened."

Meg yanked her arm out of Fletcher's grasp. "Don't tell me what to feel or who to blame. If it was so all-fired important for Ballenger Pharmaceuticals to expand into the Far East, Nick should have moved to Singapore himself. He should have been the one flying all over Southeast Asia. That should have been *his* silver coffin, not David's!"

Tears threatened again and Meg started walking, quickly this time. Fletcher followed. "I'm sorry, Meg. I didn't mean to upset you." He touched her arm. "Come on. Slow down. I won't ask you to go to Ballenger Hall. You don't have to see Nick."

She slowed her pace, but didn't stop. "I'm sorry. I shouldn't have yelled. I know you've been friends with the family for years, and you still have to work with Nick. David would have understood your loyalty and appreciated it. Let's just drop it, okay?"

Fletcher's nod was reluctant, but he apparently knew when to withdraw from the field of battle. "Have you decided when you'll be returning to Singapore? I expect I'll be here another two weeks, at least. If that fits in with your plans, I'm sure I can get you a seat back on the Ballenger jet."

Meg hesitated. She'd been dreading this from the moment she realized that her choices about what to do with her life were now severely limited. She found she couldn't look at her friend as she told him, "I'm not going back, Fletch. I left a letter of resignation with your secretary, and she's going to ship my things to me as soon as I get settled somewhere.''

Meg could feel the weight of Fletcher's surprise. "You're not serious."

She nodded. "Yes, I am."

"But...why?''

"A lot of reasons. You know as well as I do that Nick will eliminate the counselor position now that David's gone.''

"No, he won't,'' Fletch assured her. "Your job will be secure as long as I'm at Ballenger East.''

Meg shook her head. "Don't do battle with Nick on my account, Fletch. I can't go back. If I do, my work visa will be revoked regardless of what Nick does about the position.''

"For heaven's sake, why?''

Meg took a deep breath. She'd decided days ago that when this moment came, she'd tell Fletch the truth. She was going to need job recommendations and references, but more important, she couldn't lie to a good friend. She cast a cautious glance at him. "In strictest confidence?'' she asked.

"Of course.''

She looked straight ahead again. "I can't go back because physicians are required to report pregnancies to the Ministry of Health, and the government takes a very dim view of unwed American mothers.''

Fletcher stopped in his tracks. "What?''

The pain was oozing out of the cracks in her armor again. It was hard to face him, but she did. "You heard me, Fletch. I'm pregnant. About ten weeks. I found out right after David left for Thailand. That was the special homecoming I had planned—I was going to tell him we're having a baby.'' She closed her eyes and twin tears clung to her lashes for a moment, then coursed down her cheeks.

"My God... Are you sure, Meg?"

She found a fresh wellspring of composure and opened her eyes. "Ballenger boasts that its home pregnancy test is the most accurate in the world. I passed three out of three. And of course, there are the less scientific diagnostic methods—like morning sickness."

Fletch took her hand. "Oh, Meg. I'm so sorry."

"About the pregnancy or the morning sickness?" She smiled through the tears.

He smiled, too. "You know what I mean."

"Yeah. I do. Don't be sorry, Fletch. It's the only good thing I've got to hold on to right now. I'll always have a part of David that no one can take from me."

"Then you're having the baby."

"Of course."

Fletch nodded as though he'd expected no less. "When are you going to tell Nick and Eleanor?"

Meg slipped her hand out of his and started moving again. "I don't know. That's something I haven't worked out in my head yet."

"But you are planning to tell them?" he asked with obvious concern.

Meg sighed heavily. "I suppose so. Eventually."

"Not eventually, Meg. Now. You're not going to go through this alone. You need—and you deserve—the family's support."

"Oh, I can just imagine the support Nick would give," she scoffed. "Do you honestly think that the Ballengers are going to welcome a little hick from the Ozarks into the family?"

"You're not a hick, Meg."

A hollow laugh rumbled in her throat and her accent

was pure country when she replied, "Fletch-a, honey, my fam'ly was so low that bein' called poor white trash was a compliment."

"That's not funny, Meg."

She gave him a cold, hard glare. "It wuddn mint to be."

"Stop that," he snapped. "You are not a hick, Meg, and poverty isn't a crime. It's nothing to be ashamed of, either."

"Well, it's sure not something to brag about," she retorted, bringing her hill-country dialect under control. "David told me repeatedly how proud Eleanor is of her family's bloodlines—Lord Louis Ballenger was one of the first royal governors of Charles Towne, and the Tates trace their lineage back to Richard the Lion-heart. Do you really believe Eleanor is going to be thrilled by this news?"

She looked at Fletcher expectantly. A long pause and the discomfort on his face answered her question. "See?" she said. "It's not as easy as you'd like it to be, is it?"

"I admit, Eleanor is very old-fashioned," he conceded. "She's seventy some–odd years old, for God's sake. In her day, families like the Ballengers still used marriage to consolidate their wealth, power and social position. But she just lost her youngest grandson, and the only remaining Ballenger male hasn't shown any sign of providing a suitable heir to the family fortune. Even to someone as class-conscious as Eleanor, a lowborn heir is better than no heir at all."

Meg's eyebrows went up in surprise. "Lowborn?"

Fletch held up his hands. "Hey, you're the one who insisted on bringing bloodlines into this. I personally think she'll be overjoyed to know that something of David has survived this tragedy. You know how much she loved him—can you really deny her that comfort?''

Meg hadn't thought of it in those terms. David had adored Eleanor. He would clearly want to ease her pain, and if knowing that he had left a child behind would do that, Meg couldn't keep the truth from her.

On the other hand, Nick Ballenger didn't have a sentimental bone in his body. He wouldn't want to acknowledge David's child, and Meg had no intention of forcing him to. In fact, she had no intention of being in the same room with him. Telling him the truth was out of the question.

Fletch must have sensed the stiffening of her resolve because he immediately altered his tactics. ''Okay, you're not going to buy the emotional arguments. How about the practical ones? How do you plan to work and raise a child single-handedly? I'm sure you've got some money saved, but it won't last long.''

Meg had been trying hard not to think about this, because he was absolutely right. Without a job that included a strong medical plan, Meg would be broke by the time her baby was born, and an extended maternity leave would be impossible. She'd have to go back to work almost immediately.

Fletch spotted her weakness and pursued it. ''Well, Meg? What are you going to do? Who's going to take care of David's baby while you work?''

Meg dug into her purse for the keys to her rental car. It was just a few yards away, and she was glad. Fletch wasn't going to let this go. ''I don't have all the answers yet, Fletcher, but I will never go to the Ballengers with my hat in my hand. Granted, they have a right to know about the baby eventually, but I don't want anything from them.''

"You're going to do this totally on your own, then?" he asked skeptically.

"Yes."

"How?"

"I don't know!" Meg said impatiently. "I'll manage! People do it every day."

Fletch nodded. "True enough. The homeless shelters are full of people who are managing just great. And there's always welfare. I hear food stamps are—"

"Stop it!" Meg demanded. She could see that Fletch was manipulating her, but that didn't keep her anger or her fear at bay. He knew very well that her greatest fear was sinking back into the poverty she'd clawed her way out of a decade ago. "That's enough, Fletch. I don't want to talk about this anymore."

"Because you know I'm right?"

Tears welled up behind the dam again. "Because I haven't had time to find all the answers. But I will."

"The answer is obvious, Meg. You have to go to David's family. Forget pride, forget sentiment, forget how much you hate Nick. You cannot deny David's child its birthright. You cannot rob this child of the life David's wealth and social position can give it."

"I am not a beggar!"

"No. You're a lovely, intelligent, compassionate woman who's going to make a wonderful mother...who would have made a wonderful wife to David Ballenger." When a tear slipped down Meg's cheek, Fletch took her hand and sandwiched it between his. "Tell the family now. Let them help you."

Meg shook her head, fighting her tears again. "I can't. I will not beg David's family for a handout. I won't open myself to accusations that I was trying to trap a wealthy husband. I won't let Nick Ballenger or anyone else question the paternity of this child.''

"My God, Meg," Fletch gasped. "What have you got built up in your head? What do you think is going to happen if you tell the truth?"

Meg yanked her hand out of his. "More than I can handle right now!"

She whirled toward her car, and there was nothing Fletcher could say to keep her from driving away.

CHAPTER TWO

"NICK, ARE YOU SURE you want to talk business now? You still have guests..."

"It's just a few of the cousins. Getting out of there is self-defense," Nick said dismissively as he closed the door to his study behind Fletcher. Across the hall, Eleanor was still surrounded by a handful of relatives who hadn't had the good sense to leave with the other mourners. "If one more mealymouthed suck-up tells me that David was too young to die, I'll find myself up on manslaughter charges."

He didn't look as if he was making a joke, but Fletcher smiled anyway. "I understand."

Nick moved to the polished mahogany bar opposite his desk, loosening his tie on the way. "Can you believe that Selina Tate had the nerve to ask if David mentioned her in his will? She's our second cousin once removed, for God's sake. She hadn't said more than two words to David since Eleanor forced him to escort her to her coming-out party twelve years ago."

Fletch moved to the bar, too. "Selina Tate? The leggy brunette? Why on earth would she need a shotgun escort?"

"That was B.P.S.L., as the kids would say today." Nick held up a crystal decanter. "Bourbon, right?"

Fletch nodded. "Neat. B.P.S.L?"

"Before Plastic Surgery and Liposuction." Nick

poured a generous shot for each of them, then gestured vaguely toward one of the leather armchairs in front of his desk.

"I guess I've been out of the country too long. Singapore doesn't import American slang."

"You're not missing much," Nick said absently, as though dismissing that part of their conversation and the irritating relatives who had inspired it.

Fletch sat, but Nick seemed too restless to settle in one place. He moved to his desk and turned on his computer, then stood there looking down, sipping bourbon and tapping a key now and then to get to who-knew-what file.

Fletch waited. There were a million and one business details that would have to be ironed out before he went back to Singapore—not the least of which was finding a replacement for David as head of Ballenger East—but Fletch didn't think Nick's mind was on business. Not really. He had the look of someone who was being held together by willpower and wishful thinking—just like Meg. Nick's emotional seams weren't as visibly ragged as hers; his grief was bottled up and vacuum-packed, but the strain was there. Fletch was worried about both of them.

All the way over here, Fletch had wrestled with his conscience trying to decide what to do with the bombshell Meg had dropped. Was he supposed to keep her confidence and allow her to struggle through a pregnancy complicated by grief and crippling financial worries? Or should he do what David would have wanted and let the Ballenger family shoulder his share of the responsibility for the pregnancy?

"Fletcher, how would you feel about taking over as president of Ballenger East?"

The question ended the long silence so abruptly that it momentarily drove Meg's dilemma completely out of his head. The offer wasn't unexpected, though. Fletch had been David's second-in-command, after all. "I feel confident that I can run the Singapore operation and oversee the Bangkok factory," he replied, choosing his words very carefully.

"No qualms about staying in Singapore?"

Fletch shook his head. Unlike David, he was very happy in Singapore. "No. Mei Ling would throw a very Americanized hissy fit if I tried to uproot her from her family and her medical practice."

"Then you'll take the job?"

Fletch hesitated. "Possibly. But not before we talk about the expansion into Vietnam—"

"I'm tabling that for a while," Nick announced, his blue eyes betraying not a flicker of the emotion Fletch knew had to be there. They were talking about the reason David had been on that doomed jet. "I'm going to put an assessment team on it and reevaluate David's last few reports. I need to determine if he had good reason to oppose the expansion."

"That's a wise idea, Nick."

"But a little late?"

"I didn't say that."

Their gazes locked, as though Nick was searching Fletcher's face for something, but he broke the contact after only a second or two. Apparently he decided he didn't want to know after all. He looked down at the screen again. Silence made the room seem even bigger than it was.

The emotional undercurrents around them had shifted subtly by the time Nick spoke again. He didn't look up from the computer when he asked, "Have I thanked you yet for bringing David home?"

"Yes, you have. Several times."

Nick inclined his head, and a lock of thick black hair fell into his forehead. He swiped it out of the way. "Oh? Well... Good. My memory is shot to hell, but at least my manners are improving," he murmured to himself. To Fletch, he said, "I should have gone over there myself to handle things, but Eleanor..."

When his voice drifted off, Fletch nodded. "I understand how it was."

"After what had just happened to David, the thought of me getting on a plane was more than she could handle. Hell, she still paces the floor when I go out on the boat, and it's been nearly twenty years since Mother and Father died. I couldn't put her through that trauma so soon."

"I was glad to be able to help, Nick," Fletch said. "And the government was very cooperative. Once they were satisfied that the plane crash wasn't sabotage or an act of terrorism, things went very smoothly."

"But it couldn't have been easy."

"Nothing is easy at times like these."

"True enough." Nick took another sip of bourbon and ambled toward the big bay window that overlooked Eleanor's rose garden. "The last I heard, the official cause of the accident was wind shear."

"Yes," Fletch confirmed.

"Witnesses reported that the jet just suddenly dropped onto the runway." He didn't turn around.

"That's right."

"And exploded on contact." His voice was hollow and distant.

"Yes," Fletch said softly, wishing for Nick's sake

that he wouldn't pursue this line of thought. Needing to talk about it was one thing, but torturing himself with images of the tragedy wouldn't help anyone.

"It was just an accident, Nick. A stupid, senseless accident," Fletcher told him.

"But it wouldn't have happened if I hadn't sent David to Singapore."

There is was. The guilt that needed to be expressed, soothed, assuaged, exorcised.... "You didn't kill him, Nick. If that's what you're thinking, you can stop it right now. David's accident wasn't your fault."

"Wasn't it?" Bitterness bled into his voice as he turned from the window. "I made him go over there, Fletch. For his own good. Is that a laugh? I wanted to get him out of my shadow and force him to finally take some responsibility for his life."

"Which he did," Fletch assured him.

"And I still wouldn't let him come home! I rammed the Thailand expansion down his throat, then forced Vietnam on him. I played on his family loyalty to keep him in Singapore when what he really wanted was to come home.... Jesus..." Nick gulped the last of the bourbon and moved to the bar. "I'm a real piece of work, aren't I?"

Fletch felt utterly helpless. "You did the best you could, Nick."

"That isn't saying much."

"I disagree. You were more of a father to David than Nick, Sr., ever was."

"Well, if this is the best I can do in the parenting department, it's a good thing Camille and I didn't have kids."

Nick took another deep draft of whiskey, and Fletch had the strongest feeling that some other pain had just spilled into the mix—an older one, not nearly as fresh as this loss. Did Nick regret that he and his ex-wife hadn't had children?

How was he going to feel if Meg ever got around to telling him that David had left a child behind?

"It's never too late to start a family, Nick," he commented mildly.

"It is for me." Nick brought the glass to his lips, then set it down abruptly, as though he'd suddenly remembered that getting drunk wasn't going to make his pain go away. He started toward his desk. "Let's change the subject, shall we? We need to discuss—"

"No, let's not."

Nick's look of surprise was so comical that Fletch almost smiled. *No* wasn't a word that the powerful CEO of Ballenger Pharmaceuticals, International heard very often. But now that Fletch had said it and he had Nick's full attention, could he really follow through?

Telling Nick about Meg's pregnancy would be a betrayal of her confidence, but she obviously wasn't thinking straight. She needed the help and support of David's family, yet she was stubbornly determined to deny herself that assistance. She was doing exactly the opposite of what David would have wanted.

But did that give Fletch any right to take the decision out of her hands?

"Fletch?" Nick was staring at him, waiting. "You had a thought you wanted to pursue?"

Fletcher nodded, his decision made. Hopefully Meg would thank him someday. Or at least forgive him. "Did David ever tell you that he was dating someone in Singapore?"

The apparent change of subject surprised Nick. "Uh…yes. When he was home last Christmas he mentioned that he was seeing that counselor of his—Megan Linley." Nick frowned. "Where is she, by the way? I thought you were going to bring her to the house."

"She wouldn't come. I think she has visions of you accusing her of being a gold-digging hussy who was out to trap David into marriage."

Nick's black eyebrows arched in curiosity and surprise. "Was she?"

"No. She and David loved each other very much."

Nick moved thoughtfully toward the window as he digested that information. It was a moment before he answered, "Good. I'm glad he had someone in his life."

"It's a little more complicated than that," Fletch said, praying that he was doing the right thing.

Nick turned. "What do you mean, complicated?"

Fletch sighed. "I hate the thought of betraying a confidence, but maybe this will be easier for you and Eleanor to accept if it comes from an impartial third party."

"*What* will be easier to accept?" Nick demanded, clearly beginning to lose his patience.

"I think you'd better sit down, Nick. And grab another drink. You may need it."

WHEN THE STUDY DOOR opened into the dark room an hour after Fletcher left, Nick was sitting on the cushioned shelf of the bay window, staring into the deep, black shadows of the garden. When he and David were kids, he used to find his brother curled up in this window seat almost every day, waiting for their father to come home and throw him a crumb of affection or a moment's attention. He was invariably disappointed, and Nick was invariably outraged by their father's indifference.

He'd never understood why David kept leaving him-

self open to the pain of their father's rejection. Nick had
learned early that it didn't matter how well he behaved,
how many perfect papers he brought home from school,
how many goals he scored in soccer or how flawlessly
he performed at his piano recitals; Nicholas Ballenger,
Sr., barely noticed and rarely praised.

His mother, Cynthia, the busiest socialite in Charleston, had been the same. When David was born, Nick
had been only six, but he still remembered thinking,
"Why?" They barely noticed the one child they had.
Why bring another into the house for the servants to
raise?

And sure enough, within a month of David's birth,
Cynthia was back to organizing charity fund-raisers and
meddling in the historic preservation of Charleston.
Nick, Sr., hadn't paused long enough between business
deals and golf games to notice the birth. Eleanor, their
only surviving grandparent, had become a world traveler
after the death of her husband, and even when she was
in Charleston, her presence was seen but seldom felt:
she was an attentive grandparent but not a demonstrative
one.

So Nick, Jr., had made a point of spending a few
minutes every day with David. He was the one who'd
coaxed the first baby steps out of his brother. He'd read
books to him at night, taught him how to color inside
the lines, gave him his first piano lesson and taught him
the rules of baseball. In return for that brotherly devotion, David had stuck to Nick's heels like a well-trained
puppy. He'd looked to Nick for approval, for guidance,
for comfort whenever Nick, Sr., barked at him to get out
of the window seat and go to his room. Before and after
their parents' death, if David got in trouble, Nick picked

up the pieces. If David was unsure what to do, Nick made the decision for him.

That was the pattern of their relationship, and the brothers were adults before Nick realized that it wasn't a healthy one. That's why he'd sent David to Singapore. That's why David was dead.

That's why Nick had a hole in his heart so big it couldn't possibly heal.

"Nicholas?" The room was dark save for the glow of the computer monitor on the desk. Eleanor, standing just inside the door, looked uncharacteristically tentative. "Nicholas, are you in here?"

"Yes, Nan. Right here," he said without getting up.

"Whatever are you doing sitting here in the dark?" she asked in the distinctive drawl of a Carolina aristocrat.

"Just trying to ruin my eyes."

Eleanor clucked her tongue the way she always did when she was amused and trying not to show it. "Was that meant to be impertinent?"

"Yes."

"Congratulations. You succeeded." Her dry tone almost made Nick smile.

She moved to the desk and flicked on the old-fashioned banker's lamp. It bathed the surface of the desk in soft green light, but did nothing to banish darkness from the rest of the room. It did let Nick see that his grandmother had changed out of her black suit into a pair of gray slacks and a long-tailed silk blouse.

She looked softer than usual, almost fragile, in fact, but still untouchably regal. You'd never know by looking that she'd lost someone she loved very deeply. Her grief had been relegated to cold storage and would only be taken out and examined in private. Not even Nick, who knew her better than anyone, had seen more than the tiniest glimpse of her pain; nor had he been allowed the opportunity to comfort her. Not that he would have known how. David had been the demonstrative one in their tiny family.

"Has everyone gone?" Nick asked his grandmother.

"Yes. Selina wanted to stay the night but I threatened to cut her out of my will if she didn't go home and stop fussing."

Nick smiled wryly. "I'm sure that sent her flying."

"Like the proverbial bat out of Hades. I never should have told her that I was gonna leave her Grandma Jenna's rings. Now she's convinced that if she pesters me enough, I'll leave her everythin'." Eleanor moved around the desk toward the glowing computer monitor. "Nicholas, you haven't been trying to work, have you?"

"Not really. I was just getting a head start on some details that Fletcher and I will have to work out before he goes back to Singapore."

"But Fletcher left an hour ago and you're still here." She looked at the computer screen and frowned thoughtfully. "Megan Linley...?"

Nick tensed. He'd forgotten that he'd pulled up the Linley woman's personnel file. He was still in shock over what Fletcher had told him, and he didn't feel inclined to spring this on Eleanor until he decided if it was good news or bad.

"Isn't she the girl Fletcher mentioned this morning?" Eleanor asked. "The one who organized a memorial service for the Singapore employees."

"Yes. She's the personnel counselor David hired about a year and a half ago."

"And she came all the way back to the States for David's service?" she queried, her voice laced with speculation. "Wasn't Fletcher supposed to bring her to the house?"

Nick stood up from the window seat and crossed to the desk. "She had other plans, I believe."

Eleanor pursed her lips thoughtfully as she gave ground, moving toward one of the leather armchairs. "Linley...Linley... Don't we know a Linley family in Virginia? They were related to the Carolina Albersons."

Like most everyone else in Charleston society, Eleanor judged people by their genealogy. Nick didn't know much about Megan Linley's, but from what little Fletch had told him, her family tree wasn't going to hold up under Nan's scrutiny.

Nick reached for the keyboard and cleared the computer screen. "She's not one of the Virginia Linleys, Nan. Her family came from the Midwest. The Missouri Ozarks, I think."

"Oh." She clearly wasn't impressed. "Why were you so interested in her file?"

He sat in the comfortably worn leather chair. "No reason, really. Fletch said she was quitting, and I wanted to look at her credentials, her employee evaluations. She's going to need references...."

Eleanor shook her head as she sat in the chair Fletcher had occupied earlier. "I know it's been a dreadful day, Nicholas darlin', but you're usually a much better liar than this." She paused until Nick's gaze met hers over the desk. "Now, what is it you're trying so hard not to tell me?"

"Nothing."

"This Linley woman... Was she involved with David romantically?"

Nick sighed heavily. If he lived to be a hundred he'd

never understand that sixth sense women seemed to have.

"Yes," he admitted. "She and David were seeing each other."

Eleanor's voice and demeanor were completely matter-of-fact as she asked, "Is she threatening a scandal or something of that nature? Are we being blackmailed?"

"Oh, good grief, Nan. Don't be ridiculous."

"Well, it does happen, Nicholas. Unscrupulous women have been preying on men like David for centuries."

Nick glared at his grandmother. This wasn't a good day to dissect his brother's character. "What do you mean, 'men like David'?" he asked sharply.

Eleanor didn't appear the least bit intimidated by the scowl that sent Nick's employees scurrying for cover. "Wealthy young men with more libido than backbone."

"I resent that characterization."

Eleanor waved one hand airily, dismissing his irritation. "You may resent it, but it's true. David was a wonderful young man—kind, generous, loving... But he didn't have your strength, and we both know it. My greatest concern when you sent him to Singapore was that some bargain-basement Lolita would sink her claws into him."

The irony caught up with her, and drove a wedge into her armor. It didn't break, but it did crack, allowing Nick to see a tiny sliver of her pain as she said softly, "Odd, isn't it? The things we choose to worry about and the things we take for granted...."

"Yes. It is..." Nick had trouble meeting Eleanor's pale blue eyes, but he managed it. There was no reproach in her gaze, only sorrow. If she blamed him for David's death, she wasn't letting it show.

And she didn't let the sorrow show long, either. She cleared her throat, sealed the breach in her defenses and returned to the original topic. "So tell me, what is it about Miss Linley that has you ruminating in the dark?"

Nick didn't see any point in lying. "She's pregnant."

"Oh. I see." Eleanor's pause hung heavily in the air. "With David's child, supposedly?"

"I wouldn't have been sitting in the dark trying to figure out how to proceed if it wasn't," he replied dryly.

She ignored the dig. "Do we have any proof?"

"Nothing that would stand up in court, but there's plenty of circumstantial evidence. David mentioned that he was dating her last Christmas, and Fletch says they were very much in love. I know he wouldn't be party to any type of deception."

"If he were aware of it."

Nick nodded. "Yes."

"Tell me, what do we know about the girl?" Eleanor asked.

"Only what's in her personnel file and what little Fletch could tell me," Nick said as he pulled up Meg's file on the computer again. "Apparently, she's a very private person. Doesn't talk much about herself."

"Admirable. Unless, of course, she has something to hide."

He ignored the speculation. "She moved to Singapore about six and a half years ago when her employer in Missouri, Dr. Lewellyn Holmby, accepted a position as head of Family Practice at the American Clinic."

"Was she his nurse, or his paramour?" Eleanor asked.

Nick couldn't very well condemn Eleanor for being suspicious. He'd found a tactful way to ask Fletch the same question. "Holmby and his wife are a middle-aged couple who regarded Miss Linley as a daughter. They

even helped her obtain her credentials as a nurse practitioner with a specialty in psychology. She started in
Singapore as Holmby's office assistant, and eventually
began group-counseling sessions for Americans who
were having trouble adjusting to living there. That's how
she came to Fletcher's attention. His wife, Mei Ling, had
become acquainted with Miss Linley through the clinic,
and when one of the Ballenger researchers began having
marital difficulties, Mei Ling suggested that Fletch send
the couple to Miss Linley.''

"When was this?" Eleanor asked.

"Um... About four years ago, I guess. Shortly before
David took over the operation there.''

"And how did Miss Linley become a Ballenger employee?"

"When Holmby completed his five-year contract and
returned to the States, Fletcher sold David on the idea
of hiring her to counsel our employees and their families
on a full-time basis. She did employee initiations, cul-
tural counseling, helped spouses and children learn their
way around Singapore—literally and figuratively.''

"But had Fletcher not intervened on her behalf, she
would have lost her work visa, wouldn't she?"

"Yes."

Eleanor sighed delicately. "Sounds like an old-
fashioned boondoggle to me.''

"That's what I thought until I saw the results of her
work. Productivity increased and requests for transfer
decreased. Before Miss Linley, the average stay in Singapore was eight months. Now, employee turnover
among the American executives and researchers is virtually nil. If she doesn't go back, I'm going to have to
replace her.''

"And she can't go back pregnant.''

"No. She can't," Nick confirmed. "The Ministry of Health would revoke her work visa as soon as they discovered the pregnancy."

"So it's fair to say that the girl is in desperate straits."

Nick could see the wheels turning behind his grandmother's sharp blue eyes, but he hadn't a clue where she was leading. He knew better than to let himself be caught in one of her traps, though. "That might be one way to characterize it," he said cautiously.

"What about her family?"

Nick punched another key. "None. Dr. and Mrs. Lewellyn Holmby are listed as next of kin, but their relationship is given as friends."

"Then her parents are dead?"

"It would seem so. Fletcher did tell me that she grew up in impoverished conditions."

"Hmm…" Eleanor paused, digesting the information with deceptive passivity. "How far along is the girl?" his grandmother asked.

"About two and a half months. Apparently, she only discovered it herself while David was on this last trip. She was planning to tell him when he returned."

A look of surprise gave way to an unexpected sparkle of unshed tears in Eleanor's eyes. "David didn't know?"

Nick had never seen his grandmother cry, but he understood the emotion that nearly brought her to tears. It was sorrow for chances lost, for the cruel trick of fate that had robbed his brother of the joy of knowing that the woman he loved was carrying his child. The unfairness of it made Nick want to cry, too. But he didn't. And neither did Eleanor.

Instead, as she fell silent, Nick got up and moved to the bar to fix her a light gin and tonic. While he was at it, he poured a bourbon and water for himself. The effects of the last one had worn off an hour ago.

"Are you all right, Nan?" he asked, handing her the drink.

"I suppose so. I'm just terribly torn. The thought of a Ballenger heir is undeniably appealing, but to know that the child will be labeled a bastard..." She looked up at her grandson and he saw that her tears had been replaced by frosty determination. "It is unthinkable, Nicholas. Absolutely unthinkable."

He returned to his chair. "Well, there's not much we can do about that, Nan. Either we acknowledge the child or we don't. And if we choose the latter, we might find ourselves drawn into an ugly legal battle after the baby is born."

"But there has never been an illegitimate child in the Ballenger family. I am not prepared to see scandal visited on this house, Nicholas."

"Times have changed, Grandmother. An illegitimate child is—"

"Is still a bastard," she said sternly. "Do you want that stigma applied to your niece or nephew? Do you want the child to grow up hearing whispers and sniggers? To feel that censure and not know what he's done to deserve it?"

"Of course not." Nick sighed and prayed for patience. This would have been so much easier if he'd had time to decide on an appropriate course of action and presented his decision to Eleanor as a *fait accompli*. She was a strong-willed matriarch who would fight to get her own way on any issue that was still open to question, but she'd been trained to capitulate to the masculine head of the family. Once a decision was made, Eleanor respected it.

But that wasn't the case now. Nick didn't know what to do, and Eleanor was going to take advantage of his indecision.

"What are you suggesting, Nan?" he asked archly. "That we pay Miss Linley to have her baby elsewhere and never darken our door? Shall I play the villain? Maybe I should grow a mustache and start oiling it?"

"Don't be absurd. If this woman's child really is a Ballenger, he will be raised as such."

Nick leaned back in his chair, absently rolling his glass between his hands. "Then I don't see any way around the legitimacy issue. Fletch is convinced that David would have married the girl immediately, but since that didn't happen I don't know of any way to prevent this child from being labeled a bastard."

"Of course there's a way."

Nick's dark eyebrows went up in curiosity. "Oh? How?"

"You can marry the girl."

He bolted upright in his chair. "What?"

"You heard me," Eleanor said placidly.

"I heard you suggest that I marry a woman I don't even know."

Eleanor looked as innocent as he'd ever seen her. "You're not otherwise involved, are you?" she asked innocuously.

"You know very well I'm not, but that still doesn't—"

Eleanor cut him off. "It makes perfect sense, Nicholas. Think about it. Since the pregnancy hasn't advanced very far, we can claim that the two of you met and fell in love on one of your trips to Singapore. You were over there several times this past year," she noted.

"Nan, you're insane."

She ignored him. "We'll say that you've been conducting a discreet affair long distance, and this tragedy has made you realize that you don't want to be separated any longer. We can have a small, private ceremony within the month, and no one will be the wiser."

"Until the baby is born suspiciously early," he said sarcastically.

"A child conceived on the wrong side of the sheets is not nearly as scandalous as a birth out of wedlock," Eleanor countered. "You'll get the girl to sign a prenuptial agreement, of course—they're all the rage these days, anyway. Agree to pay her whatever it takes to get rid of her. Then, a suitable interval after the baby is born you can obtain a quiet divorce. She gets rich, and we retain custody of the Ballenger heir."

The total lack of emotion in her voice chilled Nick to the bone. "You can't believe she would agree to that."

"On the contrary. What pregnant, impoverished young woman *wouldn't* jump at marrying one of the wealthiest, most powerful men on the eastern seaboard. And if she refuses to relinquish custody later, we can deal with her in the courts. But by then, of course, we'll have established you as the child's father, and renouncing your paternity would only weaken the girl's position."

"Grandmother! This is ludicrous!" Nick said, coming to his feet in a masculine attempt to take control of the room.

Eleanor only regarded him calmly, completely unintimidated. "Is it? Think about it, Nicholas. You're thirty-eight years old and childless. Here's your chance to finally be a father."

He looked at her through narrowed eyes. She had just skated onto dangerously thin ice. "Don't wave fatherhood in front of me, Nan. Or family honor or potential scandals," he said flatly, trying not to betray any more emotion than necessary.

"And don't you discard this opportunity," she warned him, then softened her voice. Her eyes were almost warm when she went on, "My darlin' Nicholas, when you were a young man, you wanted only two things out of life. I robbed you of the first—"

Nick came round the desk again. "Nan, stop it. I don't want to dredge up—"

"Let me finish," she insisted. "I robbed you of the first when I forced you to take the reins of Ballenger Pharmaceuticals. Fate or biology or a cruel trick of nature has robbed you of the second—the family you always wanted."

"Nan, I never—"

She regarded him sadly. "Don't waste breath denying it, Nicholas. I know who raised David, who nurtured him and gave him the loving affection neither your parents nor I could provide. I've seen the anguish in your eyes when you look at your cousins' children. The rest of Charleston may believe that you and Camille remained childless by choice, but I know better."

Instead of denying it, Nick finished the syllogism Eleanor had started. "And since my ex-wife gave birth to a son less than a year after she remarried, the fault must have been mine," he said, moving to the bar to refresh his drink. Straight bourbon this time, no water.

"I'm not saying this to upset you, Nicholas, or to goad you," Eleanor assured him gently. "We've never spoken of it before, and I don't expect we ever shall again. But you have an opportunity here to do something wonderful for your brother's child and for yourself at the same time. There's nothing wrong with being selfish now and again, darlin'."

Nick knocked back a generous draft of bourbon. It was a smooth Kentucky blend, but it still burned his throat and brought tears to his eyes. He blinked them back, and at the same time murdered the ache that Eleanor's argument had created in his chest. "I'm not marrying Megan Linley—even assuming she'd agree to it. Which she wouldn't. Miss Linley—" He stopped abruptly.

Eleanor tilted her head to one side. "What about her?"

Nick frowned, wishing he'd never spoken. Fletcher hadn't said it outright, but Nick had gotten the message loud and clear. Megan Linley held him responsible for David's death, which meant that she probably hated him even more than he hated himself.

He couldn't bring himself to say that to Eleanor, though. "Nothing, Nan. Just trust me on this. The woman would never agree to marry me."

"Darlin', a woman will agree to anything for the right price. I'm sure this one won't come cheap, but she's obviously a schemer. Look at the way she used Fletcher."

Nick returned to his desk. "No, no. She told Fletcher about the baby in confidence after the funeral today— and then only because he pinned her into a corner. Fletch says she's proud and very stubborn. She hasn't even decided whether to tell us at all."

Eleanor shook her head wearily. "Men are so gullible," she said on a sigh. "Darlin', the girl was perfectly aware that Fletcher was on his way here, so she made a tearful confession full of protestations that she wants nothing for herself or her child, knowing full well that there's not a man alive who wouldn't feel compelled to come to her rescue. Fletcher was acting in the girl's best interest because the poor maiden-in-distress was too emotionally distraught to make the right decision for herself. Correct?''

Nick had to confirm her assumption. It was an accurate assessment of Fletch's reason for spilling the beans. But as for the woman having nefarious motives...Nick had his doubts about that. Which was damned odd, actually.

Why was he giving her the benefit of the doubt? Usually he was the one looking for misrepresentations, lies and ulterior motives; it was one of the reasons he was so successful in business. So, what made this situation different?

Guilt, that's what. Pure, unadulterated, gut-wrenching guilt. Learning that David had been in love somehow eased a little of Nick's guilt. His brother hadn't wanted to be in Singapore, but at least he hadn't been alone.

Nick wasn't a sentimental man, so he wasn't about to welcome Megan Linley into the bosom of the Ballenger family without looking before he leaped, but he wanted her claim to be genuine. He wanted the comfort of knowing that he had something more of his brother than memories. He wanted very much to believe that the mother of David's baby was a sweet, honest, loving woman who would always put the welfare of her child first. A woman who was everything his own mother hadn't been.

Okay. Maybe he was a sentimental schmuck, after all.

But what was Meg Linley? A grieving lover and mother-to-be, or a bargain-basement Lolita, as Nan had so colorfully phrased it?

"Do you really think she's a schemer, Nan?'' he

asked his grandmother. "Isn't that giving her an awful lot of credit?"

"Darlin', it doesn't take much intelligence to manipulate a man. You'd be amazed at how effective a woman can be if she's armed with the singular bit of knowledge that a man can always be counted upon to underestimate her," Eleanor replied. "Now, I suggest that you pay Miss Linley a visit and find out what she wants from us."

Nick had made that decision even before Eleanor came into the study. "Of course. But Fletch says she doesn't want anything."

"Fletcher is a man," Eleanor decreed flatly, as though that explained it all. "You, on the other hand, are a Ballenger, like your father. You won't be so easily manipulated."

The comparison to his coldhearted, ruthless father made Nick's stomach turn, but he let it roll off of him. It was, after all, deserved. "Assuming Miss Linley is a schemer."

Eleanor inclined her head. "Assuming."

Nick sighed heavily as he moved back to his chair. "I'll make arrangements to see her, Nan. But I'm not marrying her," he added firmly as he sat.

"Why ever not?" Eleanor asked. "This family has a long history of arranged marriages."

"Last century, perhaps," he conceded, "but not this one."

"Really? What would you call your marriage to Camille?"

The question brought Nick fully upright in his chair, glaring at his grandmother. How dare she? "That was *not* an arranged marriage."

"No?" Eleanor queried lightly. "What were you in

love with? Her beauty? Her wit? Her stellar intellect? Or could it have been the forty-five acres of land that you bought from her father for a pittance the week after your engagement was announced?''

Normally, Nick knew better than to let Eleanor get under his skin, but today was anything but normal. "I paid a fair price for that property, Eleanor," he snapped.

Nick only called her by her given name when he was angry, but Eleanor didn't let that faze her. "Fair, yes," she conceded. "But if you hadn't been marrying his daughter, Lewis Devonaux would have held you up for an arm and a leg, too."

"I did not marry Camille for her land!" Nick said hotly.

"Of course not. You married her because she was rich, beautiful, compliant, and she had been raised to be the perfect Charleston wife, mother and hostess. The fact that her father owned the perfect piece of land for the new Ballenger corporate headquarters was merely icing on the cake. But you will notice, Nicholas darlin', that nowhere in that list of Camille's qualifications did I mention the fact that you were madly in love with her, because we both know better."

The inescapable truth doused Nick's anger with cold water and it sputtered out of existence. After all, it wasn't Eleanor's fault that he'd married a woman for whom he'd felt little more than strong affection, respect and a moderate dose of passion. Like everything else he did, he'd chosen a wife for logical reasons, not emotional ones, and the arrangement had worked out well for the better part of a decade. In fact, if Nick had been able to give Camille the children she'd wanted to go along with the wealth and social position that went hand in hand with the Ballenger name, they probably would still have been married, and this ridiculous conversation with Eleanor wouldn't be taking place.

"Enough, Nan," he said calmly but sternly. "We're not going to dissect my marriage to Camille."

"Fine," she conceded. "I'm only trying to make the point that since you married once for practical reasons there is nothing wrong with doing so again. And I can think of no better reason than providing a father for David's child and a legitimate heir for the Ballenger fortune." She looked at him archly. "Or had you made peace with having the family name end with you now that David is gone?"

"I haven't made peace with anything, Nan," he growled. "Least of all my brother's death!"

Eleanor met his gaze with calm determination. "Then do the right thing and assure the future of David's child."

"By marrying the woman he loved?"

She ignored the sarcasm in his voice. "It's the only way, Nicholas. Merely acknowledging the child as a Ballenger won't give either one of us any say in how or where the child is raised, where he is educated, or the type of values his mother chooses to instill in him—*if* she has any values at all. Are you going to be content standing on the sidelines while a complete stranger raises David's child?"

Eleanor was finally raising arguments that made sense to Nick. Still...a marriage of convenience seemed so...so Victorian. "I'm sure some type of agreement can be reached," he said with too much hesitancy in his voice.

"At what price, Nicholas? A thousand dollars a visit? Ten thousand for a week during the summer?"

"Don't be absurd."

"I'm not," Eleanor insisted. "Unless you establish a legal claim to that child, it doesn't matter how much money you throw at the mother now or what she agrees to in principle. Miss Linley can hold this family up for any amount of money she chooses. We'll be at her mercy for the next twenty years."

"Not if I negotiate some sort of shared custody in exchange for a generous financial consideration for her and the child," Nick argued.

"And if she refuses? Takes us to court? What then?" Eleanor asked, then answered her own question with, "She gets the money, she gets custody and David's child gets scandalous tabloid coverage that will haunt him the rest of his life. Is that the legacy David would have wanted?"

Damn, but she was good! Nick had no intention of getting married, but for the life of him he suddenly couldn't see any other alternative. Eleanor was right. This *was* the perfect solution—oh, maybe not for Megan Linley, who certainly wouldn't want to marry a man she hated. And not for Nick, who'd already spent ten years of his life in a loveless marriage. But for David's child, who needed the legitimacy that only a marriage certificate could guarantee, and who deserved the love and devotion David would have freely given if he had lived.... It was the perfect solution—the only solution—to assure a secure future for the child. And in the final analysis, was there anything more important?

No. There wasn't. In fact, in Nick's head and in his heart, nothing else even came close. He had to marry David's lover and give their child the name it deserved.

But now that he'd reached that conclusion he had only one problem.

Convincing Megan Linley.

"All right, Nan," he said, coming to his feet. "You win. I'll take care of it."

Eleanor seemed more surprised by her victory than pleased. "You'll marry the girl?"

He nodded. "As soon as I can persuade Miss Linley to accept my proposal."

"Oh, that shouldn't be too difficult," Eleanor said as she rose. "The girl set her cap on a Ballenger husband and had very nearly snagged him. I expect you'll find her quite willing to accept a substitute."

Nick inclined his head noncommittally, letting Eleanor win the point without argument, but he hoped that his grandmother was wrong. He would do whatever it took to get what he wanted, but he was going to be very disappointed if Megan Linley turned out to be a cheap little gold digger.

CHAPTER THREE

"MAY I HELP YOU?" The Ballenger Pharmaceuticals receptionist had a Carolina drawl that made the question sound friendly, but the expression on her stern face was all business.

Meg refused to let herself be intimidated. "Could you notify Fletcher Matson that Meg Linley is here to see him?" she inquired, lightly shifting the note she'd received from Fletch back and forth between her fingers. "We have a ten o'clock appointment."

The receptionist nodded brusquely and reached for the phone. "Just a moment, please."

Meg stepped back from the desk and looked around the lobby. The corporate head office of Ballenger Pharmaceuticals, International, the world's third-largest drug company, was a big shiny building sitting smack in the middle of an industrial park that also bore the Ballenger name. It reminded Meg of modern-day Singapore, modular, clean and lacking any sense of history.

Somehow, that struck Meg as odd. Since the funeral last Friday, she'd avoided thinking about her predicament by exploring Charleston, matching David's loving descriptions with the real sights and smells. Not only had the exercise connected her to David, but it had brought Meg in touch with American history for the first time. When she was growing up, "old" had equaled "bad." Someone else's old clothes. Old cracked-and-peeling linoleum. An old Chevy pickup that spent more time rusting in the yard than it spent on the road.

To the best of Meg's recollection, the only old thing that had ever been treasured in the Linley house was a painted-and-embroidered crazy quilt that had been passed down from Meg's great-grandmother. And the only reason she remembered it at all was because of the way Loreen, her mother, had cried when she saw that Dub had used it to cover the engine of the old Chevy while he was trying to get the truck running one hot summer afternoon. Meg's father had returned it to Loreen saturated with motor oil, gasoline and ground-in dirt.

Crying as though her heart was breaking, Loreen had taken it out back to the dump by the old outhouse and burned it. She'd wept the rest of the day and into the night until Dub got sick of her caterwauling. He'd shut her up the only way he knew how—with a sharp slap across the face to stun her to silence, then a hard jab to prove he meant business.

Meg was only five at the time, and her father hadn't started using that particular technique on her yet, but it taught her a valuable lesson about getting attached to "old" things. It just didn't pay.

That was why she'd never taken much heed of what little history there was in Pine Ridge. To her, the pre–Civil War courthouse in the square at the center of town was just a big brick building with a broken clock on top. The turn-of-the-century houses on Elm Street were just old firetraps with broken sidewalks and shutters that hung crooked on their hinges.

But Charleston was different. David had talked about the way his family's heritage intersected the city's history, so that they were inseparable; and with both a part of the history of the entire nation. Walking the streets of Charleston with a tour book and David's words to guide her, Meg was getting a sense of her country's roots for the first time in her life. "Old" wasn't "bad." On the contrary, it was something to be embraced, treasured.

That's why Ballenger headquarters seemed odd. The company was old, but it was housed in a building without a sense of the past. Was that by accident or design? she wondered. Nick had commissioned the building eleven years ago, consolidating the factory and executive suites into a high-tech complex with ample room for growth, away from one of the older sections of the city. Why had he chosen not to give the building any character? she wondered.

"Miss Linley?"

Meg turned back to the glass-and-chrome reception desk. Another stern-faced woman—this one a decade older than the receptionist—was standing to one side of the counter, glowering at her as though Meg had committed some horrible social gaffe.

Was the main office always this grim, she wondered, or was it a response to David's death? "I'm Meg Linley," she informed the woman.

"You're expected, Miss Linley. If you'll come with me I'll show you up."

"Thank you." They rode an elevator in silence to the executive suites on the sixth floor, where the woman escorted Meg down a plushly carpeted corridor. She opened one of a pair of polished oak doors and stepped back.

"If you'll wait in here, please. It won't be long."

Until what? Meg wanted to ask. Instead, she said, "Thank you," again and stepped into a boardroom that was larger than her apartment in Singapore. An enormous oak conference table filled the center of the room. Smoke-colored floor-to-ceiling windows took up two walls, and painted portraits adorned the others.

"Please make yourself comfortable." The door closed with a soft but firm click.

Comfortable? She felt like Jonah in the belly of the whale. She'd come to think of Nick Ballenger as her enemy, and that made this enemy territory. If she hadn't needed a letter of recommendation from Fletch, she never would have set foot in the place.

Too uneasy to sit, she put her purse on the near end of the long conference table, then ambled down the neatly aligned row of padded chairs wondering which one had been David's during the four years that he had worked out of this office after graduating from William and Mary.

The oak table didn't offer any clues, but the head of the table had to be Nick's. She could tell by the position, and the chair. The back was taller; the seat, wider.

"Nothing but a throne for King Nicholas," she murmured.

She turned her attention to the portraits. All the men who had ruled the Ballenger empire were represented, going back to Lord Louis Ballenger. Most were at least borderline handsome, and all of them bore the distinctive Ballenger cleft chin—the only significant feature David and Nick had shared. The last three generations had identical blue eyes rimmed with impossibly long, thick black eyelashes, but Nick was the most handsome; his jaw was more chiseled, his features more classic. He was also the most stern, forbidding and humorless; a man who hated his life.

The insight startled Meg. It wasn't the first time she'd speculated that Nick had forgotten how to have fun—if he'd ever known—but she was a long way from feeling the slightest bit of sympathy for him. He had chosen his life, but he'd had no right to force the family business down David's throat.

Bitterness welled up all over again, and Meg turned away from the portraits. She was tired of hurting and hating, but couldn't see an end to either. She moved on to the windows that overlooked the manicured courtyard outside the lobby, and forced her mind to go blank.

"Hello, Miss Linley."

Meg whirled toward the voice, startled because she hadn't heard a door open. When she saw who it was, her surprise was displaced by the hatred that had become her constant companion. Nick Ballenger was closing a side door that Meg hadn't noticed. His suit was dark blue today, but otherwise he looked exactly as he had at the funeral—tall, handsome and as cold as stone.

He was also wearing the same arrogant self-assurance that had rattled Meg from the first moment they met in Singapore. It was an air of divine right, an expectation that the world would bow to him, and that women, most especially, would recognize and respond to his power and the sensuality that came with it.

"Do you have the hinges oiled so that you can sneak up on your employees?" The words slipped out before she could censor them, and it was the CEO who looked startled this time.

"I apologize. I didn't mean to catch you unawares."

Meg took a deep breath and reined in her anger. She had no desire for a confrontation with Nick Ballenger. "Don't apologize. There's obviously been a mistake," she said, moving quickly toward her purse and the door. "Someone put me in the wrong room."

"No, she didn't," Nick countered. "That was my secretary, Patrice Williamson. She brought you up here at my request.''

Meg stopped and glared at him. What on earth was going on? "Why? Where's Fletcher Matson?'' she demanded to know.

''Fletcher left on Monday to spend a few days with his family in Abbeville. He'll be back next week.''

''But I have a note from him.'' Meg realized it was still in her hand and she held it out to Nick. ''It was left at my hotel yesterday while I was out.''

Nick shook his head as he moved to the head of the table. "That note was my doing. Fletcher knows nothing about it. He was already gone when you called on Tuesday to mention your need for references. The message was forwarded to me.'' He placed a small stack of manila folders on the table.

''You mean *you* wrote my reference?'' Meg asked. *Great. That'll do me a world of good,* she thought sarcastically. But she was also a little relieved. Nick was just playing one of his power games with her—making her sit up, roll over and fetch before he gave her the letter of recommendation, but that's all that was going on. For a moment, when he first appeared, she'd been afraid that Fletcher had told him about the baby.

Nick pushed one of the folders across the table toward her. ''Your recommendation is in here, and I think you'll find it's quite a good one. Though I hope that you won't need it.''

''Why wouldn't I?'' Meg asked cautiously. ''I have to work somewhere, and you've obviously gleaned that I'm not returning to Singapore.''

''Fletcher told me that, yes.''

Oh, God... What else had Fletcher told him? Had she been relieved too soon? Meg picked up the folder and slipped it into her oversize purse. "Then I'm sure this will be helpful in my search for new employment."

"Actually, Miss Linley, I'm hoping that you'll accept a proposition I'm about to make."

She told herself she didn't want to hear anything Nick Ballenger had to say, but she couldn't keep from asking, "What proposition is that?"

"It's something my grandmother suggested last week," Nick replied as he stepped to Meg's side of the table and pulled out the first chair to the right of his. "Won't you have a seat, Miss Linley?"

"No, thank you. I prefer to stand." *As far away from you as I can get.*

"As you wish." Nick stepped to the head of the table once more, rested his elbows on the back of his throne and continued as though he hadn't interrupted himself. "Frankly, when Grandmother proposed the idea, I thought she'd gone round the bend. But after I had a chance to think about it—and discuss it with my lawyer, of course—I changed my mind."

"About what?" Meg asked impatiently. This meeting was taking on the same discomfiting timbre of their first encounter in Singapore, when he'd raked her over the coals without ever raising his voice or betraying so much as a flicker of emotion. He'd been perfectly calm and chillingly pleasant as he'd ripped her to shreds.

His eyes were the same cold-as-ice blue today. He reminded Meg of a hunter setting up his prey for a kill.

Nick slid another of his folders from the neat stack, but he didn't push this one toward her. "My lawyers and I have put together an agreement," he informed her. "Something eminently sensible and legally binding."

Legally binding? What reason did Nick have to want a legal agreement with her unless...

A shudder of terror rippled down Meg's spine. Fletcher had told Nick everything. And Nick's response had been to call his lawyers to figure out a quiet way to get rid of the little tramp who'd gotten knocked up by his brother.

For the first time since she'd discovered she was pregnant, a wave of shame washed over Meg, followed by a fresh wave of hatred for Nick for making her feel dirty.

"You know, don't you?" she asked, her jaw clenched tighter than her fists.

"About your pregnancy? Yes," he confirmed with a nod and a look that might have passed for sympathetic if it had come from anyone but Nick Ballenger. "Fletcher didn't want to betray your confidence, but he was deeply concerned for your well-being—and that of the baby, of course."

"Of course," Meg said sarcastically, then made a concerted effort to shove aside her anger at Fletch. She'd deal with his betrayal later. Right now she needed all of her wits to escape the trap Nick was laying for her. *Welcome to my parlor...*

"Please try not to be too angry with him," Nick was saying. "He doesn't know that I used his name to get you here. He thinks that we're going to talk to you together after he returns from Abbeville."

"Frankly, I don't care what he thinks," Meg snapped. "And I don't much care what you think, either. If Fletch told you about the baby, then he surely told you that I don't want anything from the Ballenger family. There's no need for lawyers or papers or intimidation tactics. I'm not going to cause trouble."

Nick's full lips pursed in a thoughtful frown. "It wasn't my intention to intimidate you, Miss Linley."

"Oh, please. You lured me under false pretenses into

your territory, where all the advantages are yours—including that of surprise. You knew exactly what you were doing.''

"You're right," he conceded. "But given the things Fletcher told me, I was afraid you might bolt if I contacted you outright and asked for a meeting.''

"And you couldn't wait for this alleged meeting that Fletcher thinks we're supposed to have when he gets back?'' she asked shrewdly.

Nick couldn't help but smile in appreciation. Meg Linley was one sharp lady. Even distraught, confused and angry she had the backbone to stand up to him. He wished more of his executives had her kind of guts.

He was a little puzzled, though. David's taste in women usually ran toward tall, buxom, leggy blondes who knew how to play dumb whether they were or not. This pretty young woman with hair like cornsilk spun into gold and eyes like sparkling emeralds looked as delicate as fine china, but her fire and quick wits proved that she wasn't half as fragile as she looked. Singapore had matured David even more than Nick had thought if he'd grown up enough to realize that real treasures came in packages like Megan Linley.

"Touché," he said with a gentlemanly tilt of the head. "You're absolutely right. I did want the home-field advantage. And I did want to eliminate Fletcher from this discussion. What I have to say is just between the two of us.''

The smile that had made his eyes crinkle at the corners was gone, and Meg was glad. Slapping the smirk off his face had been too tempting. "Then why don't you spit it out and get it over with?'' she suggested.

"All right." Nick picked up the folder he'd separated from the others. "This is a contract, Miss Linley, and like all good business deals, it has some points that are negotiable and some that are not."

"I won't negotiate, Mr. Ballenger, because I'm not signing anything," she told him flatly.

"Not even for the benefit of David's child?"

"You don't have to buy me off!" Meg exclaimed in frustration.

Nick very deliberately matched his tone to hers. "That is not my intention!" He quieted his voice. "If you will just hear me out."

"Then quit dancing around and tell me what you want! Get to the bottom line."

"Very well." Nick placed the contract folder on the table and extracted a tiny, black velvet ring box from his jacket pocket. He moved around the table and his quarry tensed as he flipped open the lid and glanced at the contents before turning it toward her.

Meg didn't know anything about diamond rings, but this was the most beautiful she had ever seen. And the biggest. The square center stone sparkled as though lit by some inner fire, and a tier of sets around it glittered like stars.

It must have cost a fortune, she thought as her stomach turned sickeningly.

"What is this? A bribe to get rid of me?"

Nick sighed patiently. "No, Miss Linley. It is not a bribe. It's a proposal. If you are, indeed, pregnant, and the child is, indeed, a Ballenger, he will be raised as such. But he will *not,* under any circumstance, suffer the stigma of illegitimacy."

Meg looked at him incredulously. "Then just what, *indeed,* are you suggesting?"

"An alliance. For the good of David's child." He

took the ring from the box and held it out to her. "We're getting married, Miss Linley. Temporarily."

Meg stared at him. That handsome face with its cold blue eyes stared back expectantly, and the brittle core of grief at the center of her soul snapped. Grief over losing the man she loved, over the knowledge that her child would never know its father, over the loss of the life she and David could have built together, all bubbled up and boiled over.

Nick Ballenger was making a mockery of her grief, and in that moment Meg hated him more than she'd ever thought it was possible for her to hate.

"You're insane," she said, sneering.

"I assure you, I'm not," Nick replied calmly. "I made some discreet inquiries among David's friends and colleagues in Singapore. It was their unanimous opinion that my brother was very much in love with you. Marriage had even been discussed, according to one of my sources. Is that true?"

Meg only glared at him. "Go to hell. My relationship with David is none of your business!"

She whirled to leave, but Nick grabbed her arm and spun her back toward him. The cold calm in his eyes had been replaced by something harder and hotter. "Your relationship with my brother is very much my business if you're carrying his child. Now, *are* you pregnant, Miss Linley, or were you just playing mind games with Fletcher?"

Meg snatched her arm out of his grasp. He towered over her looking stern and forbidding, but she held her ground. "I don't play games. That's your favorite pastime, not mine."

"Then you are pregnant."

She wasn't about to deny it because doing so would

have meant denying the only part of David she had left.
"Yes."

"And what do you plan to do about it?"

"Have my baby and raise it as far away from you as
possible!"

Nick shook his head as he placed the engagement ring
back into its box and snapped the lid closed. "No, Miss
Linley. You will not. That's your anger talking. Fletcher
says you blame me for David's death. I certainly don't
hold that against you, but for some reason you also per-
ceive me as a threat, and in that you are very much
mistaken. Why would I want to bring harm to the only
thing I have left of my brother?"

"To save your precious family from scandal."

"This is a tragedy, not a scandal," Nick argued. "If
word got out that David died just minutes before learning that the woman he loved was carrying his child, the
press would be nothing but sympathetic."

"Then why would you propose something as ludicrous as a…a marriage?" She could barely bring herself
to say the word.

"Sympathetic or not, the society in which David and
I were raised still brands its illegitimate children with
the mark of scorn. They're never treated quite the same
as other children. Marriage to me is the only way to
assure that this child will have the best opportunities in
life." Nick backed away from Meg, cooling the heated
air between them.

He placed the velvet ring box on top of the contract
folder and moved toward the massive windows, his
voice calm and dispassionate as he explained, "Miss
Linley, I have every reason to believe that if David had
lived, he would have married you and used the impending birth as leverage to convince me to allow him to

come back to Charleston. David would have brought you to Ballenger Hall and proudly introduced you to his family and Charleston society. He would have supported you through your pregnancy and made certain that you had the finest prenatal care money can buy. When your child was born, it would have come into the world with all the prestige, privilege, tradition and power that attend the Ballenger name. And it would have been blessed with two parents who loved it beyond measure.

"That child could have had anything in the world, Miss Linley. *Been* anything. Done anything. Achieved anything."

Nick turned and found that his portrait of what could have been had reduced Megan Linley to tears. She was standing rigidly upright, glaring at him with pride and defiance, but the horrible pain in her eyes made Nick realize that there was someone in this world whose grief was as deep as his own. He had an odd, incomprehensible urge to go to her and comfort her, and to find comfort in sharing their pain, but he knew better than to try it. She didn't want his comfort, and he didn't deserve hers.

And besides, it didn't fit in with the strategy he'd plotted out. Instead, he remained a safe, impassive distance away, trying to ignore the tender feelings that curled inside him as Megan found her voice.

"Is there a point to this, or are you just trying to see how much more pain you can cause me?" Her voice was ragged with emotion.

"I don't mean to cause you pain," Nick replied gently. "But I do have a point. You see, I don't have any children, Miss Linley. Nor do I ever expect to. In essence, the child you're carrying, be it male or female, is the sole heir to the Ballenger fortune."

Meg glared at him defiantly. "And you think that matters to me?"

"It should," Nick said, coming closer to her. "What loving, devoted mother wouldn't want that kind of advantage for her child?"

"Is that what you're offering? The advantages of wealth and privilege?"

Nick nodded. "Yes."

"At what price? I give you David's child in exchange for a fat financial settlement?"

Nick tensed. "Is that all it would take?"

Nick's instincts told him that if he'd been closer, she would have slapped his face. "I won't give you my child for *any* price."

He relaxed. She was either a smart negotiator or a good mother, and he still chose to believe the latter. "What *are* you willing to do for your child, Miss Linley?" he asked her.

She opened her mouth as though to give him a quick retort, but apparently she realized the trap he'd laid. Nick had hoped she'd swear her willingness to do anything for her child. Instead, she shook her head.

"I have a better question, Mr. Ballenger," she countered, wiping at the moisture on her cheeks, her composure regained.

Nick spread his hands in invitation. "By all means, ask it."

"What *are* you willing to do for the Ballenger heir?"

"I thought I made that clear. I'm willing to do everything my brother would have done for this child—including legitimizing his claim to the Ballenger name and fortune by marrying his mother."

She'd been outraged the first time he mentioned marriage; now she merely looked distrustful. "You want to marry me?"

"I want David's child to grow up confident and secure. I want him to know his place in the world, and I most emphatically do not want him to bear the stigma of being a bastard. The only way to accomplish that is for you to marry a Ballenger. Regrettably, I am the only one available."

Meg's gaze was locked with Nick's. "Yes. Regrettably," she echoed, and almost smiled with satisfaction when he looked away.

He didn't give ground long, though. A second later he met her gaze again. "Well? Are you at least willing to hear my offer?"

Meg couldn't believe it, but she was. The whole idea was outrageous. Ludicrous. Unthinkable. But it was also the only possible way to give her child everything that David would have wanted him to have—well, everything except a father who loved him. But that was lost to her child whether she married Nick or not.

All she had to give David's baby was love, and Meg wasn't so naive as to believe that love was all it took to raise a child. She understood poverty only too well, and she knew what it was like to grow up as an outcast, having people look down their noses at her; never feeling worthy and not knowing why.

She would do anything in the world to spare her child that pain and confusion. But could she really marry a man she despised?

For her child's sake, she had to at least consider the possibility. "What if I don't like your offer?" she asked.

Nick shrugged. "We'll negotiate."

"And if I still refuse?"

Nick paused a fraction of a second, calculating his

options. What would she respond to? A good guy who swore he had only the best interests of her and the child at heart, or a ruthless bully who would do whatever it took to get his way?

As much as she obviously hated him, it seemed unlikely that she'd buy Nick as a benefactor. She was already afraid of him; his best chance for success was to use that fear.

"Then I'll hire a battery of private detectives to dig into your life and find out everything there is to know about you, Miss Linley," he threatened in the coldest, most calculating manner in his arsenal of negotiating stances. "And when they're done, I'll turn over their findings to my lawyers and let them tear you to shreds in court. By the time I get finished, I'll have sole custody of David's child and you'll be lucky if you get one court-supervised visit a year."

The terror that flickered through her eyes was there and gone so quickly that Nick almost missed it. She believed that he could do it—that he *would* do it, take her child away from her. But did she think it was because he had power and political clout in Charleston, or because there was something in her past he could use against her to prove she would be an unfit mother?

He couldn't tell which, but he had to admire the way she refused to give in to her fear. Nick had sat across the bargaining table from seasoned businessmen who couldn't control their emotions half as well as Megan Linley.

Her chin was up, her fear was buried, and she was ready to do battle. "You're not going to bully me into doing something I don't want to do," she swore.

Nick regarded her calmly. "You asked for a worst-case scenario, Miss Linley. You wanted to know how far I would go if you refused to negotiate. Now you know. I have no intention of being cut out of this child's life, and if destroying you is the only way I have of watching my niece or nephew grow up, then by God, I'll destroy you. Don't think I won't.''

It was clear from the fear in her eyes that she believed him. It was also clear that she hated him more than she had when he'd come through the door. If she did agree to marry him, Nick was going to have a devil of a time proving to his wife that he wasn't a monster.

He wondered if he was a good enough actor to pull it off.

''Well? Shall we start negotiating?'' he suggested.

Meg looked at the contract folder on the table. ''This is it? Your deal?''

He touched his fingertips to the edge of the manila folder and slid it across the table to her. The black velvet ring box went along for the ride.

Her hand was trembling as she reached for the folder, and a sickening wave of self-hatred washed through Nick for having created a fear that deep. When she picked up the folder, the box rolled quietly onto the polished oak table like a spotless black die.

''Why don't we sit down and discuss the terms of the contract,'' he suggested, pulling out his chair.

''No, thank you. I can read a contract without your help, Mr. Ballenger, and if I have any problems interpreting the fine print I'll let my own attorney explain it to me.''

Though it wasn't the answer Nick wanted, his respect for her went up another notch. Her instincts were telling her to get away from him so that she could consider the offer without being bullied or manipulated. Nick could have found a way to stop her, to force her to go over the contract point by point with him, but he didn't. He'd abused her enough for one day.

"Very well," he said, easing his chair back up to the table. "When do you anticipate having an answer for me?"

"I'll call you tomorrow," Meg replied.

Nick had given up something, now he had to get something back to reassert his control of the situation. "I have a better suggestion, if I may offer it. David's grandmother wants to meet you, Miss Linley. Why don't you come to Ballenger Hall for supper tomorrow night? You can meet Nan, and then you and I can retire to the study afterward to discuss the contract."

Meg regarded him hesitantly. "She knows about the baby?"

"Yes. As I said before, the idea of a marriage of convenience was hers."

Nick could see the wheels turning as she thought it over. It was a moment before she finally made a counteroffer. "I'll come to the house and meet her, but dinner is a little too...civilized for these circumstances. After dinner," she suggested.

"All right," he conceded, wondering if she was a trained negotiator or a natural-born one. A good businessman never accepted any offer without revision, and the negotiator who made the last concession was generally considered to be the loser.

That's why Nick reasserted control again, and this time didn't offer her a choice. "I'll send a car to your hotel to pick you up at eight."

"That won't be necessary. I can find my way there without your help."

Nick looked at her with a touch of impatience. "It's a courtesy, Miss Linley. Accepting my gesture doesn't diminish you or your bargaining position."

"No, but it seems to irritate you, so I'll stick with saying thanks, but no thanks." A ghost of something that might have been a smile played around her lips and Nick realized that if she ever turned that smile loose she could go from "pretty" to "irresistible" in a heartbeat.

Nick resigned himself to losing this round. He spread his hands and gave a small, courtly bow. "As you wish. I'll look forward to seeing you again tomorrow night."

She didn't bother with a reply, but moved off to the door with such purpose that Nick felt confident their meeting had ended. She surprised him when she turned back and looked at him hesitantly. "This agreement we're talking about," she began, holding up the contract folder. "It would be a marriage in name only, right?"

Nick nodded, but found himself strangely reluctant to answer. "Of course. I'm not asking you to sell yourself or your child, Miss Linley."

"Just so we understand that from the start."

"We do."

"Then you'll have my answer tomorrow."

She turned and left Nick standing at the head of the big oak table.

He reached out and picked up the velvet ring box— the first of several tests David's lover had passed this afternoon. She hadn't even given the enormous rock a second glance.

"Your Megan is quite a woman, little brother. What I wouldn't give to bring her back to you," Nick whispered.

A band of pain constricted his heart as he felt his brother's absence as keenly as he'd ever felt his presence. Was David somewhere looking down at him with approval? Nick wondered.

Or was he damning him to hell?

CHAPTER FOUR

MEG READ and reread Nick's marriage contract detached from the reality of what she was contemplating.

In some respects it wasn't a bad deal at all. She and Nick would be married in a quiet civil ceremony, after which Meg would move into her own quarters at Ballenger Hall, separate but adjacent to Nick's. All her medical expenses would be paid, and after the baby was born, she would continue to live with Nick for a minimum of three years, at which time they would begin a legal separation.

As terms of the separation and subsequent divorce, Meg would receive a fully furnished and staffed home, plus a trust that would give her a lifetime income of a hundred and twenty thousand dollars a year regardless of her subsequent marital status. An equivalent irrevocable trust would be established for the baby but would remain under Nick's control until the child's twenty-first birthday. In addition, all decisions regarding education would rest solely with Nick.

A vague morality clause enjoined Meg from engaging in any illegal or immoral behavior, but the only real restriction placed on her life after the divorce was the single requirement that she could never take the child out of the state without Nick's knowledge and permission.

There was also one final clause that had the power to

supersede all the others. In lieu of alimony and a home in Charleston, Meg could, at any time within a year of the birth, opt for a single payment of ten million dollars and leave the city permanently so long as she vacated her parental rights, turning the baby over to Nick entirely.

No bargaining, no negotiation, just cold cash and a quick getaway.

Meg was rational enough to appreciate the finesse of the contract's construction. Nick was hoping she'd jump at the idea of a quick settlement, but he'd placed that clause last, giving it the appearance of an afterthought so that Meg wouldn't be outraged at the insinuation that she was nothing more than a common tramp who would sell her child.

The cash offer wasn't even worth thinking about, but as for the rest, Meg had learned enough about dealmaking to know that Nick had salted the contract with bargaining chips. There was plenty of room for give-and-take, but the bottom line was that she could raise her child in the city David loved and never have a single worry about the baby's financial future. With interest and careful investments, her child would be independently wealthy—a millionaire several times over—by the time he graduated from college.

There was just one catch in an otherwise perfectly workable arrangement. The contract stipulated joint custody. The exact timing would be determined later, but each parent would have "possession" of the child six months of the year. And while Meg was prevented from leaving Charleston without Nick's permission, she was granted no similar privilege. In fact, the contract was worded so that it gave Nick generous visitation rights

while the child was in Meg's custody without any reciprocal provisions for her.

A sixth sense told Meg that this was Nick's deal-
breaker. It was the one point on which he wouldn't negotiate.

Well, neither would Meg. She had no intention of giving the Ballengers that much control of her child. She
might consider allowing them to hold the reins to his
financial future and his education but Nick wasn't going
to take her child away from her six months a year and
use that time to poison his mind against her.

She couldn't agree to the contract under those terms.
But she couldn't reject Nick's offer, either, and it didn't
have anything to do with financial security or custody
rights. The real bottom line was Nick's threat. If Meg
didn't agree to marry him, he'd start digging for anything he could find that would prove Meg was an unfit
mother.

If he dug deep enough, he'd find a gold mine.

With the Ballengers' wealth and political influence,
they'd have an advantage in court even if Meg's past
was as pure as the driven snow—which it wasn't, not
by a long shot. No judge would give custody of a baby
to trailer trash like Meg Linley if the truth came out.
Rejecting Nick's offer and forcing him to take her to
court would be Meg's quickest route to losing her child.

On the other hand, if she gave Nick what he wanted,
he might not dig into her past. He was so anxious to
avoid a scandal that he was willing to marry a woman
he knew despised him. If she was reasonable and could
carry off the pretense that she had nothing in her past to
be afraid of, Nick would have no reason to sic private
detectives on her. She would be at his mercy for the next
twenty years. Her life would be one long compromise

with Nick calling the shots, but it would be worth it if it meant giving her child a sense of his own worth and his place in the world.

She could make that sacrifice, couldn't she? Wouldn't David *want* her to make it?

For the next twenty-four hours, Meg thought, prayed and pored over the contract, plugging up loopholes, planning strategies and drafting counteroffers that were three layers deep. By the following night, she had made her decision. If Nick agreed to her minimum requirements, she would marry him.

But not once did she allow herself to think realistically about how she could live under the same roof as a man she detested.

THROUGHOUT HER COURTSHIP with David, Meg had formed a formidable image of Eleanor Tate Ballenger as a great and grand lady, the perfect high-society matron who was as cold and remote as a marble statue.

Meeting Eleanor that next night did nothing to change Meg's preconception. Fetridge, the Irish-immigrant butler who was half of the husband-and-wife team that had been with the family for forty years, showed Meg into "Mr. Nick's study" where he said "the family" was waiting. Nick rose from his chair behind the desk, taking command of the room, filling it with his presence in a way that irritated Meg immensely. Eleanor remained seated in one of the two high-backed leather wing chairs. Fetridge disappeared, Nick welcomed her and performed the introductions.

"It's nice to finally meet you, Mrs. Ballenger." Meg prayed that her voice sounded steady. She knew a lot about fear, but couldn't recall ever having been frightened in quite the same way as she was tonight. "David told me so much about you."

"I wish I could say the same," Eleanor replied, looking her over from head to toe with a detached disdain that made Meg feel like an indentured servant on the auction block.

"So do I," Meg managed to reply. "It would make this meeting much easier for both of us."

"I've discovered that very few things in life are easy, Miss Linley."

"Please have a seat, Miss—may I call you Megan?" She nodded. "And please call me Nick," he said, giving a serious thought to strangling his grandmother. Couldn't she see how nervous Megan was? How much she wanted Eleanor's approval? The pretty young woman was impeccably dressed in a plain gray business suit and low-heeled pumps. Her hair was pulled away from her heart-shaped face into a loose but carefully tamed bun. Her jewelry was inexpensive but tasteful, and her makeup flawlessly done.

It was obvious that she'd put a great deal of thought and care into her appearance because she'd wanted to make a good impression. Since she loathed him, the effort certainly hadn't been made for his benefit. She was trying to be someone Eleanor would approve of. Couldn't Nan see that and unbend just a little?

Of course not. That would be like asking winter not to come.

"May I get you something to drink?" he offered.

"No, thank you." Meg settled into the chair that mirrored Eleanor's and prayed that her heart would stop pounding so ferociously.

"Did you have any trouble finding us?" Nick asked solicitously.

"No," she answered. "Ballenger Hall is highlighted in all the guidebooks. It would be hard to miss." She didn't add that she had walked by the elegant old three-story white brick Georgian mansion several times while exploring the historic district. The brick-and-wrought-iron fence draped in wisteria had prevented her from seeing more than tiny slivers of the ground floor and gardens, but that hadn't kept her from detouring by the house every time she was in the neighborhood.

"Nan and I have been discussing opening the house to the public during the fall historic-homes tour," Nick said pleasantly as he returned to his chair behind the desk.

"It's a great bother, but David always thought it was important," Eleanor explained. "We haven't participated since he went to Singapore."

He didn't just *go* to Singapore, he was *sent, banished,* Meg wanted to remind her, but in the interest of maintaining the peace, she let it pass.

"That would be a fitting tribute," she said, not allowing herself to become emotional. "Sharing the history of Ballenger Hall was one of David's favorite things."

Nick nodded. "Yes. It was. I always told him he would have made a great museum curator."

But instead you forced him to become a businessman and he hated it. Meg bit her tongue again and managed to confine her response to a simple statement of truth. "David was proud of his heritage."

"Unfortunately, he chose a rather inauspicious way of honoring it," Eleanor said, her voice loaded with enough frost to turn the room into a meat locker.

Meg felt as though she'd been slapped. "I guess this means the pleasantries are over," she muttered.

Eleanor inclined her head. "I beg your pardon?"

"Nothing." Meg squared her shoulders and got ready to do battle. Actually, she'd expected Nick to fire the first shot, but this didn't surprise her. He conducted meetings the way a general conducts a battle—letting his lieutenants go in first to sniff out the enemies' weaknesses. "Let's get down to business," she suggested.

Eleanor's delicately arched eyebrows went up in affected surprise. "Is that what this child is to you, Miss Linley? Business?"

"That's what you and Nick have made him," Meg retorted. She'd wanted this meeting to be polite and civilized, but if Eleanor wanted to take the gloves off, Meg was only too happy to oblige. "This marriage contract wasn't my idea, Mrs. Ballenger—it was yours. If you've changed your mind about meddling in how and where I choose to raise my child, I'll be only too happy to leave."

"I don't think anything has changed, Megan," Nick said, his tone conciliatory. "And I don't believe my grandmother meant her comment as an attack. These last two weeks have been difficult for all of us." Nick cocked one eyebrow in Eleanor's direction expectantly.

She looked completely unrepentant. "Nicholas, darlin', I have no intention of apologizing to you or to Miss Linley. This young lady's situation is not of my making, and I have every right to question her motives."

"I had no *motive* for becoming pregnant, Mrs. Ballenger, but I'm not sorry," Meg retorted, unable to hide her irritation. "And I have every reason to believe that David would have been thrilled, too."

Eleanor regarded her so calmly that Meg's comment seemed like a hysterical outburst in comparison. "I presume you're referring to the marriage proposal supposedly tendered to you by my younger grandson."

Meg nodded. "David had asked me to marry him. We'd discussed it several times, actually."

"But you hadn't agreed to wed?"

"No." Meg looked down and smoothed the hem of her skirt over her knees.

"Why not?" Eleanor asked. "By all accounts, the two of you were very much in love..."

Meg looked up and met the old woman's cold gaze evenly. "I was afraid you wouldn't like me. That you wouldn't think I was good enough to marry your grandson."

Apparently, honesty didn't mean a great deal to Eleanor. She waved one hand as though clearing the air of it. "I'm afraid the circumstances have rendered that issue moot. You are here and your claim that you carry David's child must be addressed. Are you prepared to do the right thing and marry Nicholas?"

Well, that was blunt. "No. But I am prepared to discuss the terms of his contract," Meg countered. "I want one thing understood, though. I didn't ask for anything from you people, and I wouldn't be sitting here now if I had a choice."

"Megan, there are always choices," Nick told her.

"You've threatened to take me to court and you've got enough money to buy any verdict you want," Meg said. "Marry you or lose my child. Some choice."

"Why don't we focus on the positive, not the negative," Nick suggested. "You have a lot to gain from marriage, Megan. And even more for your child. Legitimacy, social position, financial security... Those are the things you should concentrate on."

"Oh, I have considered them," she assured Nick. "You've dangled some sparkly carrots in front of my nose, and if I walk away I'll look like the worst mother in the world.''

''Then you're looking favorably on the marriage contract,'' he adjudged.

''It's a very generous offer—if I'm nothing more than a gold digger out to make a quick buck. But since I have no intention of selling you my child, we're a long way from reaching any type of agreement.''

Nick opened a leather folder in front of him. ''I look forward to hearing your suggestions,'' he said by way of invitation.

Meg darted a quick glance in Eleanor's direction, but the dowager showed no signs of getting up to leave. Apparently, she considered herself part of the contract. Meg tried not to let it rattle her.

''All right. We'll start where you're hoping I'll start.''

''Where's that?'' Nick prompted.

She opened the notebook that contained all her notes, and balanced it across her lap. ''With the question of alimony.''

A small frown dug a furrow between Nick's black eyebrows. ''What about it?''

She met his stern gaze placidly. ''All payments to me will terminate on the child's twenty-first birthday.''

Nick's countenance went from stern to astonished to mildly amused. ''I don't think you understand how this process works, Megan. You negotiate for *more* benefits, not fewer.''

''I know exactly what I'm doing, so you'd better take this while you can get it,'' she replied. ''Because it's the only thing I'm giving up. The rest of the concessions will be yours.''

The threat didn't sit well with Nick. ''You think so?'' he asked with a dangerous edge to his voice.

Meg knew better than to flinch. He was trying to intimidate her. "I know so."

"And if I don't agree to your concessions?"

She met his hard-edged glare evenly. "I'll walk out of here and go to the first abortion clinic I can find." Meg heard a sharp intake of breath from Eleanor's direction, but she didn't take her eyes off Nick.

"You would do that?" he asked her.

"In a heartbeat," she promised, fully aware that she'd only sworn to go to the clinic, not to have an abortion. She could never terminate David's child, but it was important that Nick not know that.

Apparently, he bought the bluff. "Why don't you outline these concessions I'm supposed to make," he suggested. "We'll see if we can reach a compromise that won't force you to do anything drastic."

Meg tried not to look relieved by her temporary victory. She consulted her list. "All right. We'll start simple. I'll agree to the education clause if you'll stipulate no military academies, prep schools or other institutions that require the child to board away from home."

"Fair enough." Nick made a note on his copy of the contract.

"And the morality clause goes."

He looked up from his writing, clearly searching for some sign of weakness. "You have something to be concerned about?"

Meg shrugged. "I'm pregnant and unmarried. If you decide to use that clause against me, what more ammunition would you need? Besides, we both know that it's virtually unenforceable. Unless you're willing to define exactly what you mean by 'proper moral standards' and apply them equally to yourself in all respects, the clause has to go."

Nick drew a diagonal line across the bottom of one page and turned to another. "Score two for Miss Linley." He looked at her expectantly. "Next?"

"The length-of-marriage clause. Three years after the baby's birth is absurd. I'll agree to three *months*, but no more."

Nick shook his head. "Two years."

"This isn't an auction."

"No, it's a negotiation. You give a little and get a little, remember? I won't agree to looking like a bastard for divorcing my wife and a three-month-old baby."

Meg paused a moment, letting Nick think she was reconsidering, when actually she had known he would object and already had her counteroffer planned.

"Well, what about this...?" she began thoughtfully. "I'll stay married to you and live in Ballenger Hall for six months after the birth, then move out. The terms of legal separation will go into effect, but I won't file for divorce for another two years—or until you give your consent, whichever comes first. If appearances are so important to you, this will allow you to claim that we're trying to work things out."

Nick was silent and completely unreadable for a long moment, then he nodded his head. "All right. Six months."

Hallelujah! Her first real victory. This might work out, after all.... She tried not to let her exultation show.

"As to custody... First and foremost, everything has to be reciprocal. If I can't take the baby out of the state without your permission, the same has to apply to you."

Nick nodded. "That's fair." He made another note.

"You won't think this is. For the first three years, I have sole custody," Meg said, diving headlong into the issue that was going to make or break the negotiations.

"I don't want my child bouncing around from one address to another."

"That's absurd," Eleanor finally interjected herself into the negotiations. "You can't deny Nicholas access to the child for that length of time—studies show that the first three years of a child's life are the most formative."

"Really?" Meg swung her attention away from Nick for the first time. "How much did you see of your son the first three years of his life?"

The sharp retort caught Eleanor completely by surprise. "I don't know what that has to do with anything," she said haughtily.

"According to David, he and Nick were raised almost exclusively by servants and a succession of nannies, following the tradition you established with their father," Meg explained. "Why should I give a nanny custody of my child for six months out of a year?"

Nick intervened. "I have no intention of forfeiting my parental influence to servants, Megan. You should be very clear on this—I plan to be more than a father in name only."

Meg swung back on him. "Then that's an even better reason to oppose the terms of the custody agreement."

Eleanor gasped. "Miss Linley!"

"Grandmother—don't," Nick cautioned her, his voice quiet and calm. "We can't blame Megan for having a low opinion of me. I wasn't very kind or fair to her at our first meeting in Singapore, and I didn't give her any reason to see me in a different light yesterday."

"Still, considering your generous offer—"

"There's nothing generous about this offer, Mrs. Ballenger," Meg argued. She wasn't about to let anyone cast her in the role of a beggar accepting the largesse of the great and noble Ballenger family. "You're not *giving* me anything. If you could find a cheap, scandal-free way to take this baby away from me and pretend I never existed, you'd do it in a flash. Let's at least be honest about that."

Meg had the sudden sensation that she had ceased to exist. Eleanor looked blankly past Meg, then focused on her grandson as she rose slowly. "I think I should leave these negotiations to you, Nicholas. You seem better able to deal with Miss Linley without evoking emotional outbursts. I do hope you'll keep me apprised if you come to an agreement."

"Of course, Nan." Nick rose as well and escorted his grandmother to the door. Meg watched them go, feeling that she should apologize but not knowing how. She was in the middle of a game with stakes higher than anything she could have imagined, and despite all of Eleanor's pretentiousness, the haughty old dowager wasn't really a part of the game.

Meg let her go without comment and waited until Nick had closed the door behind her. "I just made an enemy, didn't I?"

Nick shrugged as he returned to his desk. "Possibly. Though she may come to respect you for standing up to her."

"I can't worry about that now," Meg said, letting go of her concerns about Eleanor. "I do want to apologize to you, though. What I said about your desire to be a real parent—I shouldn't have said that. It was cruel."

Nick sat and leaned back in his chair. "For what it's worth, Megan, I won't ever fault you for speaking your mind. I'll take honesty over hypocrisy any day of the week."

Meg actually believed he meant it. An unwanted feeling of warmth for Nick began to unfurl within her. "Then I'll be honest with you," she told him. "If you genuinely want to be a father to this child, to provide him with love and emotional support, I won't do anything to impede that."

Nick tilted his head to one side, studying her closely, struck once again by how deceptively delicate she looked. He was assaulted by an image of her as she would appear months from now, seriously pregnant, radiantly beautiful. The protective urge that swept through him was as powerful as any emotion he'd ever felt.

"You really mean that?" he asked her.

Meg nodded, astonished to find that she did. "David loved you. He used to tell me that when you weren't being an arrogant son of a bitch you were the best man he knew. If you want to show that side of your personality to this child, I won't do anything to stand in the way."

"Considering how much you obviously hate me, that's very generous of you."

"I don't want to hate you, Nick," she said quietly. "Maybe someday when I've worked through the grief and the anger..."

She let the thought trail off, but Nick understood.

"You'll be able to forgive me for causing David's death?"

She nodded. "Yes."

Nick looked down at his leather folder and flipped to a new page. "Well, when you figure out how to do that, Megan, please let me know," he said, distancing himself from Megan and his own emotions. "I'll be more than a little interested in learning the technique. Now, shall we get back to custody? Three years without joint custody is unacceptable," he informed her, bringing the conversation back to formal battle positions. He looked at her. "I hope you have a fallback position."

Meg collected her thoughts and her emotions, but it wasn't easy. Nick's admission of guilt had taken her by surprise, as did the distance he had just placed between them. "I don't have a counteroffer and I won't compromise. We're not going to pass this baby back and forth like a football," she said flatly. "Bonding is too important during those years."

She could see Nick about to protest and went on quickly, "However, in exchange for maintaining the child in *my* home, I'll give you unrestricted visitation. If you want to stop by and give him his bath every night or read him a bedtime story, that's up to you."

"That's generous, but it's not the same as being able to walk up the stairs of my own home and kiss my son good-night," Nick said.

David's son! Meg wanted to shout. The warmth she'd begun to feel for Nick had vanished, but she kept calm. "Maybe not, but it's the most I'm willing to concede for those first three years."

Nick cocked his head to one side and regarded her curiously. "If you're amenable to putting up with me on a daily basis, why not just agree to stay married for three years?"

Meg bit her tongue, counted to five and weighed her answer carefully. "I don't mean to question your good intentions, Nick, but I seriously doubt that you'll be making a daily commitment to *David's* child."

"You think the more difficult you make it, the less likely I'll be to put up with the obstacles?" he asked suspiciously.

Meg shook her head. "No obstacles, Nick, other than

the distance between two Charleston addresses. I swear. I don't want to be difficult. Just realistic.''

He tented his fingers as he leaned back in his chair, deep in thought. "If I agree to your proposal, what happens after the first three years?'' he asked finally.

"I'll agree to joint custody. But for only three months a year, not six. And your twelve weeks will be taken in increments of one week a month, with your visitation in the alternate time limited to twice a week. Plus, I'll have at least one visit during each week that you have custody. When he gets older, I can foresee working out other arrangements—longer blocks of time, vacations out of the state, things of that nature.''

"But only a week a month until then," he said skeptically.

Meg could see that he wasn't going to go for it. "This is my child, not yours," she reminded him.

"But the whole purpose of this marriage is to keep anyone from knowing that," Nick countered. "By establishing myself as the father, I'm assuming the full parental rights that David would have enjoyed.''

"Three months a year is a typical and acceptable custody arrangement in divorce settlements.''

"But it's not acceptable to me," he said with a deep frown cutting furrows into his forehead.

"Four months. In twelve weekly increments plus one full month every year, providing I have unrestricted visitation—daily if I choose.''

Meg held her breath as Nick thought it over. *God, what am I doing?* she almost cried aloud. She hadn't intended to give away so much. Was she going to hate herself for this someday? Worse, would her child hate her for the deal she was forging on his behalf? Should she walk out now and take her chances in court?

No, she had no chance in court. It was compromise or lose everything.

"All right, Megan. Four months a year."

Something that wasn't quite relief ebbed through her. "And my other conditions? You'll agree to those, as well?"

Nick glanced over his notes. "I don't see anything here that I can't live with." He looked at her for a long, long moment and everything grew still as though all the air had suddenly been sucked out of the room. "Well... It would seem that we're getting married," he said almost to himself.

Meg could barely breathe. "I suppose so."

They stared at each other through the long silence. Nick finally broke it. "Funny. This should be a moment for celebration."

"How can it be when we both know that it's David I should be marrying?"

"True enough." Nick closed his contract folder and stood up. "My lawyer will revise the agreement and have it ready for you to sign by Monday afternoon."

"Fine." Meg closed her own notebook as Nick came around his desk.

"Tell me something, Megan. Where did you learn your negotiation skills?" he asked with something resembling a faint, friendly smile on his lips.

"From you."

He looked astounded. "Me?"

Meg nodded. "Every night before David went into any kind of negotiation, you'd call and talk strategy."

Nick grunted and his smile turned sardonic as he remembered. "Over the speakerphone."

"Yes. It was very educational."

He chuckled darkly. "No wonder some of your negotiation moves seemed so familiar.'' When Meg didn't comment, Nick rested one hip on the edge of the desk and changed the subject. ''I suppose we should discuss wedding arrangements...''

Meg shook her head. That was one obscenity more than she could bear. ''I'll leave that up to you. Given the circumstances, there's no reason to make a fuss. City hall would be fine with me.''

''Actually, I'd prefer something less impersonal, if you don't mind,'' Nick countered. ''A small, quiet ceremony here in the garden a week from Saturday. Would that be acceptable to you?''

Meg hesitated. ''Define small.''

''Fifteen or twenty relatives and family friends.''

She nodded. ''All right.''

''What about you? Is there anyone on your side of the family you'd like to invite? Parents, siblings...?''

''I don't have anyone,'' Meg replied tersely, hoping he wouldn't pursue the subject. There was no way he'd want any of *her* family at his fancy dog and pony show.

''Friends?''

Meg hesitated. It would have meant the world to her to have Dr. Holmby and his wife here. They were back in Missouri now, retired, with plenty of time on their hands. If she called, they'd be only too happy to come.

But they both knew about her relationship with David and she didn't think she could bear to see the disappointment in their eyes when they learned what she was doing and why.

It would be better to go it alone. ''I've been out of the country for so long that I really don't have any friends on this side of the world,'' she told Nick after the moment of hesitation.

''What about Fletcher?'' he asked.

A flash of anger rippled through her. "That traitor? You can invite him if you want, but don't seat him on the bride's side."

Nick frowned at her. "I hope you'll reconsider that, Megan. Fletcher only did what he thought David would have wanted him to do. He threw the ball into my court, and it's not his fault if I've handled things less than tactfully."

"He betrayed my confidence," Meg argued. "Would you trust a friend like that?"

That sardonic half smile played around Nick's lips again. "Probably not, but I have a feeling you're a better person than I am."

"Thank you," Meg said somewhat dubiously. Considering her opinion of his character, it wasn't much of a compliment. She gathered up her purse and notebook, and started to rise. "I think I should go now. You'll want to let your grandmother know what we've decided."

Nick came to his feet, and the movement had the desired effect of forcing Meg to ease back into the chair. "In good time," he said. "There are one or two final items we need to clarify first."

All of Meg's senses went on alert. "Such as?"

"Things that I couldn't put into writing," he answered, easing back onto his desk perch. "I'm sure you noticed that the contract was worded very carefully."

Meg nodded. "There was no mention of David at all. You wanted it to have the appearance of being a prenuptial agreement."

"That's right. If, God forbid, the contract should ever be made public, at worst it will appear that you and I entered into a marriage because I had gotten you pregnant and wanted to provide for you and my child."

"I understood your intent when I read the contract," Meg replied.

"Then you have no qualms about making a verbal commitment."

"To what?"

"For one thing, a pregnancy test," he answered. "Purely as a matter of formality. You need to get started on your prenatal vitamins, and—"

"And you need to be certain you're not buying swampland in Florida."

Nick inclined his head deferentially. "You really were paying attention to my lessons in business negotiation," he said lightly. "If it's all right with you, I'll make an appointment on Monday—"

"I've already seen an OB-GYN," Meg interrupted him. "Dr. Robert Michaelson."

Nick nodded. "I know him. He's one of the best in the city. If you don't mind asking him to release his records to me, we can skip the trip to my family physician."

"I'll go by his office Monday morning," she assured him. "What else?"

He hesitated. It was only a fraction of a second, but it was long enough for Meg to know she wasn't going to like what he was about to say. "The birth certificate. I want it made perfectly clear that I'll be named as the father, not David."

The other shoe fell with a sickening thud.

Meg hadn't even thought of the birth certificate. Falsifying it was more than perpetrating a legal lie. Nick was asking her to deny David entirely—to herself, to his family, to the world, to the law, and most especially to the child himself. If Megan agreed, David's child would never know any father but Nick. The wonderful, kind, loving man who had given him life would be just a vague notion—his Uncle David who had died before he was born.

The price was too high.

"No," Meg said, shaking her head emphatically as she fought back tears. "I won't agree to that."

"Megan, our contract is a private document that can be kept confidential for as long as you and I agree to do so, but the birth certificate is a matter of public record. If it doesn't bear my name, we might as well tear up the contract right now because the truth will come out some-day."

Meg rose. "Then tear up the contract. I won't agree."

Nick came to his feet, towering over her. "Then what, exactly, did you think you were agreeing to in the first place?"

Meg refused to back down or be intimidated. "A public appearance of propriety that would keep my child from openly being labeled a bastard. But I never intended that the truth would be kept from him. I assumed that when he got old enough to understand, we would tell him about David."

"Well, you assumed incorrectly," Nick said flatly. "You can't have it both ways, Meg. If you agree to marry me, this becomes *my* child. And if you *don't* agree, I'll see you in court."

Meg tossed her head defiantly. "What good will court do you? You'll make his parentage a matter of public record and a national scandal at the same time. The baby would know who his father is eventually, no matter what lies you tell him."

"But you won't be around to see that momentous day," Nick promised her. "If you force this issue into court—"

"Don't!" Meg practically shouted. "Don't make that threat again."

"And don't you even think about threatening me with an abortion clinic," Nick warned her, his dark eyes glittering dangerously. "We both know you'd never abort David's child. So what's it going to be?"

They glared at each other, the air in the room sizzling with electricity. He had called her bluff and Meg was out of options.

"God, how I hate you," she murmured under her breath but more than loud enough for Nick to hear.

Nick felt none of the exultation he normally experienced when he'd browbeaten an opponent into submission. He got up and moved back around his desk. "Join the club, Megan. Join the club."

CHAPTER FIVE

NICK HAD NEVER seen his grandmother any more remote than she was when he joined her in her private sitting room on the second floor of the east wing.

"It's settled," he announced as he closed the door behind him. Megan was gone, but he wasn't ready to broadcast any of this to the servants. "We have an agreement in principle."

Eleanor closed the book on her lap and slipped off her reading glasses. "What are the terms?"

As he gave an abbreviated version of what had happened, Nick fixed himself a watered-down bourbon from the small collection of spirits Eleanor kept in her room. He outlined all the concessions he had made, but his grandmother stayed suspiciously quiet.

"Well?" he prompted, when she made no comment even after he finished. "Aren't you going to tell me I gave away too much?"

Eleanor reached for the eyeglass case on the side table and folded her reading glasses into it. "What you agreed to in principle is irrelevant, Nicholas. It's obvious the girl will have to go."

He scowled at his grandmother as he stepped closer to her chair. "What do you mean?"

She looked up at him, nonplussed. "You know exactly what I mean. I won't allow that woman to raise my grandson."

"And how do you propose to stop it?"

"We'll begin by hiring a private detective. Marilyn Tillison found a very good one last year. He handled that messy business with her granddaughter quite discreetly. It shouldn't take him long to learn why Miss Linley found the morality clause so objectionable."

Nick heaved an exasperated sigh. "Grandmother, she found the clause objectionable because it was an objectionable clause! I put it in there specifically so that I could be magnanimous and give it up."

His rationale bounced off her like bullets off steel. "Well, it doesn't really matter. With or without the clause you can still investigate her," Eleanor told him. "That girl has a past. She's hidden it behind a facade of manners, but she's as common as clay."

Nick had expected that assessment, but it still infuriated him. "I disagree," he retorted. "Megan Linley is about as uncommon as any woman could be. She's numb with grief, but she still had wits enough to stand up to both of us—and we didn't make it easy for her."

"On the contrary, you made it exceptionally easy," Eleanor retorted. "If I didn't know better, I'd say you actually had feelings for the girl."

"I do," Nick admitted hotly. "I *like* her. I think David did a damned good job of choosing a woman to love, and if I hadn't just buried him last week I'd say he was the luckiest man alive!"

Nick sucked in a deep breath of air and retreated to the other side of the room. Behind him, he heard Eleanor rise, and he fought the overwhelming urge to flee from the room, from his grandmother, from the house. From his life.

But he'd made his choices years ago, and whatever his other faults, Nick Ballenger didn't run from anything.

He stayed where he was, mastering his anger as Eleanor crossed the room to him.

She didn't reach out to touch him, of course, but she did come near, and her voice was as close to kind as he'd ever heard it. "Nicholas darlin', I know you feel a misplaced responsibility for David's death, but you're carrying guilt to the absurd if you let it blind you to the reality of this situation. You've obviously romanticized your brother's relationship with this young woman into something to be envied…perhaps even sought after. If you're not careful, you're going to fantasize yourself into falling in love with her, and that must not happen. You must be more clearheaded now than you've *ever* been."

Nick made a mental note to talk to someone in Genetic Research when he got to work tomorrow. He wanted tests done to see if he could find out exactly when the Ballenger family's blood had mutated into ice water.

He was completely calm—on the outside, anyway—when he turned to his grandmother. "Listen very carefully, Eleanor. We are not hiring an investigator, and I don't want to hear any more about it. Unless Megan Linley does something to prove that my faith in her is grossly misplaced, no one is going to try to dig up dirt. No one is going to even *think* about taking this baby away from her. I negotiated a contract in good faith, and by God, I'm going to honor it—and so will you."

"But Nicholas—

"I said no, Eleanor! The subject is closed. I suggest you make peace with it, because we have a wedding to plan!"

ELEANOR DIDN'T believe in challenging authority. She couldn't recall a single instance in her childhood when she'd openly defied her father, and only once in her thirty-five-year marriage to Harlan Ballenger had she refused to accede to her husband's wishes. Of course, there hadn't been any reason to rebel; Eleanor's father had raised her to be a dutiful daughter and it was her good fortune to have had a mother who taught her to be clever.

It was Eleanor's strong opinion that a woman had no need to openly oppose the men in her life if she understood the value of subtle manipulation. Fathers were notoriously easy for their daughters to control, and husbands, even more so. Sons were more complicated because the use of girlish or womanly charms were out of the question, but even so, Eleanor had never had any difficulty controlling Nicholas, Sr.

Grandsons were another thing altogether. Through the course of wedding preparations the next week, Eleanor watched hers behave with an irrationality that was appalling. Nothing she said to him made the slightest dent in his determination to give the benefit of the doubt to the little tart who had seduced young David.

Every scrap of her grandson's considerable common sense seemed to have flown out the window. His marriage contract had been absurdly generous and he was taking a keen interest in the planning of this wedding, which certainly had *not* been true of his first, legitimate marriage to Camille Devonaux. As for his refusal to have the girl investigated...

His attitude was simply beyond Eleanor's comprehension.

It had been nearly two decades now, but this wasn't the first time Nicholas had tried to defy her. He hadn't been successful then, but he had been a young man of only nineteen; no match for a woman with fifty years of experience in getting her own way with three of the most powerful men in the Carolinas. Still, forcing Nicholas to take the reins of Ballenger Pharmaceuticals after the death of his father had been the hardest battle Eleanor had ever fought in her life.

At the time, she'd been so certain that she was right— her son's tragic death in the prime of his life had left his company and the Ballenger fortune on shaky ground. Eleanor had seen too many family dynasties fall in her lifetime; she wasn't about to let hers succumb to the same fate. David had been too young to be of any practical use to the company. There had simply been no other solution but for Nicholas to take charge, and Eleanor had done everything necessary to force him to see his duty and do it.

She had no regrets about it now, but her certainty in the rightness of her actions had been shaken in the dark days that followed, when late in the night she would hear Nicholas downstairs in the conservatory, pouring his anguish into the music she had taken away from him.

She'd never let him know that she could hear him, of course. She had robbed him of his concert halls. She refused to take away any private joy that still remained inside him.

But the music had eventually stopped. She made certain that the magnificent grand piano in the conservatory was regularly tuned, but as far as she knew, it had been more than a decade since Nick had set foot in the room that had once been his heart and soul. If he missed whatever satisfaction he'd received from playing, it didn't show, and she doubted that anyone even remembered now that her grandson had once been heralded as the most promising piano virtuoso of his generation. The past was buried along with her grandson's incredible talent.

But now Eleanor had a different battle on her hands and there was nothing she could say to convince Nicholas of the insanity of taking Megan Linley at face value. He was obviously besotted with David's paramour. His guilt and his grief had robbed him of his good judgment, leaving Eleanor no choice but to take matters into her own hands.

That's why, on Friday morning, as Fetridge chauffeured her through a dozen errands that all related to last-minute wedding preparations, Eleanor included a stop at a high-rise on Pierson Avenue. Fetridge didn't expect or receive an explanation for the stop, and since the busy office building housed business and professional offices of every kind, Eleanor was confident that no one would notice or question her reason for being there.

Still, she wasn't exactly comfortable entering the reception area of Hamilton Security Services, nor was she pleased to be asked to wait. She sat in the lobby in her somber gray Chanel suit and a choker of pearls, hands folded in her lap, ankles crossed demurely. Waiting, and trying not to question the wisdom of defying the authority of the head of her family.

It was a great relief when she was finally ushered into the private office of James Hamilton. The investigator was athletically built and seemed to be effectively staving off middle age with vigorous outdoor exercise. He was fit, tan and moderately handsome, but not so vain that he felt it necessary to camouflage his prematurely silver hair.

Eleanor was also impressed by his etiquette when he met her at the door and showed her to a chair. So many younger men were completely oblivious to the fact that it was ill mannered to shake hands with a lady unless she initiated the gesture.

He didn't extend his hand, and Eleanor didn't offer.

"Mr. Hamilton, I won't waste time by protesting that I've never done anything of this sort before, nor will I explain my motives for soliciting your services," she began bluntly as soon as they were seated.

"I don't need either, Mrs. Ballenger," he replied in a reassuringly southern drawl. "I need only to know how I can be of assistance to you."

"I want you to investigate a young woman. Miss Megan Linley." Eleanor put a manila envelope on the desk between them. It contained a copy of the personnel file she had printed from the computer in Nick's study. "This is everything I know about her. It's not much, as you can see," she commented as Hamilton glanced through the sheets.

"It's enough to start with," he assured her. "What sort of information do you want me to collect?"

"Whatever you can find," Eleanor said as though it should be perfectly obvious.

"Past or present?" he asked.

"I beg your pardon?" she said testily, hating the feeling of being out of her depth.

"Am I to dig into her past? Do what amounts to a comprehensive background check," Hamilton explained. "Or do you want Miss Linley put under surveillance to determine what her activities are on a daily basis?"

"Oh. Full-time surveillance won't be necessary at present," Eleanor replied. "The girl is marrying my grandson tomorrow and will be living at Ballenger Hall. I should be able to keep her daily activities under observation myself. My concern is her past. In particular, her secrets.''

"I understand," he replied, though Eleanor wondered if he really did. "Miss Linley has been living in Singapore?" he asked, looking over the file again.

"Yes. Though I hope it won't prove necessary for you to go there to obtain a complete picture of her life. The American community in Singapore is quite close-knit. If you ask questions about Miss Linley there, word will eventually get back to my grandson, and that must not happen. I would much prefer that you start in her hometown, a place called Pine Ridge, Missouri.''

Hamilton gave her a reserved smile. "I prefer to start at the beginning, too, so to speak. I'll get on this first thing Monday morning, and get back to you—''

"No," Eleanor cut him off. "I will contact you for a report in a week's time. You are never to visit my home, nor will you call me unless you have information of a time-sensitive or critical nature.''

The investigator frowned. "Mrs. Ballenger, I fully understand your concern for confidentiality, but my work often takes me out of this office. I can't guarantee that I'll be available to report to you anytime you call. May I suggest an alternative?''

"You may *suggest*," Eleanor said skeptically.

"If you phone and I'm not available, I will return your call using the name Phillip Henderson and identify myself as a member of the Charleston Art League. I believe that is one of your favorite civic organizations, is it not?''

Eleanor was surprised and impressed that he knew so much about her. "Yes.''

"If my call proves to be an inconvenience, just ask

me to call back and specify an appropriate time. Would that be acceptable to you?''

Eleanor couldn't find any reason to object. ''Perfectly.''

''Good.''

''Now. As for your retainer...''

Hamilton quoted a rate, and Eleanor paid him from the cash withdrawal she'd made at her bank on one of her stops earlier that morning. Until she had ammunition to use against Megan Linley, Eleanor wanted to leave no trace of her transaction with the private investigator. Hamilton's secretary brought in a receipt, and they were done.

Eleanor rose to leave, offering her hand this time to seal their deal, and the investigator escorted her to the door with one final assurance.

''Don't worry, Mrs. Ballenger. If Megan Linley has anything to hide, I'll find it,'' he promised, and Eleanor left, assuaging her conscience with the certainty that she was only doing what Nicholas should have done the moment he learned of Megan Linley's pregnancy.

Eventually, he would thank her.

CHAPTER SIX

"DEARLY BELOVED, we are gathered together to join this man and this woman..."

Judge Nathaniel Warren's tie tack was a tiny gold golf tee. As he began mouthing the words of the wedding ceremony, Meg stared at it the same way she'd stared at the stone cherub at David's funeral. It was the best method she could think of to recapture the numbness she would need to get through what would surely be the longest afternoon of her life.

As Nick had promised, their wedding was a quiet, tasteful affair in the rambling garden at Ballenger Hall. There were two dozen people fanned out behind the bride and groom—not counting the servants, photographer and the musicians in the string quartet that had played an airy selection of classical music for a full hour before the ceremony began. The retired federal judge officiating the ceremony was an old friend of the family, chosen, Meg had no doubt, as a reminder of the Ballengers' influence in the state of South Carolina.

She was beyond caring. She was doing what was right for her baby, and to assure herself a place in the child's life. If that meant marrying Nick, pretending this was his child and playing the chameleon to convince the world that she loved a man she actually detested, then so be it. Meg had learned her survival skills the hard way, and the one thing she knew how to do better than anything was pretend. She would defy anyone to look at her standing beside Nick and think she was anything but a beautiful, happy bride.

The *beautiful* part was none of her doing, of course. Her designer wedding suit, a gift from Eleanor, was a sheath of champagne-colored satin with a matching jacket that had hundreds of seed pearls swirling along its high, stand-up collar and down the open lapels. Her legs—which she'd always thought were stumpy and un-attractive—were magnificently showcased by sheer silky stockings, three-inch moiré satin high heels and the short skirt of the Armani dress.

Her hairstyle had been carefully sculpted by a professional stylist, crimped and curled and artfully pinned up, with feathery tendrils left hanging to brush against her throat and face. Her makeup had been applied with equal care by a makeup artist, who had approached her face with the enthusiasm of a painter approaching an empty canvas.

How could she not be beautiful with such expensive attention lavished onto her? Nothing but the very best for the soon-to-be wife of Nicholas Ballenger.

And nothing but the best for Nick, either. She could see him out of the corner of her eye, in his perfectly tailored black tuxedo, looking as if he'd just stepped out of the casino scene in a James Bond movie. His thick black hair was combed back, and only one unruly lock had the temerity to creep onto his forehead. Even Meg had to admit that he was the epitome of masculine elegance.

She also had to admit that he had been very considerate of her this past week, keeping her apprised of decisions and wedding arrangements but maintaining his distance at the same time, as though giving her the opportunity to adjust to his presence in small doses.

She knew it was a calculated strategy on his part, but it had worked fairly well. She didn't trust him, of course, but she had decided days ago that as long as he was being courteous she would at least respond in kind. Meg firmly believed that a mother's emotions during pregnancy had a profound effect on the unborn child, and she had no desire to bring an angry, bitter baby into the world. And, as Nick had pointed out, since they were going to have to pretend to like each other in public, they might at least try to be civil to each other in private.

It was a formula that had worked fairly well. Meg's dislike of Nick made her too blunt sometimes, but they'd managed to get through the week without any major blowups.

Now, if she could only make it through the ceremony without thinking about the Ballenger brother she *should* have been marrying.

The judge mentioned something about rings, and Meg forced her attention away from his tie tack and onto his words. This part required her participation. Nick produced a slim gold wedding band, and Meg turned to give him her hand.

"Do you, Nicholas Tate Ballenger, take this woman to be your lawful wedded wife?"

Meg held her breath, waiting for more vows, for Judge Warren to ask, "Will you love, honor and cherish her, and forsaking all others, keep her only unto you until death do you part?"

But he didn't say the words and Nick didn't have to swear to do anything more than take her as his wife. His softly spoken "I do," held just the proper amount of conviction to convince those assembled that this was something more than an elaborate photo opportunity.

He slid the ring onto her finger next to the magnificent diamond engagement ring he'd cajoled her into accepting earlier in the week.

And then it was Meg's turn. She took Nick's wide gold band from the tiny pocket set into her jacket lining and accepted the hand he held out to her.

"And do you, Megan Rae Linley, take this man to be your lawful wedded husband?"

She tried to match her tone to Nick's, but it came out as barely more than a whisper. "I do."

She slipped the ring onto his finger and noticed with an odd detachment that his hands were bigger than David's, his fingers longer, more tapered. They were beautiful hands, masculine, but elegant, too. The ring went on smoothly.

"Then by the power vested in me by the state of South Carolina, I now pronounce you husband and wife."

There. It was over. She had sold her soul to the devil, and there was no turning back.

Meg wanted to cry, for David, for herself, for the baby. For the loss, the pain...the lies.

"Nick, you may kiss your beautiful bride."

Meg fought hard to locate the strength that had gotten her through David's funeral, but it was nowhere to be found—until she looked into Nick's eyes. There was compassion in them, and sorrow, as though he knew her pain, understood it...shared it. The monster Nick was gone, and in his place was a man with a heart and a soul.

Meg caught her breath sharply as he took her face in his hands and pressed a kiss to her lips that was as tender as the look in his eyes.

His lips were warm. Surprisingly so. And sweet.

The tears she had managed to control for more than a week got away from her. Two coursed down her cheeks, but when Nick raised his head he brushed at them gently and leaned close again to whisper in her ear, "It'll be all right, Megan. I promise. I promise."

He straightened and stepped back. When she looked into his eyes again, she almost believed him.

"Friends and family, may I proudly present to you Mr. and Mrs. Nicholas Ballenger."

More tears threatened, but Meg found the strength to fight them back when Nick took her hand and squeezed it firmly. They turned to the guests and accepted their applause.

Finally, the travesty was over.

Now, the really hard part could begin—meeting Nick's relatives and friends for the first time, smiling, pretending, accepting their good wishes and deftly handling their rampant curiosity.

Nick and Meg had rehearsed their story, of course. After a champagne toast, they made the rounds of their guests and answered the questions.

Yes, their decision was sudden, but David's death had made them realize how foolish it was to waste precious time.

Where had they met? Why, in Singapore, of course, on one of Nick's frequent trips abroad.

Was it love at first sight? Naturally. How could you even ask?

As they circulated, the reception took on a relaxed garden-party air, but the curiosity directed at her made Meg feel like a bug under a microscope. Through it all, Nick's hand at her waist kept her close, suggesting an intimacy that didn't exist, but providing an unlikely source of strength that Meg didn't examine too closely.

"Are you all right?" Nick asked quietly as they moved away from the gazebo where Nick's great-aunt Ophelia Ballenger Currant was holding court. Their unspoken strategy was to never stay too long with any conversational group. So far, the ploy was working, but Meg still felt like a long-tailed cat in a roomful of rocking chairs.

She took a deep, steadying breath. "I suppose so," she replied. "But I know now what my mama meant when she usta say she was bein' held together by spit and Scotch tape." Meg heard herself then and almost groaned aloud. She had lost complete control of her dialect. She stopped in her tracks. "Oh, Lordie, how long have I been doing that? I sound like I just stepped offa Sugar Creek Road."

"This is South Carolina. Who's going to notice?" Nick said with a smile. He'd done quite a lot of that with his relatives this afternoon, but this smile actually reached his eyes. Meg had to admit, it did wonderful things to his face.

"Everyone," she answered.

"No they're not. Don't worry about it. Eleanor's drawl is thicker than yours," he said.

"Yes, but it's an elegant, educated drawl. When I revert to the hills, I sound like a moonshiner cussin' out a Revenue man."

Nick chuckled. "Oh, come on. How many moonshiners have you known in your life, Megan?"

"You might be surprised," she murmured.

"Well, no one's noticed your accent, and you're doing brilliantly."

Something inside her blossomed under the light of

approval in his eyes. "Thank you," she murmured, then felt an overpowering burst of irritation. How could she feel such warmth and gratitude for the man who had forced her into this farce? It was obscene. "Come on. We should get back to your guests," she said shortly.

But Nick didn't move. "Not until you tell me what's wrong. We were doing so well."

Damn him. He was entirely too sensitive to her feelings today. Lying seemed pointless. "I was just struck by the irony of being grateful for the support of the man who put me in this ridiculous situation."

"Funny. I was struck by how gracious and resourceful you've been."

Meg looked at him for a long moment and decided that it would be idiotic to start World War III over something as inconsequential as a compliment—or, more accurately, the way his compliment made her feel. "Sorry. We should get back to the guests."

"As you wish." They moved along the meandering flagstone path to the arbor where Eleanor and the other Tates were conversing with Judge Warren and his wife, Vivian.

"There they are! The guests of honor!" Judge Warren intoned bombastically. His face was a little florid from all the champagne he'd imbibed. "I don't think I've ever had the privilege of marrying a more handsome couple. Tell me, Nick, where are you taking your lovely bride for your honeymoon?"

Oh, boy. This was something they hadn't discussed at all. Meg stiffened, but Nick's hand on the small of her back moved ever so slightly, like a horseman gentling a skittish mare, and she knew—somehow—that everything was under control.

"I'm afraid we don't have time for a real honeymoon,

Judge. I've given Megan an IOU for a month in the Caribbean this winter, but in the meantime we're going to spend a few days at Cat's Eye. Loll around the cottage. Take the *Rhapsody* out for a sail.''

"Oh, Nicholas, must you?" Eleanor asked.

He nodded patiently. "Yes, Nan. We must. We're leaving right after the reception. I want to get to the island in time to check out the boat before dark."

"But darlin', there's really no need. I'm going down to Savannah to spend a week with Mariel," she said, nodding in the direction of Selina's mother, "so that you and Megan can have the Hall to yourselves. The servants are here, and no one's been at the cottage since last year. I'm sure it's—"

"It's fine, Nan," Nick assured her. "The caretakers know we're coming. Buck and June will have everything ready."

"But—"

"Nan, please," Nick said quietly, but with an authority that silenced his grandmother.

Meg was astonished by the exchange. Eleanor was genuinely upset by the thought of Nick going sailing, and it could be for only one reason. She'd lost her only son and daughter-in-law in a sailing accident. She didn't want to lose her grandson, too.

Eleanor suddenly seemed a little more human. The woman had emotions after all.

"Megan, do you share Nick's passion for sailing?" Vivian Warren asked, drawing her attention away from the quiescent Eleanor.

"I've been out a few times," she replied noncommittally.

"Off Cat's Eye?" Selina Tate asked with deceptive innocence. Thus far, Nick's twenty-eight-year-old cousin had been the most skeptical of all the relatives. Or perhaps just the least subtle. Meg knew she would have to be careful where the nosy brunette was concerned.

"No. In Singapore. David kept a sloop off Sentosa Island." This time it was Nick who stiffened imperceptibly. Meg sensed it and almost shook her head in exasperation. Did he really think she was going to betray their charade? She smiled at Selina and explained, "Everyone at Ballenger East used to joke that if you didn't sail, you could kiss your promotion goodbye. Excursions were mandatory for all the executives."

Meg felt Nick relax. He hugged her closer as he added, "And of course I commandeered the *Sea Witch* the last time I was there so Meg and I could go out alone. She's quite a good sailor."

"What did you do at Ballenger East?" Mariel asked.

"She was David's personnel counselor," Nick replied. "I'm not being prejudiced when I say she did a marvelous job. Our employee-turnover rate plummeted thanks to her work."

Meg barely covered her surprise, but his praise seemed genuine. No. It *was* genuine. Maybe it was all those hours she'd spent listening to his conversations with David, or maybe it was just that he'd told so many lies this afternoon, but she was already getting an instinct for when Nick was telling the truth and when he was fabricating. The difference was nothing more than a tiny shift in the timbre of his voice, but Meg could hear it when he lied. And it wasn't there when he complimented her contribution to Ballenger East.

"You must be delighted to be back home," Vivian Warren said.

Meg leaned lightly on Nick and smiled. "How could I not be happy to be here?"

"You know, Megan," Selina drawled, "I have the strongest feelin' that I've seen you somewhere before."

"This is my first trip to Charleston. I don't see how that's possible."

"But weren't you at David's funeral?"

Oh, no. That was another contingency Meg and Nick hadn't discussed. She knew better than to lie. "Yes. I was."

"But you weren't with Nick," Selina said pointedly.

Oh, brother. The nosy little witch wasn't going to stop until she hit pay dirt or drew blood, which ever came first.

"Megan arrived late from Singapore," Nick lied. "I didn't even know she was here until after the service."

"But you didn't come to the wake, either," Selina pressed. "Considering your relationship with Nick, I would have thought you'd—"

"I attended the funeral to say goodbye to David," Meg interrupted her, keeping her voice perfectly calm and even. "I didn't feel comfortable intruding on the family."

"You and David were close then?" Selina asked.

"Yes," Meg replied before Nick had any chance to intervene. She was being forced to lie about a lot of things, but she wasn't about to let *everything* be taken away from her. "David was a good friend and the best boss anyone ever worked for. If I was successful at Ballenger East it was because David created an atmosphere of trust and cooperation that made people want to work for him."

"His death was tragic," Judge Warren said solemnly. "Just tragic."

"Yes. It was." Nick looked at Meg. "Darling, why

don't we go speak to the caterer? I imagine it's about time to cut the cake.''

''Certainly. Excuse us, please,'' she said to the others, then went willingly as Nick guided her back down the path.

''I hate to tell you this, Nick, but Cousin Selina isn't buying the charade,'' she said, keeping her voice low.

''Don't worry about her. You handled her brilliantly. Selina may be suspicious, but she's not going to do anything to jeopardize her place in Eleanor's will. None of them will.''

Meg stopped on the walkway between a bed of wildflowers and a fountain statue that obscured them from the view of many of the guests. ''You mean, what they think of our marriage, what they think of *me*, is irrelevant?''

''To a degree,'' he admitted.

''Then why did you invite them? What was the purpose of all this?'' she asked incredulously.

Nick bent his head to hers. To anyone looking, they seemed like newlyweds sharing an intimate moment alone. ''These are some of the most socially influential people in Charleston. Inviting them today makes them part of our lives as a couple—and by extension, our child's life.''

''You mean you're circling the wagons so that when the baby is born, shall we say…early, the family has a stake in supporting our story. Whether they believe it or not.''

He shrugged. ''Essentially. I'm the head of the family, and they all have a vested interest in sucking up to me. Usually, they're the ones who need me—for a loan, to back a business deal, to contribute to a charity, to show up at a fund-raiser that might otherwise go unattended.''

"But you need them now, and this is your way of telling them so."

"Exactly. Now, forget about my family," he said dismissively, taking her hand again. He straightened and smiled. "I'm just sorry you don't have any of your own here to drive you crazy."

Meg didn't dare comment on his sweet sentiment. "There's always Fletch," she said with false good cheer, glancing across the garden. He was in an enclave of business associates camped near the champagne fountain. She hadn't spoken to him since he returned from Abbeville, though he'd tried to contact her several times. "With friends like him, who else could I possibly need?"

Nick didn't smile at her joke. "I know you're being facetious, Meg, but I really wish you'd talk to him. He still hasn't forgiven me for going behind his back. I actually thought he might quit his job. He's very concerned about you."

"And I'm supposed to forgive him because he's concerned? I can't, Nick. He betrayed me."

Nick's forehead creased in frustration. "Is that really such a bad thing?" he asked softly, searching her face. "Is marriage to me the end of the world?"

"No," Meg replied without rancor. Something warm, like pleasure, sparked in Nick's eyes until she continued, "David's death was the end of the world. My world, anyway."

The pleasure in his eyes died and Nick regarded her gravely. "For now, maybe, but hopefully not forever. If you give me the chance, I think I can make your life better, Megan. Not better than it would have been with David, but certainly better than it would be without this marriage. For you and the baby."

It was everything she could do to hold his gaze steadily and without tears. "You may be right, but I'm not ready to let go of what should have been, Nick. And I may never be able to let go of what *was*." She took a deep breath to stave off the pain, and Nick reached for her hand.

"It's all right. I miss him, too."

All his sympathy and understanding threatened to undo her carefully constructed composure. She turned and stooped to examine the bed of wildflowers because it wouldn't do for anyone to read her body language right now.

"Don't do that, Nick," she warned him softly. "Not unless you want to see me fall apart in front of your family."

Nick crouched beside her and they looked at the flowers instead of each other. "I'm sorry. I didn't mean to upset you. I just feel that we have so much to say to each other."

She slanted a glance at him. "About David?"

"About everything. I don't know you, Meg, but I want to," he said with a quiet urgency that was convincingly sincere. "I think you're a remarkable person."

She found that hard to believe. "Why?"

He smiled. "Do you know how hard I have to work to find someone with the guts to stand up to me?"

She blushed and glanced away. "That's because most people have the good sense to get out of the way when they see a steamroller coming."

He chuckled. "I don't mean to roll over people, Meg."

"Then don't do it."

"That's easier said than done."

She leveled her gaze at his. "I guess being a bully

gets to be a habit," she said, and watched him bristle with irritation.

"Is that how you see me? As a bully?"

"It's what you are, Nick. It's what you are with your employees. What you *were* with your brother. It's what you were with me until these last few days."

He looked as though he was about to defend himself, then shook his head. "Of course. How else could you see me?" He pinched off a sprig of cornflowers and handed them to her. "Come on. Let's get the cake thing over with. Our guests won't take the hint and go home until we do. I want to get to the cottage before dark."

"So you said," she murmured as they started down the path again. "You know, Nick, it would have been nice if you'd given me a little warning about that."

"I'm sorry. I wasn't sure until last night that we'd be able to get away at all with Fletch leaving for Singapore on Monday. Do you mind?"

"I don't know. Do your caretakers live on the property?"

"Oh, no. They're a couple of island residents who make their living tending places like mine. June takes care of the houses, and Buck maintains the boats. I doubt we'll even see them unless there's a problem."

"Then I think it makes a great deal of sense." She lowered her voice even more. "Being alone, I mean. If we stay here it's going to be obvious to the servants that we didn't, well…you know, consummate the marriage."

A quiet, shuttered look closed over Nick's features. "That was my thinking as well," he replied, but Meg had the strongest feeling that he was lying.

But what was he trying to hide?

THE STRING QUARTET was playing an airy Mozart piece as the guests gathered round the "bride's table" to watch Nick and Meg feed each other cake. The photographer snapped endless pictures, and there were more toasts and good wishes before the first guests finally started making noises about leaving.

Nick and Meg dutifully thanked them all for coming, but when Judge Warren declared that he and his wife were departing, Nick left Meg alone for the first time that afternoon to see them off.

Alarm rippled through her as soon as he left her side, and Meg chided herself for being foolish. Forging a truce, as they seemed to have done, was one thing, becoming dependent on him...that was something else entirely. But when she turned and found herself face-to-face with Fletcher Matson she would have given a month of her life to have Nick beside her again.

"Well! I was beginning to wonder if I was ever going to get a chance to kiss the bride," he said with forced good cheer. There were still a half-dozen guests who had yet to depart, and most of them were close by.

Meg submitted to a quick kiss on the cheek. "Thank you for coming, Fletcher. Are you about ready to leave?" she asked a little too pointedly.

"Not until we've had a chance to talk," he whispered. He tucked her hand through the crook of his arm and Meg had two choices—go with him or pull away and make a scene. Together, they sauntered into the shade created by a grove of fragrant magnolia trees.

"Why have you been ducking my calls all week?" he asked bluntly as soon as they were alone.

"Because I didn't want to hear your lame apology."

"Well, I've got a news flash for you, Meg. I didn't call to apologize. I only did what I felt certain David would have wanted me to do. But *you*—"

She could see where this was headed and shook her head at him. "Don't preach at me, Fletch. This is your doing!"

"No, no. This wasn't what I had in mind when I told Nick the truth. I wanted the family to support you emotionally and financially, not swallow you whole and force you to live a lie. How can you do this, Meg?" he asked incredulously.

She refused to look at him. "I'm doing what's best for the baby."

"And what about you?"

"I don't matter."

"Don't be stupid, Meg. Of course you do. You have a right to—"

"Stop it," she hissed. "It's done. I don't want to hear any more."

"I'm sorry," Fletch said, gentling his tone. "It's just that I've been so damned worried about you. I'm returning to Singapore soon, and I have to know that you're going to be all right."

Meg felt herself softening toward Fletch and realized she didn't have enough friends that she could afford to throw one away who cared as much about her as he did.

"I'll be as right as I can be, Fletch," she told him quietly. "Can we leave it at that?"

He sighed, then nodded reluctantly. "But if you need me, you only have to call."

She almost smiled. "And you won't run to Nick again?"

He crossed his heart and raised his hand. "I swear." He lowered his hand. "I have to say that seeing the two of you together today has been something of a revelation. Have you actually made peace with Nick?"

"After a fashion," she replied. "It's hard to be actively hostile to someone who's treating you like a fairy princess. At the moment, we're operating under a flag of truce.''

"And tonight? On your honeymoon?''

Meg stiffened. "This isn't going to be *that* kind of honeymoon, Fletch. Nick and I are very clear on that point.''

"Are you sure? I mean, what I'm sensing from the two of you is—''

"Whatever you're sensing is just the result of good acting. End of story,'' she snapped, then changed the subject. "Has Nick made you president of Ballenger East?''

He nodded. "He made it official at the board meeting yesterday.''

"I suppose I should say congratulations, but I don't envy what's ahead of you,'' Meg said as they emerged on the other side of the magnolia grove and began following the looping path back toward the house. She noticed Selina alone at the arbor on the other side of the back lawn sipping champagne and watching them with considerable interest. Meg smiled politely as she continued, "I hope Mei Ling is prepared for what this promotion is going to do to your lives.''

"You're thinking about the Vietnam expansion,'' he guessed.

"You won't have a life anymore, Fletch,'' she warned him.

"Yes, I will,'' he replied. He lowered his voice confidentially. "This isn't official yet, but Nick has postponed the expansion.''

Meg stopped dead in her tracks. "What?''

Fletch turned to her, nodding. "You heard me. He spent most of last week taking a second look at David's reports and he's thinking about killing the project permanently.''

"He's not... David..." Meg couldn't form a coherent thought, let alone a sentence that made sense. David had complained for months that expanding into Vietnam would be a mistake, but Nick hadn't listened. Now, when it was too late, he finally started paying attention?

Every kind thought and warm feeling Meg had for Nick evaporated in the space of a heartbeat.

"That bastard," she whispered.

Fletch put out one hand to her, frowning with concern. "Meg? Are you all right? I'm sorry. I didn't mean to upset you."

She shook off his hand. She was too furious to cry, but she wasn't in any shape to play blushing bride. "Oh, I'm just dandy," she said as she turned back toward the magnolia grove again.

Fletch took a quick double step to catch up with her. "Where are you going?"

"Inside. Through the conservatory so that I don't have to run the gauntlet of Nick's wedding guests. I don't think any of them need to know my opinion of my new husband right at this moment."

"But...but what should I tell Nick?" Fletch stuttered.

"Tell him the honeymoon's over."

CHAPTER SEVEN

NICK HURRIED up the stairs, concerned by Megan's sudden departure from the reception. Selina Tate had come looking for him to inform him with speculative delight that his new wife had disappeared into the house after an "intense" conversation with Fletch. Nick wasn't worried about his cousin's obvious suspicions about the authenticity of his marriage, but if Fletch had done anything to upset Megan, Nick was going to murder him. She may be a tough negotiator but physically she was so tiny. And she was pregnant.

It didn't show, of course. Today, the attractive young woman he'd browbeaten into signing a marriage contract had turned, butterfly-like, into the most beautiful creature he'd ever seen in his life. The satin dress showed off her figure to perfection, and her makeup made her green eyes as vivid as sparkling emeralds. And her hair... The curls and spirals looked so soft and touchable. It had been everything Nick could do all afternoon to keep from burying his hands in it.

His new wife was so completely, totally and utterly magnificent that he was having a hard time remembering she was his wife in name only. Every time he did forget, though, Megan was only too happy to remind him. That was as it should be, he supposed, but there had been times today when he'd felt such a bond with her that it had been easy to believe there was more between them than Megan's dormant hatred and his guilt.

As to what that *something* was...

Don't go there, Nick, old boy, he warned himself. *This way lies madness....*

From the sweeping curve of the cantilever staircase, Nick emerged on the second-floor landing into the hall-way that bisected the house into east and west wings. Meg's room was the second on the right; the first would soon be converted into a nursery, the third was Nick's. Two huge bath suites and a connecting parlor sat between their respective quarters. A hallway branched off to the left of the stairs, leading to Eleanor's suite, guest rooms and the service stairs that ran from the kitchen vestibule up to the third floor.

Nick knocked on Megan's door and waited. He knocked again, more insistently as his concern mounted, but finally he heard a clipped, "Come in."

He opened the door. "Megan?"

No answer.

He closed the door behind him and looked around the room that, like almost every other room in the house, could easily have been a museum exhibit. The bed, with its towering canopy of intricately carved mahogany, was an eighteenth-century work of art; the creamy satin brocade fainting couch predated the Civil War. The lamp on the bedside table was Tiffany. A delicately carved Queen Anne desk sat on the wall between enormous sash windows.

The only thing missing was a barricade of red velour ropes to protect the room from the trampling feet and curious fingers of visitors. Its very formality invited one to look, but not linger.

Nick had wondered even before Megan moved in this

morning whether she would love the antique elegance as much as his mother, grandmother and ex-wife had, or if she'd share his discomfort with living in the past.

If Megan was anything like David, she wouldn't want to change a thing. Somehow, the thought was disappointing.

Megan's satin shoes were right inside the door, and her beaded jacket was lying neatly on the bed, but his new wife was nowhere to be seen.

"Megan?" He was beginning to grow alarmed. "Megan?"

"What?" she snapped as she popped out of the dressing room. Her hair was still a jumble of perfect golden curls, but she'd changed into a pair of white slacks and an emerald silk shirt. She was carrying a padded hanger, and she barely glanced at him as she moved toward the bed.

"Are you all right?" he asked.

"Why? Don't I look it?"

"You look…" She looked beautiful. And angry. All her defenses Nick had so painstakingly worked to erode this past week were back in full fighting mode. He was so disappointed he could actually taste it. He leaned against the door and gave his bow tie a yank as he donned a little emotional armor.

"You look angry," he said finally, with a flippancy that would probably make her even madder. "I don't know you well enough to tell if it's a murderous rage or you're just royally pissed off, but obviously something is wrong."

He was right. His cavalier tone only enraged her more. She whirled on him, hurling the padded satin hanger onto the bed. Nick knew he was lucky it hadn't come sailing toward his head. "Don't make fun of me, you son of a bitch."

"Ah. The pendulum is swinging toward murder," he muttered sarcastically. "Enlighten me, Megan. What have I done now?"

"Fletcher says you're canceling the Vietnam expansion."

Nick was surprised. He hadn't known what to expect, but it certainly wasn't this. "That's a strong possibility," he admitted cautiously. "I'm running feasibility studies based on some of the projections in David's last few reports."

Meg glared at him. "Which you rejected repeatedly over the last three months."

He nodded slowly. Her anger began to make sense. "Yes."

"Damn you," Meg hissed. "Why didn't you listen while he was alive? Why didn't you trust his judgment just a little? He might not be dead now if you had!"

Nick started piling on more armor, protecting himself from the arrows she was slinging, because every one was finding a home. "I didn't listen because the expansion would have been good for the company," he replied, looking for a place to hide, but there wasn't one. He knew the truth as well as she did.

"You mean it was good for company profits."

Nick spread his hands. "One and the same."

"Well, what has David's death done for profits?" she said, sneering. "How are you going to compensate for that loss?"

The question excavated a gigantic hole in Nick's cool exterior. "I can't," he said after a moment, his voice thick with emotion. "The company will survive without him, Megan, but there are nights when I wonder if I will.

Contrary to what you obviously believe, I loved my brother more than anything else in the world.''

That didn't say much about his ability to love. ''Then why did you send him away?'' she demanded to know, trying not to be moved by the pain and guilt in Nick's eyes.

Nick sighed and ran one hand over his face. God, he was tired. Megan was asking the questions he'd asked himself a million times in the last month, and the answers were going to sound as lame to her as they did to him. ''I did it for his own good,'' he replied.

''His own good?'' Meg echoed incredulously. ''What gave you that right?''

''David did. When he decided to join Ballenger Pharmaceuticals.''

Meg advanced on him, furious. ''Damn you! He didn't *decide*. You forced him!''

Nick drew back as though she'd slapped him. Surprise and excruciating pain were so clear on his face that Meg almost wished she could call the words back. But she was only telling the truth. Didn't someone have to make Nick face what he'd done?

But Nick didn't fight back this time. He didn't try to justify or rationalize. ''David told you that I...*forced* him to join the company?'' he asked haltingly, achingly.

''Yes.''

Nick's face turned to stone and right before Meg's eyes he retreated to a place so remote that she wondered if he'd ever be able to find himself. ''Well, he lied.''

He started toward the door to the parlor that separated their rooms, but Meg jumped in front of him. ''David wasn't a liar!''

''Then you misunderstood him,'' Nick thundered. ''Because I would never have forced David into a career

he didn't want. He had choices, Megan. I made damned sure of that! It's not my fault that this is what he chose!''

"He didn't choose Singapore!" she retorted.

Nick's righteous indignation faded and he backed away a step. "I know."

"And you didn't care that he was miserable."

"Of course I cared!"

"Then why didn't you let him come home?" Meg implored, her heart breaking all over again.

"Because I sent him to Singapore to get him out of my shadow. I was determined not to let him come home until he'd matured enough to stand up to me. Or to stand on his own without me, which ever came first."

"You did it for his own good?" Meg said derisively. "That's rich, Nick. Rich."

He stepped toward her again. "No, Megan. It's tragic. I did what I thought was right, and it got him killed. Now I have to live with that. Every day. For as long as I live. You may have loved him for a year, but I loved him all his life," he said softly, then stalked off, disappearing through the parlor into his own quarters.

Meg stayed where she was, her anger gone. In its place were things she'd never expected to feel for Nick Ballenger.

Compassion. Sympathy. Even a little *em*pathy. Like her, Nick was in pain. Soul deep, and devastating. His cold heart wasn't so cold, after all. In that instant, Meg learned a valuable lesson.

It was hard to hate someone once you'd glimpsed his soul.

In fact, it was damn near impossible.

THE MORNING SUN glinting off the ocean made it impossible for Meg to sleep much after dawn the next morning, which was unfortunate considering how little she'd slept.

Late yesterday afternoon, she and Nick had arrived on Cat's Eye, one of the most exclusive of the residential Sea Islands off the Carolina coast, where million-dollar beachfront properties were strung along the sandy white coast like shining pearls.

The Ballenger "cottage" was one of the shiniest of them all; a two-story stone-and-glass beach house that was as contemporary as Ballenger Hall was historic, and a lot more inviting.

The ground floor was one gigantic great room, where everything that wasn't oak was the color of sand. Sand-and-white checkerboard tiles formed the kitchen countertops. The appliances were café au lait. The living area had sand-colored carpets; an overstuffed sofa and chairs were upholstered in bone-and-cream stripes. The recreation area had a massive oak bar trimmed with sand-colored padding and brass rails. The baize on the pool table matched the decor, and even the paintings on the walls were of sand dollars and seashells framed in oak with ivory mats.

Here and there, the monochrome was relieved by a splash of brown.

It was also beautiful, and the absence of structure gave it a relaxed air that certainly didn't exist at Ballenger Hall.

Unfortunately, the house was about the only welcoming thing at the cottage. Nick had been politely remote on the one-hour drive from the city, and had barely seen her settled in before he went off to the marina. Though he claimed it was only to check on his forty-two-foot ketch, the *Rhapsody*, Meg had been certain he was just trying to get away from her.

Despite the heat of their argument, there was no anger in his behavior toward her, just an irritating courtesy that made her miss the other Nick—the one who'd kissed her so sweetly and stayed at her side during the wedding reception, comforting and soothing her with no more than the lightest pressure of his hand against her back.

She could hardly blame him for putting up walls, though. She was the one who'd decimated their truce. At first, she'd justified her actions by rationalizing that she'd only been confronting Nick with the truth, but as the night wore on and Meg grew more and more haunted by the horrible wounded look in his eyes, she began to question just how truthful she'd been.

David's dislike of Singapore was something that only those closest to him had been aware of. One of the things that had made him such a wonderful boss was that he never once let any of his employees feel the impact of his dissatisfaction. And even fewer people knew that David would have preferred to be a teacher, a historian, an archeologist...anything, in fact, but a businessman.

When Meg asked him why he was stuck in a career he hated, he'd said only that he hadn't had a choice, and Meg had assumed the obvious—that Nick had forced his brother into the family business.

But that look on Nick's face... He'd been devastated. Almost...betrayed.

That kind of shock couldn't be faked. In his own mind, he obviously believed that David's career decision had been voluntary.

So where was the truth?

Meg couldn't begin to guess, but she did come to realize how little she knew about her new husband. David had talked endlessly about the Ballenger family history, but not much had ever been said about the more recent generations—particularly Nick.

Meg realized now that the oversight was her fault. She had been so resentful of the way Nick ruled David's life that she hadn't wanted to know more about him. It had been easier to think of him as a ruthless dictator than admit that David shared at least an equal amount of blame for allowing his brother to dominate him.

That admission made Meg feel like a traitor, but looking for reasons to continue despising Nick was insane. She was married to him now, and though the union would only last for a year, she had given him a place in her child's life that would last forever. Peace between them was imperative. And friendship with him, while not an absolute necessity, could enrich her life and her child's beyond measure.

But achieving that meant being fair to Nick, when what she really wanted to do was forget about David's faults and enshrine his memory in her heart. But Meg didn't have the luxury of clinging to an image of a perfect David. She had to make peace with Nick, and that meant trying to understand him.

She'd spent a big part of the night trying to put together the pieces of what she came to think of as "the Nick puzzle." Who he was, how he could be cold and remote one minute, then warm and generous the next. Whether he'd been born a ruthless dictator, or if someone had made him into one. What had motivated him to force her into marriage when it would have been so much easier to offer her money to simply disappear?

Meg didn't have enough pieces to put even a fraction of the puzzle into place, but she'd had plenty of time to consider the questions, because Nick hadn't returned to the beach house until long after she had turned in for the night. She'd heard him come in, known when he climbed the stairs.

He'd paused outside her closed door, and Meg had listened tensely, wondering if he would try the knob and discover that she had forgotten to lock it. But then he'd moved on to his own room down the hall.

Once or twice Meg thought she heard a noise on the deck that connected the upstairs bedrooms to the deck below and the beach beyond, but it was never anything more than a vague creaking that could have been the wind. Even after the house grew quiet again, it had still been hours before Meg fell asleep.

Now the sun wouldn't let her catch even a short cat-nap and she wasn't ready to face what lay ahead. Her morning ritual, which included an increasingly nasty bout of morning sickness, grew longer every day because she had discovered weeks ago that creeping around at a snail's pace made the nausea much less severe. If she moved delicately and chased a soda cracker with a cup of ginger tea she usually got by without throwing up.

Unfortunately, her tea was still in her overnight bag, the hot water was downstairs in the kitchen and there wasn't a cracker in sight.

To avoid the inevitable, she rolled over and found herself looking at the boxes that were piled high on the bureau. She'd discovered them yesterday after Nick left, stacked neatly in the closet with a note that read:

Dearest Megan,
   I know it may be some time before the rest of your belongings arrive from Singapore. Please accept this trousseau as my wedding gift.

                                        Fondly,
                                        Nick

P.S. Everything should fit. The fashion coordinator who helped with your wedding dress also worked on assembling the trousseau.

The contents of the boxes were pure magic. Everything imaginable, from swimsuits to business suits. Loungewear, sportswear, a cocktail dress. Slacks, shirts, dresses, shorts, a hat, sweaters... Plus purses and shoes to match, all from the finest designers and the most expensive shops in Charleston.

Meg couldn't be bought, but the wardrobe of treasures in the guise of a "wedding gift" had been hard to resist. Like anyone who'd grown up wearing charity castoffs and rummage-sale hand-me-downs, Meg loved new things, beautiful things. Now, an entire wardrobe of incredible clothes was right at her fingertips. The question, though, was whether she should accept them.

Ultimately, it was the thought of at least trying on something from Nick's treasure trove that finally gave Meg the incentive to crawl out of bed. She was going to have to face the morning sickness eventually. It might as well be now.

Steeling herself, she sat up slowly.

As soon as she was vertical, a mild queasiness hit her. By the time she inched her way across the plush salmon-colored carpet to the door of her private bath, the nausea was of the please-God-let-me-die variety.

By the time she finished in the bathroom, she didn't have the strength to do more than sit on the edge of the bed praying that a cup of ginger tea would materialize in front of her.

"Only two more weeks. Maybe three. Only two more weeks. Maybe three..." She chanted it like a mantra to remind herself that the morning sickness would pass shortly after she moved out of the first trimester. At least that's how it had been the first time.

Meg knew what to expect from her pregnancy only too well. In a few weeks, her morning sickness would abate and before another month was out, her abdomen would start to swell like a balloon. Backaches would hit her long before most women succumbed to that particular malady, and in three months she'd look like a beached whale, from her puffy face to her swollen ankles and everything in between.

But that was as far as her personal experience reached. Everything she knew about the last trimester came from her secondhand experience as a nurse. Her first child— a boy—had lived inside her only six months.

Meg put a protective hand on her abdomen. She'd been little more than a child herself the first time she became pregnant, and that mistake had set in motion a chain of events that would haunt her to the day she died.

No matter what it took, this child was going to survive. He wouldn't be born prematurely because a drunken brute thought that using his fifteen-year-old wife as a punching bag proved he was a man. This child would live inside her for nine months, not die on a tiny respirator in a sterile plastic hospital incubator. Meg would hold this child in her arms and protect him. Love him. And he would never know poverty or brutality or scorn or shame. Whatever it took, *this* baby would live and be well and be happy.

If his mother could survive a few more weeks of morning sickness.

Damn Nick and his pretty clothes! This was all his fault. If she'd just stayed in bed...

"Megan?"

There was no knock, but Nick was clearly on the other side of the door.

"Go away," she moaned. "This is not a sight for the faint of heart."

"I think I can handle it. Are you decent?"

"Why? Are you thinking of sticking that morality clause back in our contract?"

She heard a muffled chuckle before he warned her, "I'm coming in." Something bumped against the door and the knob rattled repeatedly before the door swung open. Meg slitted one eye in his direction and saw the problem. He was carrying a tray.

"What's this?"

"Breakfast."

Meg groaned and finally gave in to her intense need to lie down. She turned her back on Nick and curled into a tight ball of misery. "You bring breakfast in bed to a dying woman? What kind of a sadist are you?"

"Don't be so quick to judge. This is a real gourmet delight. Ginger tea and unsalted soda crackers."

Meg opened her eyes and looked over her shoulder as he put the tray on the bedside table. "How did you know?"

"Dr. Michaelson. When I talked to him last week he said this was the remedy of choice for your morning sickness."

"This, and time."

"Just another week or two, right? Until you're out of the first trimester?" He plumped her pillows and propped them against the headboard.

"Good Lord willin' and the creek don't rise," she muttered, but even sick, she couldn't help but be impressed by his knowledge. And his concern.

"Here. Scooch up and lie back on the pillows," he instructed.

Meg was too miserable to do anything but comply. She pulled her robe tighter around her and folded the tail demurely across her legs, but as she reached for a cracker she realized that she was more modestly dressed than Nick. In fact, when she took a good look at him, she was downright shocked.

In the time she had known him, Meg had never seen Nick in anything less formal than trousers and a white shirt with the cuffs rolled up a notch or two. This morning, the upturned cuffs were on a pair of white walking shorts, and the polo shirt that hugged his broad shoulders was the exact hue of his dark blue eyes.

He hadn't shaved yet, so dark stubble accentuated the perfect angles of his jaw, and his barely combed hair, still damp from the shower, was so attractively disheveled that it made him seem almost human.

And...well...*sexy.*

Even her morning sickness couldn't undermine the disconcerting way this lean, muscled, masculine Nick made her feel.

Meg nibbled on a cracker and searched for something other than her husband to look at as he poured a cup of tea for her.

"I see you found your wedding present," he commented, nodding toward the boxes on the dresser.

She took the cup he held out to her. "Yes. It was quite a surprise. But I suppose if I'm going to pretend to be your wife, I have to look the part, don't I?" Meg hadn't intended to greet his gift with sarcasm, but that's how it came out.

Nick heaved an exasperated sigh. "Gee...can't you

give me credit for having at least *one* altruistic bone in my body? Maybe in a toe, or a little finger?''

Meg was ashamed of herself. "I'm sorry." She sipped her tea. "Everything is just beautiful. Considering the circumstances, a maternity wardrobe might have been more practical, though."

"You can cross that bridge when you come to it. I've set up accounts for you at a dozen or so shops and department stores. I want you to get whatever you need, whenever you need it."

"Nick..." Meg tried not to frown. "Our agreement didn't include—"

"No, it didn't," he said, cutting her off. "But it should have. I didn't put things like a clothing allowance or a monthly stipend into the contract because I assumed you'd negotiate for them. You didn't, so I'm free to handle those issues as I see fit. And I see fit to provide you with the same considerations that my first wife enjoyed. So, the real issue here is, do you like the clothes in your trousseau?"

Meg had the strongest sense that despite his cavalier attitude, this was important to him. He needed her to accept his generous gift as a gesture of friendship. Meg was stubborn, but she wasn't cruel—or stupid.

"Yes. I love the clothes. Thank you."

Nick nodded a little too solemnly. "You're welcome. Wear them in good health."

Meg laughed and moaned at the same time. "Was that a pun? Why, Nick! I didn't think you had a sense of humor."

"Neither did I," he admitted, grinning.

Meg inched toward the center of the bed as a wordless invitation for him to sit. The tea was settling her stomach and she felt better already. "How was your boat? Everything shipshape?"

Nick accepted her invitation and sat on the edge of the bed, facing her. "Everything's fine. She's ready to sail. But I suppose it was foolish of me to think that you'd be up to—" He imitated the troughs and peaks of ocean waves with his hand, and Meg slapped it away.

"Don't do that unless you want to take another shower this morning."

"Sorry," he muttered, but didn't look it in the least.

"Actually, my morning sickness is aptly named," she informed him. "Once I get past this part of the day, it usually doesn't come back."

"Even on—" He made the wave-motion again, and Meg chuckled.

"Even on. I just need an hour or so to shower and sip and get dressed. But I hope you realize, Nick, that I'm only a second-rate sailor. I didn't grow up spending my weekends at the Pine Ridge Yacht Club."

Nick's dark eyebrows went up in surprise. "There was a yacht club in the Ozarks?"

Meg rolled her eyes. Didn't he know sarcasm when he heard it? "Oh, yeah. A nice one. Called Bubba's Bait and Tackle."

"How colorful," Nick said with a grin. "What did they call the local country club?"

"Jeanie's Putt-Putt. Had a windmill hazard that was a real beaut," Meg said dryly.

Nick cocked his head to one side. "Does that mean you do play golf, or you don't?"

She looked wounded. "I'll have you know I have a handicap of four."

He whistled appreciatively. "I'm impressed."

Meg shrugged. "That's one of the pastimes the Singapore government approves of. In fact, there are a couple of world-class golf courses over there.''

"Would you care to put that handicap to use?" Nick asked. "I have memberships all over the Sea Islands. I could get us a tee-off time at Wild Dunes this afternoon, or we could sail down to Seabrook tomorrow.''

"That would be wonderful," she said, genuinely excited about the prospect of playing on one of the most famous golf courses in the world. "I didn't know you played. David hated golf.''

"It's a law here," Nick replied. "If you want to conduct business in Charleston, you have to play golf.''

"Well, I guess that explains why David hated it," Meg said wryly.

Nick stiffened and Meg realized that he'd taken her comment as yet another condemnation of him. He stood. "Well, I'll see about getting us—"

"Nick, wait, please. I'm sorry. I didn't mean that the way it came out.''

"Don't worry about it," he said, but there was a wall of stone between them now that hadn't been there a minute ago. Meg didn't think she could bear it. She liked the funny, kind, easygoing Nick. It was a nice variation on the gentle, supportive man who'd guided her through their wedding reception yesterday, and she wanted him back.

He was headed for the door, but Meg couldn't let him go like this. "Nick, please. Wait. Can we talk for a minute? About what I said yesterday…''

He stopped and turned, looking as though he was steeling himself for a nuclear attack. "What about it?''

"I spent a long time last night thinking about our argument," she admitted.

He inclined his head formally. And coldly. "As did I."

"I also spent a lot of time trying to remember David's exact words. He wasn't happy with his life as a businessman, but he never said you forced him into it. He said he hadn't had a choice, and I just assumed that you were responsible."

Meg could see the layers of armor fall away from him. Most of the pain she had caused him left, too. He frowned, but there was no anger in the expression, just confusion. "Those were his words? He didn't have a choice?"

"Yes."

"Then maybe I only *thought* I gave him options," he said more to himself than her. He sat on the bed again and looked at Meg. "Did he ever tell you what he really wanted to do?"

She shrugged. "I'm not sure he knew. 'Anything but peddling pills,' he said once. I think he would have enjoyed working in some area of historic preservation, but he never seemed to view it as anything more than hobby material."

"That was our father's doing," Nick told her. "Mother spent more time on her historic-preservation charities than most people spend on their careers, but Dad always called it 'Cynthia's little hobby.' Maybe that affected David's perception of it."

"Sometimes we get more from our parents than we like to think." An image of her own father flashed into Meg's head, but she pushed it away. She was back in America, but she was still a thousand miles away from that son of a bitch. She didn't have to let him back into her life—or her thoughts.

What she was learning from Nick was much more

important, anyway. "You know, Nick, I always believed that David could have been happy in Singapore if there had been a visible history for him to study, but everything there is so new and so untouched by the past." She looked at him. "And you're telling me that all he had to do to escape that was say, 'Damn it, Nick, I'm coming home whether you like it or not.'?"

"Yes."

Meg looked at him skeptically. "As easy as that?"

"Pretty much."

Meg didn't want to believe him. If he was telling the truth, David would still be alive if he'd just had the gumption to stand up to Nick as Meg had begged him to a dozen times. But instead of taking her advice, David had always shaken his head and said, "Honey, you don't understand. I have to do what Nick wants. I don't have a choice."

It was stupid and tragic and it didn't make a lick of sense.

To either of them. "Megan, why did you tell me this?" Nick finally asked.

She pulled herself into the present, away from the senseless speculation. "Because I could see how much I hurt you yesterday. I don't know why David felt as he did, but he never blamed you directly for anything but sending him to Singapore. I couldn't let you think otherwise if it was going to cause you pain."

"Thank you."

"You're welcome."

They looked at each other for a long moment, then Nick cleared his throat self-consciously and rose. "Well, listen...I'll get out of here and let you do whatever it is you have to do."

"I just need to shower and get dressed. I won't be too

long," she assured him as he backed toward the door. "In fact, choosing what to wear from all these beautiful things will take the most time."

Nick grinned. "At least you can't claim that you don't have a thing to wear."

"How true," she said, her face lit up with delight.

Nick caught his breath. He remembered thinking once that if Megan ever let loose with a smile, she would be irresistible. How right he had been. The genuine pleasure in her eyes made her positively breathtaking. "God, what a beautiful smile you have. No wonder David fell in love with you."

Meg's smile faded and a blush swept up her cheeks. She looked down at her almost-empty cup because it was too hard to hold Nick's gaze. "Thank you."

"It's the truth. Well... See you downstairs." Nick moved toward the door quickly before he could do something very foolish, like taking her in his arms.

He shut the door behind him and took a deep breath.

If this was the effect his new wife was going to have on him, their two-day honeymoon might turn out to be the longest forty-eight hours in recorded history. And living a year under the same roof with her...?

Nick wondered how many cold showers a man could take before he caught pneumonia or went stark raving mad.

CHAPTER EIGHT

OUT OF DEFERENCE to the possible return of Megan's morning sickness, Nick kept the *Rhapsody* in sight of land on their leisurely cruise up the coast. She helped him get under way, proving to be a better sailor than she'd given herself credit for. Nick could tell she was happy, though, when the fore-and-aft-rigged ketch was under sail and she could stretch out on deck to work on her tan.

Nick didn't mind a bit. His wife sunbathing turned out to be the most breathtaking view on the Carolina coast that afternoon. She was wearing a gold one-piece bathing suit that had been part of her trousseau. The shimmering fabric caressed her rich curves, and with her hair tumbling recklessly out of a golden clip, she looked like Aphrodite and Helen of Troy all rolled into one.

He'd helped her apply a strong sunscreen before they left the cottage, but she turned over frequently, and seemed to feel no need to converse. The silence was companionable and relaxing, but after an hour of it, Nick had had about all he could stand.

"Would you like to take the wheel for a while?" he called out to her as she rolled onto her stomach for another "basting" as she'd called it earlier.

Meg popped up on her elbows and looked at him over the top of her sunglasses. "You got a yen to visit Tokyo?"

Nick laughed. "Not today."

"Then you keep the wheel."

"Only if you'll come over here and keep me company."

Meg looked surprised, but she sat up nonetheless and gathered up the golden sarong skirt that had been spread out under her. She had been sunning on the deck that formed the roof of the main cabin below. She climbed down carefully, tied the sarong at her waist and joined Nick on the padded bench behind the wheel.

"You said earlier that you usually sail alone—I figured you'd prefer peace and quiet," she said as she settled next to him.

"Not today. I'd rather talk."

"About what?"

"You."

She looked startled again. "What do you want to know?"

The blue-and-white sails above them crackled as the wind shifted ever so slightly, and Nick adjusted their course to keep the sails full. "Oh, the ordinary stuff, I guess. What your childhood was like. Why you went into nursing. How you ended up in Singapore."

Meg relaxed. There was no harm in answering him, so long as she was careful. "Fletcher told you that I grew up poor, didn't he?"

"Yes," Nick replied. "In rural Missouri."

"Then you can pretty much guess what my childhood was like. We lived way out in the country on a no-account piece of land that had been in my father's family for generations."

"Did your father have a trade?"

Meg shook her head. "My grandfather ran a sorghum mill most of his life, but the market for sorghum molasses dried up in the sixties and seventies. When Grandpa died, Daddy could have found a market if he'd wanted to, but he didn't. He'd lost the use of his left arm in a mill accident when he was a teenager, and that became his excuse to never work another day in his life.'' She hesitated before making the admission that was still uncomfortable for her. ''We lived on welfare and church charities.''

She looked at Nick to see his response, if he was judging her, condemning her. He wasn't. In fact, she saw just the opposite. Respect. ''Do you ever marvel at how far you've come, Megan?'' he asked in the gentle voice that she was finally becoming accustomed to.

She smiled and nodded. ''Oh, yeah. I spent my first three years in Singapore learning etiquette, traveling when I could to soak up culture, shedding my hillbilly accent... Basically trying to pretend that I was someone other than a little hick from nowhere.''

''Do you still pretend?''

''Every chance I get,'' she said wistfully. ''But it's hard to escape who you are. You can leave the past behind, but you can't hide from the things that shaped you. Particularly not when you're counseling. I mean, how can you ask other people to face *their* demons if you aren't willing to face some of your own.''

''Is that why you became a counselor? As a way to face your demons?'' he asked gently.

''Umm...sort of,'' she said after a moment. ''I became a nurse because I didn't want to live on welfare or wait tables in a bar for the rest of my life. Nursing was the only respectable profession that seemed even remotely within my grasp.''

She went on to explain how she'd worked her way through nursing school at the community college, and

eventually got a job in a family-practice clinic run by
Lewellyn Holmby.

Though she had an odd yearning to be completely
honest with Nick, she left out huge chunks of her life,
skipping over the nightmare years. Something inside her
wanted to trust him, but she didn't dare risk giving him
any ammunition he might use against her later. She
needed him to assume that she had simply finished high
school and headed straight to college; to her great relief,
he did.

"It was Dr. Holmby's idea for me to become a nurse
practitioner with counseling credentials," she told Nick.
"He said if I was going to spend so much time yakking
with the patients trying to solve their problems, I might
as well be earning money for myself and the clinic. He
financed my degree—sent me off to Washington Uni-
versity in St. Louis for a year and a half to study psychology. Then I went back to Pine Ridge and set up a
counseling center at the Holmby Clinic to pay off the
debt."

"Until Holmby went to Singapore?"

She nodded. "Lew and his wife were looking forward
to traveling when he retired. Spending a few years in
the Far East sounded too exotic to pass up, so he sold
his practice."

"Which put you out of a job," Nick assumed.

Meg let him. "Yes. He knew I didn't have anything
to hold me in Pine Ridge, so he invited me along to be
his office nurse again."

Meg knew Nick was familiar with her work history
in Singapore because he'd grilled her about it when David had hired her. The question he asked next, though,
startled her.

"Was it love at first sight?"

"What?"

"You and David," he said casually, looking up to study the sails, as though he'd asked a question that was of no real consequence. "Was it love at first sight?"

The very idea seemed absurd to Meg. "Heavens, no. He was David Ballenger."

Nick looked at her then, curiously. "What does that have to do with anything?"

"He was a rich, powerful, handsome American aristocrat," she said again, as though it should be perfectly obvious. "He was so far above me that it never occurred to me to think of him in romantic terms."

"When did you?" he asked.

Meg smiled. There was pain and loss mixed in with her memories, but it felt good to be able to talk about David. "I think it was right after he kissed me for the first time."

He stared at her in disbelief and shook his head. "David must have been losing his touch if you didn't know he was attracted to you until then."

She chuckled. "Well, in retrospect I realized that there were plenty of clues. I was just afraid to see them for what they were. David was more than just a great boss. He was like the perfect big brother—kind, protective, encouraging, sheltering... I used to wonder who he used as a—"

When she stopped so abruptly, Nick raised his dark eyebrows. "As a what?" he prompted.

"Nothing. Listen," she said brightly, "since we've established that it wouldn't be a good idea for me to steer, why don't I slip down to the galley and fix us a sandwich for lunch." She started to stand, but Nick took hold of her arm to keep her in place.

"What were you going to say, Megan?"

It was a long moment before she finally turned to look at him. When Nick saw the guilty flush on her face, he didn't need an answer.

She had wondered how David could be such a great big brother when all he had for a role model was Nick.

The awareness passed between them on an invisible wire, and Meg would have given anything to call her thoughtless words back. The last thing she wanted at this fragile stage of their relationship was to hurt Nick again. "I was an outsider looking in—from halfway around the world, no less. I'm sorry if I was unfair to you."

"That's all right," he said, turning his attention back to the sea. "You could only judge by what you saw, and I didn't cut David much slack these last few years."

Meg could hear the pain in his voice and knew exactly what he was thinking. "Guilt isn't going to bring him back, Nick. In the long run, it's only going to eat you alive."

"Don't you think that's exactly what I deserve?"

"What I think doesn't count."

He looked at her then. "Yes, it does."

He meant it. Meg could see it so clearly in his eyes.

"I'll tell you what counts, Nick. It's the only thing I know for sure." Very gently, she reached out and placed her hand on Nick's arm. "David loved you. It would hurt him immeasurably if he thought you were torturing yourself with guilt. If you want to honor your brother, accept what happened as the tragic accident it was, and let go."

Meg couldn't read anything in his face. She had no idea whether or not her words had made an impact on him. But, she realized suddenly, she believed what she was saying. David's death *was* an accident.

"If you really know what David would be thinking

now, tell me something, Meg," he said softly, without rancor. "Would he approve of our marriage?"

Meg glanced away. "I can't answer that, Nick. I can't even ask myself the question."

"I'm sorry," Nick said apologetically.

She turned to him. "We're doing the best we can. That has to be good enough for all of us—including David."

He tilted his head to one side and the wind blew his dark hair onto his forehead. "Do you still hate me for forcing you into this marriage?"

She held his gaze as she searched her heart for an answer. "Hate you? No," she said finally. "I didn't know you when I said that, Nick. I still don't."

"That's okay," he said with a wistful smile. "I don't think I know myself right now."

Meg smiled, too. "Well, if it's any consolation, a man who serves his pregnant wife crackers and ginger tea in bed definitely qualifies as one of the good guys."

"Why, thank ya, ma'am," he drawled, grinning broadly as he tipped an imaginary Stetson to her.

"You're welcome, Tex," Meg replied dryly. "Now, why don't I mosey on down to the chuckwagon and rustle us up some grub before the sun gets any higher over the yardarm."

"Talk about mixing your metaphors!" Nick said with a laugh that was swept away by the breeze, and for today, anyway, the sadness and guilt he carried inside him was swept away, too.

JIM HAMILTON HIT the jackpot on Megan Linley his very first day on the case.

On Monday morning, he started the investigation at his computer as usual, first conducting a credit check on his quarry and following the leads that yielded. The second step was always a hit on the Internet's National Newspaper Morgue site to see if the target's local newspaper had an on-line archive that could give him the date of any issue that contained a reference to his case subject.

That was where Hamilton got lucky. Megan Linley's credit check was mundane in the extreme, but her hometown newspaper, the *Kerry County Enterprise,* had an on-line morgue going back twenty years. No text was provided, of course; only the date of the issue, the page on which the target's name was mentioned and the type of reference—news article, legal notice, advertisement, or community service, which included obituaries, hospital admittances, etcetera. News items also gave the general subject of the article, usually in the form of a headline, as well as a list of cross-references.

Hits on the name Megan Linley—and there were several—didn't give Hamilton many concrete details, but they did allow him to make some very interesting inferences. One hit under Legal Notices, for example, told him that his case subject and one Russell Corday had been granted a marriage license on May 4, 1983.

From that, Hamilton inferred that his quarry had been married at the age of fifteen, a supposition that became a confirmed fact when a subsequent hit showed a Grant of Divorce between the couple in January 1985. Another Legal Notice in that same issue granted Mrs. Corday the right to resume the use of her maiden name.

Under a Community Relations hit, he learned that Megan Linley had been hospitalized in August of the year she was married. There was also a hit for an article relating to a nursing-school graduation in 1988; another in 1991 listed the subject "Holmby Clinic Offers Counseling Services''; and one final hit in 1993 proclaimed "Local Clinic Closes," and listed cross-references to Dr. Lewellyn Holmby and Singapore.

Under most circumstances, Hamilton would have considered that a very good day's work, but he didn't stop there. He broadened his search from Megan Linley to anyone with that last name, and hit a veritable gold mine of articles and legal notices relating to multiple arrests of one George "Dub" Washington Linley, and the death of one Loreen Linley in 1981.

It was only a guess, but Hamilton would have bet the farm that these were Megan's parents except for one important inconsistency. According to the information provided by Eleanor Ballenger, both of Ms. Linley's parents were dead. Loreen Linley qualified, certainly, but George Washington Linley's name appeared regularly on the police blotter for Drunk and Disorderly Conduct, with the most recent hit in December of last year. There was also a two-year gap in his D&D arrests that was preceded by an arrest and conviction on assault charges in 1993, which told Hamilton that Mr. Linley had done at least two years of hard time.

It was possible, of course, that the convicted felon was a distant relative or no relation at all, but Hamilton's P.I. instincts told him otherwise. If he was right, Ms. Linley had lied to her prospective in-laws. But maybe she'd had a reason. Since Jim didn't believe in coincidences, he had to wonder: Was there a connection between Linley's 1993 assault arrest and Megan's 1993 departure for Singapore?

Unfortunately for Eleanor Ballenger's pocketbook, finding out was going to take a lot more than a simple surf on the Internet. He had to go to Pine Ridge and read the text of those newspaper items. He'd have to visit the county courthouse to look at court records, talk to the local law enforcement officials, and he might even have to get the actual trial transcripts—a process that took weeks, sometimes months, depending on the efficiency of the county clerk's office.

But it was all doable. By Wednesday of the week after the Linley-Ballenger wedding, Jim Hamilton was in Pine Ridge, Missouri, asking questions about Megan Linley and telling anyone who questioned his motives that Ms. Linley had applied for a high-level management position at a company that required an extensive security check.

Eleanor Ballenger had said she wanted her new granddaughter's secrets, and Hamilton sensed he was well on the way to providing them.

CHAPTER NINE

MEG AWOKE confused and disoriented, not sure where she was or what had awakened her. Relief hit her first, along with gratitude that whatever had disturbed her slumber wasn't another vivid nightmare about David's plane crash.

Realization followed the relief. She was back in Ballenger Hall. She had returned from her honeymoon with Nick late this afternoon, and because they had spent four days on Cat's Eye instead of two, Nick had been forced to go straight to the office with an admonition that she not wait up for him.

With Eleanor still in Savannah, Meg had taken advantage of the opportunity to explore the first floor of the Hall, and had shocked the butler and housekeeper by insisting on having supper with them in the kitchen. Mrs. Fetridge—Effie, as she was called by everyone in the household but Eleanor—had then insisted on helping Meg unpack her things, and would have actually "drawn the Missus' bath" if Meg had permitted it.

But Meg wasn't comfortable being pampered, and she knew better than to *get* comfortable with it. A year seemed like a long time now, but it would pass quickly and then she'd be on her own again.

That seemed like a dismal prospect already, considering the amazing four days she'd spent with Nick. Their talk had broken all the ice between them, and they'd had fun. Lots of it. After their Sunday sail, they'd returned to the cottage to barbecue steaks on the deck just like a regular married couple. The next day they'd sailed down to Seabrook Island to play eighteen holes of golf on the famous Crooked Oaks course. Meg had won, but Nick was too competitive to let her victory stand. They already had a date to try out the Harbor Course at Wild Dunes on Saturday.

On Tuesday when Nick should have been returning to work to prepare for an end-of-the-week meeting with a representative from the Food and Drug Administration, they played hooky instead, walking on the beach, swimming, making each other laugh, and in general behaving like two people who genuinely liked each other. Nick had shown her a playful side that Meg wasn't even sure *he* knew existed.

Like Nick, she had hated to see the vacation end, but he had responsibilities he couldn't shirk. Meg only hoped that returning to his company didn't also mean that he would return to being that stern, unhappy man in the boardroom portrait.

Still wondering what had awakened her, she sat on the edge of the bed with one ear cocked toward Nick's room. It seemed quiet, but she got up anyway and opened the parlor door. No light showed under the door to his room. Either he wasn't home, or he'd already turned in.

She closed the parlor door, and that's when she heard the music, very faint, and obviously not coming from Nick's room. Curious, she slipped into the diaphanous white peignoir that had been another of the treasures in Nick's trousseau, and moved into the hall, listening.

Through the circle of the staircase to her left, Meg could see a faint light shining up from below. She hadn't noticed a stereo or CD player in her exploration of the first floor, but the music was stronger now. A solitary piano. Playing Chopin. One of his études.

Even from here, it was beautiful. Haunting. Brilliantly played, but not by an artist that she recognized.

Meg had heard all the great pianists. Not in person, of course, but on the finest recordings money could buy. Lew Holmby had been a classical music buff, something of an oddity in Kerry County, Missouri. His wife, Betsy, tolerated his passion, as well as his mediocre piano playing, but when he learned that Meg had a secret passion of her own for music, he'd taken her under his wing, taught her about the classics and the composers, the great pianists.

Meg missed the Holmbys terribly. They had been more than just friends to her—they were everything she'd ever wished her own parents had been. The music wafting upstairs made her sadly sentimental, and she followed the sound as it reached a crescendo. It wasn't until it died away that she realized she wasn't hearing a recording. No sound system on earth could reproduce the percussion of live music.

Nick was playing the piano? It seemed completely incomprehensible, but Meg couldn't think of any other explanation. Eleanor was still in Savannah, and neither of the Fetridges would have touched the piano—they would have considered it presumptuous.

That left Nick creating the exquisite music that began again in the conservatory. Another Chopin piece, one of Meg's favorites this time. The *Prelude in D-Flat*, a piece with gorgeous melodies anchored by the repetition of a single note that drove the piece forward.

The conservatory doors were shut, but a pencil-thin shaft of light bled out of the dining-room next door. Meg slipped inside and found the pocket doors between the two rooms were slightly ajar. Nick must not have noticed them when he sat down to play.

Unable to resist, Meg squeezed through the opening and retreated silently into the shadow of one of the huge columns that marched around the perimeter of the enormous conservatory that had once been half of the largest ballroom in Charleston.

Nick was on the far side of the room, his broad shoulders bent over the keyboard, his profile silhouetted by a single fan-shaped sconce set into the wall between two of the four sets of French windows that opened onto the garden.

Even in the faint light, Meg could see the fierce concentration on his face. She pulled deeper into the shadows and sank to her knees, marveling at the music that came not just from Nick's hands, but his whole body. His soul.

The sweet, lyrical melody floated around and through Meg, but it soon gave way to a variation that was as murky as the shadows she was hiding in. The sound built slowly to dark, pulsing chords that struggled against the restraint of Nick's strokes until the music finally burst free, taking Meg's breath away with its intensity and dark beauty.

Then it grew still and restrained again, delicate as summer air, leaving Meg enthralled, completely unaware of the tears that coursed down her cheeks.

THE ECHOES of the prelude died and Nick looked down at his hands with something akin to amazement.

God, how could anything that sounded so horrible *feel* so good? he wondered. How many years had it been since he'd been drawn to this room, compelled by a force he still didn't understand to let the music out?

Too many years, obviously. It took practice to play with the precision he'd perfected decades ago. More importantly, though, playing required an investment of emotion. In order to play music, you had to feel, and that was something Nick hadn't done for a very long time. Not since he'd been forced to bury the music and assume the reins of his father's company. The only way he'd been able to survive the loss was to squeeze every last drop of emotion from his hands. And from his heart. This room, this piano, became relics from another lifetime, and as long as Nick's heart stayed cold and dead, the music had stayed buried.

But then David had died, and Nick hadn't had any choice but to feel again. The pain of losing that precious part of his life had been too overwhelming to be ignored. With the pain came other feelings, too, and that's when Nick had realized how much he'd missed emotion. Not the pain and the anger, of course. But passion and excitement, joy and love...

Nick hadn't experienced even one of those feelings for nearly two decades, until the woman who had represented all of those things to his brother walked into his life, carrying the child he'd always wanted, bringing light into the dark corners of his heart and music back into his lifeless soul.

He was feeling again, beyond the grief, and it was as terrifying as it was exhilarating. And it was all because of Megan. He had come home tonight well after midnight, fighting the urge to wake her just for the simple pleasure of seeing her face.

The very idea had been too foolish for words, of course, so he'd poured a drink and wandered the house, too restless to sleep. Somehow he'd found himself in here. He'd opened the keyboard cover and run two fingers over the cool ivory. He'd pressed a key, felt the percussion of the note run up his arm, and before he knew what was happening he was playing. Feeling. Soaring.

Nick tightened his hands into fists, then stretched the fingers again. He brought them to the keys and they drifted into an arpeggio from Chopin's "Revolutionary" étude....

Too slow. Too clumsy. He tried again, and before he knew it the violent beauty of the "Revolutionary" was pouring through him like a storm-tossed ocean and he was lost again until the last chord died away.

He caught his breath and waited for the exhilaration to ebb, too. That's when he heard a rustling to his left, and he turned on the bench, peering into the shadows.

There was Megan sitting on the floor, a gossamer-white peignoir pooled around her like a cloud of mist, an expression of wonder on her face, her cheeks stained with tears.

Embarrassment flooded through Nick, he felt like a kid whose mother had caught him with a copy of *Playboy*. It was a fair analogy because every judge who'd ever awarded him a prize and every critic who'd ever reviewed his performances had praised his work for its sensual beauty. Sometimes, when the music was perfect, it was almost like making love.

Megan had caught him at his most intimate, his most vulnerable, and Nick wasn't accustomed to exposing his throat to anyone.

"What are you doing here?" His voice sounded gruffer than he intended, but he couldn't deal with her right now. He'd just spent four days torn between the sheer joy of her company and the exquisite torture of discovering that he wanted a woman he couldn't possibly have. He didn't need to see her like this, wearing a soft and sensual nightgown and peignoir that had been chosen for her by a fashion consultant who hadn't known that their marriage was one of convenience instead of romance.

"I'm sorry," she said, rising to float like a wraith across the ballroom floor toward him. "I didn't mean to disturb you, but I heard the music and couldn't resist."

Nick turned back to the piano. "I woke you. I'm sorry. Eleanor has always said you can't hear the piano on the second floor."

"I'm not sure what woke me," Megan replied. "The music was so faint I could barely hear it."

She appeared on his right, moving between him and the light, completely oblivious to the way it silhouetted the fullness of her breasts, her waist and the flare of her hips beneath the filmy robe. He'd seen far more of her in the beautiful golden bathing suit she'd worn aboard the *Rhapsody*, but there was something forbidden about this sensual glimpse of her silhouette.

Nick almost groaned at the sweet heat of arousal that stirred him.

"I didn't know you played, Nick," she said with the same wonder he'd seen in her face.

"I don't. Not anymore."

"That's not the way it sounded to me."

"Then you have a rotten ear for music," he snapped. He rose to move away from the piano, but Meg grabbed his arm.

"I'm sorry. I've made you angry. I didn't mean to intrude," she assured him. "Please don't stop on my account."

Stop on her account? It was because of her that he was playing again; that light and air and music were flooding back into his life whether he was ready for them or not. But it wasn't her fault that he'd spent the last twenty years in an emotional vacuum.

"No. I'm sorry," he said with a strained smile. "I haven't played in years and to say I'm rusty would be an insult to iron oxide."

Meg leaned against the piano. "Well, you missed a few notes in the 'D-Flat,' and that first arpeggio in the 'Revolutionary' was atrocious, but the emotion of your playing, the sheer...*passion* of it... It was the most beautiful thing I've ever heard."

Nick sat again, a little stunned. "You know Chopin?"

"He's my favorite composer." She told him about Dr. Holmby's lessons in music appreciation, and Nick shifted the piano bench, making room for her to sit.

"Do you play?" he asked her as she settled onto the bench beside him.

Meg laughed. "Me? Not even 'Chopsticks.' But when I was a kid, I used to sneak into the auditorium after school while I was waiting for my bus. The high-school music teacher taught an advanced piano course, and I'd hide in the back and listen to this incredible music—some of which was incredibly *bad*, but I didn't know that until years later when Dr. Holmby introduced me to the real thing."

Nick smiled at her and wondered, not for the first time, what her life had been like as a child. Music had been the center of his privileged childhood. For her, it was something she'd had to steal. No wonder she'd been content to listen to him play from a hiding place in the shadows.

"Megan, if you'd like to take lessons, I can arrange—"

"No, no," she said, shaking her head. "It would be a waste of time and money. Dr. Holmby tried to give me lessons once, but even he had to admit that I was hopeless. I was born to be a lover of music, not a practitioner."

Nick's thoughts stuck on the word *lover*. He started to close the keyboard, but Meg reached out a hand to stay him. "Please, play something else. Please."

Nick wondered if it would be possible to refuse her anything. "What would you like to hear?" he found himself asking.

"*Rhapsody on a Theme of Paganini*," she said without hesitation.

It was a beautiful and blatantly romantic piece of music, but unfortunately Nick had never fully committed it to memory. "I'm sorry. That was never in my repertoire. However..."

He got up and moved across the room to a wall panel that looked no different from any other in the expansive room. But when he pressed lightly on this one, it sprang open and a light came on automatically to reveal the floor-to-ceiling shelves of a music library.

Fascinated, Meg followed Nick. There were records and reel-to-reel tapes and a stack of thin black velvet boxes like the ones jewelers used for expensive necklaces, but the majority of the library consisted of folders of sheet music.

What casual piano student kept hundreds of scores squirreled away like this? she wondered. It made about as much sense as an international business tycoon who played the piano like a rusty virtuoso.

"Does Van Cliburn know you've been pilfering his rehearsal hall?" she asked in amazement.

Nick laughed as he thumbed through the files for the one he wanted. "Trust me. There are no ill-gotten gains here. Though they are being wasted," he said, pausing thoughtfully. "I really should donate these to…"

He turned to look at Meg. His voice failed him and whatever thought he'd been about to express flew away like doves released from long captivity. The bright, white light above them cast a shimmering halo around Meg, turning her into an etherial angel. Only she wasn't some distant, ethereal seraph. She was right beside him, so close that he could see tiny flecks of gold mixed into the emerald of her eyes. He could smell the faint floral scent of her perfume.

"My God… You are so beautiful," he whispered.

Her eyes widened just a fraction, partly in surprise and partly in something Nick couldn't name. Before he even realized that the intent was there, he cupped Meg's face in his hands, and kissed her.

She was too stunned to protest, and Nick took advantage of her surprise, brushing his tongue between her parted lips, then probing deeper, slanting his mouth across hers, deepening the kiss with an urgency that he hadn't felt since he discovered that girls had secret charms even more intoxicating than his music.

OH, GOD, what is happening to me?

The thought flitted through Meg's head. Something she'd never experienced before and didn't know how to control was careening around inside her. David had been the first considerate, gentle lover Meg had ever had, but this was entirely different. There was nothing harsh or cruel in Nick's kiss, but there was nothing gentle in it, either. It had wildness to it—a hint of danger that was too seductive to resist.

When he gathered her into his arms, Meg wanted to pull away, but she couldn't. She wanted to tell him to stop, but he was stoking a fire that was too consuming. When he pulled her against him and she felt the hardness of his arousal, she wanted to tell him that what they were doing was wrong. What she was *feeling* was wrong.

But it didn't feel wrong. His hand moved over her, down her flank and up again to cup her breast, brushing the hardening crest through the sheer fabric of her gown, and it felt exquisitely right. His mouth plundering hers was something between the sweetness of heaven and the torture of hell. He made love to her mouth in an imitation of an even more intimate coupling, setting Meg on fire because she wanted that coupling. The raw whimpers in her throat had to be telling him so, as did her hands woven through his thick black hair as she arched into his hand at her breast.

It was madness. There was no question about that. The father of her child had been dead little more than a month. What kind of a woman could turn so quickly into the arms of another man—one whose callousness had brought about the death of the man she loved, who had all but blackmailed her into an unwanted marriage? How could she possibly burn to feel a man like that inside her? What possible joy could there be in a meaningless sex act, for how could coupling with Nick be anything else?

He pulled her against him tighter, and for a moment Meg didn't care if it was mindless or meaningless. She wanted the passion to run its course...wanted to find out if something that started this wild could end in a new plateau of pleasure she'd never reached before. It was wrong, but she wanted it.

A hoarse cry of protest was lost in a moan of ecstasy when Nick's mouth finally left hers to work dazzling magic at her breast. It took every bit of strength she had to gasp, "No. Please, stop. Nick... Stop. Please..."

She pushed at his shoulders and wrenched away, stumbling back, barely able to stand. Stinging tears, part shame and part frustrated longing, flooded onto her cheeks, but when she looked at Nick's face as he stood there, gasping for breath and sanity, she'd never seen so much heat and desire in any man's eyes. Even David had never looked at her with so much wanting.

Meg was ashamed, humiliated by what she had let Nick do to her—and what she still wanted from him.

"You promised me, damn you," she gasped out, unable to fight the tears and the shame.

Nick took hold of the edge of the open wall panel, grasping it so hard that his fingers turned white. Frustration made it hard for him to think beyond the need that coursed through him. "I'm sorry," he managed to say.

"You promised," she said again, an accusation that cut through him, but did nothing to dull the ache in his loins.

"And I said I was sorry!" he snapped at her. "What more do you want? Blood?"

"I want you to swear that you'll never touch me again!"

"Fine! I do so swear!" he practically shouted, stepping forward to tower over her. "But if you expect me to keep our vow of marital chastity, don't flaunt your assets in sexy nightgowns at three in the morning. Despite what you may think to the contrary, I'm not made of stone!"

The accusation struck home. "It wasn't...I didn't..." Excuses failed her. She couldn't very well take the moral high ground when she'd wanted to make love with Nick as much as he'd wanted her.

"You're right," she said finally, swiping at her tears. "It won't happen again. Play your damned piano alone in the dark for all I care. I won't disturb you ever again."

She whirled and all but ran out of the conservatory, leaving Nick behind. She took the shame and the confusion with her, though.

CHAPTER TEN

As FAR AS MEG could tell, Nick engaged in no more late-night concerts. As a matter of fact, he didn't engage in much of anything for the next six weeks except the work at Ballenger Pharmaceuticals, which gave him an excuse to leave the house early in the morning and not return until very late at night.

Meg's husband became little more than a ghostly presence in her life.

At first she welcomed his absence. It allowed her to get her shame under control and put what had happened in the conservatory into perspective. Actually, it wasn't all that incomprehensible.

Nick and Meg had both lost someone they loved, which had created an emptiness inside them. Since Nature abhorred a vacuum, it was only logical that they would subconsciously look for some way to fill the void. Combine that with their recent effort to become friends, and it wasn't hard to see how they might stumble across a line they would never have otherwise traversed.

It was very sound psychology, and it tied up what had happened with a nice, tidy, nonthreatening bow. The only problem was, Meg couldn't get rid of the feelings Nick had evoked. She couldn't make herself stop thinking about how exciting his kiss had been any more than she could stop missing the kind, funny Nick from their honeymoon.

Unfortunately, he'd been swallowed whole by the cold, remote man who'd first cornered her in his company boardroom with a marriage contract; but even so, whenever she saw him now, she was aware of him in a way that made her feel like a teenager in the throes of her first schoolgirl crush.

With Nick essentially out of her life, Meg had been left to the not-so-tender mercies of Eleanor, who had returned from Savannah two days earlier than planned and apparently found nothing surprising about the tension between her grandson and his faux wife.

Under the guise of introducing her to "all the right people," Eleanor took control of Meg's life with a vengeance, trying to turn her into a sort of Stepford Socialite by attaching her to the most boring civic organizations imaginable. Meg liked flowers, certainly, but the white-haired ladies of the Rose of Charleston Garden Club weren't just from another century; as she sat sipping tea with them and listening to remedies for aphids, Meg sometimes felt as though they were from another planet.

It wasn't just age or horticulture that separated Meg from Eleanor's contemporaries. Or class or wealth or privilege, for that matter. It was the simple fact that Meg was accustomed to making a difference in people's lives.

Though she went along with Eleanor, Meg seriously suspected that the dowager's persistence had very little to do with seeing that Meg was socially accepted, as she claimed. It was purely a matter of controlling Meg and making her perform like a trained seal.

Because it was in her child's best interest that she not offend the matrons of Charleston, Meg cooperated with Eleanor for four weeks as word of her marriage to Nick became common knowledge. She tolerated the manipulation for two more weeks, but by the end of six, she was ready to rebel. She wasn't foolish enough to think that defying Eleanor would be simple, though. She needed a plan. And an accomplice.

That's why she chose to make her stand in Nick's presence. Now that her morning sickness was a thing of the past, she joined Eleanor for breakfast every morning in the dining room. Two weeks ago Nick had started putting in an appearance, as well. He was cool and distant to her, but unfailingly polite. The man who had looked at her with fire in his midnight-blue eyes might never have existed.

Meg hated his coldness, but she knew she couldn't have it both ways. If being friendly with Nick meant more episodes like the one in the conservatory, then erecting walls and leaving them up was the only logical thing to do.

Wasn't it?

On the morning she chose as her own personal independence day, she made a point of arriving early and discovered that Nick and Eleanor were already "at breakfast" as they called it. As Meg entered, Eleanor was telling him, "I'll send your regrets as usual, but you might want to phone Richard with a personal explanation—how busy you are with the FDA drug trials, or something of that nature. People *are* beginning to wonder."

"Wonder about what?" Meg asked as she assumed her usual place across from Eleanor, with Nick on her right at the head of the table.

"Nothing, my dear, nothing," Eleanor said quickly, clearly startled by Meg's sudden arrival.

"It didn't sound like nothing," Meg commented mildly. She looked at Nick. "What 'regrets' is Eleanor sending?"

Nick folded his newspaper and laid it beside his plate. "We've been invited to a bon voyage party for some friends of mine, Richard Constable and his wife, Laura. They're leaving for Europe in two weeks."

Meg raised her eyebrows. "*We* were invited...?" she asked, curious to know which "we" he meant.

"You and I," he elaborated. "Nan is sending our regrets."

Meg remembered Eleanor's exact words. "As usual?" she pressed. "How many more invitations have *we* declined? Is that what people are wondering about—our failure to be seen together in public?"

Eleanor sighed delicately, a sure sign that she thought her new granddaughter was being difficult. "Yes. Nicholas receives an average of twenty to thirty invitations a month during the summer social season. That number fell, naturally, in the month after David's accident, but the announcement of your marriage has brought a flurry of invitations from friends anxious to meet his new wife."

"I see." Meg rose thoughtfully, digesting this information as she filled her plate at the sideboard. It was, perhaps, naive of her not to have realized that she and Nick had been receiving invitations to parties and charity events. Given the current friction between them, it made sense that Nick would be reluctant to squire her about the city.

But this new knowledge raised a host of disturbing questions. If the Charleston social circle was curious about her, why hadn't she received any personal invitations? In the last few weeks she'd read newspaper accounts of two charity luncheons, and had wondered why someone as socially prominent as Eleanor wasn't in-

volved in them. Now she wondered why the wife of
Nicholas Ballenger hadn't been invited, as well.

Meg returned to the table and sat. "Just out of curiosity," she began mildly. "How many regrets has
Eleanor sent on *my* behalf alone?"

Nick looked baffled, but Eleanor's already-perfect
posture came a little more erect. "I didn't think it was
appropriate for you to be seen in public without Nicholas
until he had introduced you in a proper social setting."

Meg leveled an angry gaze at her. "In other words,
you let me *think* I was being introduced to society when
actually I was just being paraded in front of little pockets
of your friends—women you could control, who
wouldn't ask the wrong questions and would only report
to their family and friends what you wanted them to
report about me."

Eleanor didn't bother denying it. "And you have ac-
quitted yourself quite nicely with them, my dear."

Meg glanced at Nick. "Did you know about this? Did
the two of you agree that it wouldn't do to let David's
little tramp loose on proper Charleston society?"

Meg saw a nerve twitch in Nick's stiffened jaw. "No,
Megan. Frankly, I hadn't given your social activities a
moment's thought. But if I *had*, I wouldn't have taken
you for the sort of shallow social climber who cares
more about her standing in the community than the
causes she purports to serve."

He was comparing her to his mother, and that was an
association Meg wanted no part of. She realized she was
fighting the wrong battle just because her pride had been
wounded. "You're right. I don't give a fig about finding
a rung on the social ladder, but you made me your wife
to legitimize the child I'm carrying and to secure *his*
place in Charleston society. If people are beginning to

ask why Nick Ballenger hasn't been seen in public with his new wife, don't you think it would be wise to put their questions to rest?''

There was a long pause as Nick looked down, carefully folding his napkin. Finally, he told Eleanor, ''Go ahead and send our regrets to the Constables, but call the Women's Civic League and tell them I've changed my mind about attending the AIDS fund-raiser Saturday night. My wife and I will be attending the ball, after all.'' He looked at Meg. ''This is one of the most formal events of the season. You'll need an evening gown.''

''Preferably something that minimizes your condition,'' Eleanor added. If she had an opinion about Nick's decision, she wasn't letting it show.

It was the first time either of them had acknowledged the fact that Meg's pregnancy was becoming obvious. At barely four and a half months, camouflaging it for another few weeks would be difficult, but not impossible. ''I'll go shopping today,'' she told them.

''Good,'' Nick replied. ''And from now on, Eleanor will see that all of your invitations reach you personally. I'm sure her social secretary, Mrs. Burns, will have time to help you with your responses.''

Nick didn't see Eleanor's frown, but Meg did. ''I don't think it will be necessary to burden Mrs. Burns,'' she told him, more for her own benefit than for Eleanor's or the secretary's. Mrs. Burns was so dour that she made Eleanor look positively chipper, and Meg knew what their combined assistance was like. She had spent hours with both of them ''helping'' her respond to the hundreds of wedding gifts she and Nick had received, and the process had almost driven her insane. ''I can handle my own correspondence,'' she assured Nick.

''Fine.'' He started to rise, but Meg had other plans.

Nick had already freed her from Eleanor's clutches in one sense. There would never be a better time for her to announce her total independence.

"Please don't go yet," she said, putting out a hand to stay him, then withdrawing it quickly.

He looked coldly at the withdrawn hand, then at her, and resumed his seat. "What?"

"I've decided to go to work," she told him, earning a dark scowl.

"I beg your pardon?"

"I made some calls last week," she explained, her words coming out in a nervous rush. "I don't think it's wise for me to return to full-time nursing, but there are any number of organizations that could use the services of someone with my credentials. I've decided to volunteer as a counselor at the women's shelter—it's a safe house for victims of spouse abuse."

"You can't be serious," Eleanor said. "That is completely unacceptable."

Meg wanted to ignore her because she knew that Nick was the one she really had to convince, but she couldn't bring herself to be rude. "Why? Because the Ballenger women don't sully their hands with the problems of the common people?"

"I think Nan means it's unacceptable because you're pregnant," Nick replied. He frowned at his grandmother. "At least I hope that's what she means."

"Counseling isn't hazardous duty, if that's what you're getting at," Meg informed him reasonably.

"No?" Nick said archly. "Tell that to the director of the shelter who was nearly bludgeoned to death in the parking lot last year when the husband of one of her clients came looking for his wife."

A wave of nausea crashed over Meg, but it had nothing to do with her pregnancy. It was a "been there, done that" recollection of what had happened to her in a dark parking lot. Pain, fear and humiliation all crowded in on her, and she knew that her reaction had to be registering on her face because Nick was suddenly looking at her with genuine concern.

"Megan? Are you all right?"

She collected herself and tried to smile. "Fine. I've just been wrestling with a bout of morning sickness, that's all. This wave caught me by surprise."

Nick eased his chair back. "Sit still. I'll get you a cup of ginger tea." He moved to the sideboard, where Effie kept a pot steeping every morning for just such emergencies.

"Thank you," she said when he returned with the cup.

"Now, where were we?" Nick asked as he resumed his seat.

"You were doing a very good job of presenting the dangers of volunteer work," she reminded him. Only he had no idea *how* good.

"Sorry. I'm just trying to be realistic, Megan. I know that you would never willingly place yourself and your child at risk."

He was right about that. No risk was acceptable, not when it could cost the life of her child. "You're right, of course," she conceded. "But I refuse to participate in any more of Eleanor's garden parties and I'll go stark raving mad if I have nothing to do but sit around the Hall and watch the houseplants grow."

"There are all those invitations you'll be receiving," Eleanor reminded her with an irritating edge to her voice.

"Wanting the right to answer my own mail doesn't

mean that I plan to become a social butterfly," Meg retorted, then turned her attention back to Nick. She hadn't realized until that moment how important it was that he understand where she was coming from. "Nick, there are dozens of organizations in the city that do wonderful charity work—like the Women's Civic League you mentioned—but I would be absolutely useless helping organize parties and fund-raisers."

Something in Nick responded to the soft urgency of Meg's tone despite his best efforts to keep the wall up between them. "Don't underestimate yourself, Megan," he said gently.

"I'm not," she assured him. "But I know what it is to need help and have nowhere to turn. That's why I became a counselor. I like helping people one-on-one. Please support my decision."

"And if he doesn't?" Eleanor interjected.

"Nan, please—"

"No, it's a fair question, Nick," Meg cut him off, though she was undeniably pleased that he'd jumped in to protect her from his acerbic grandmother. "If Nick forbids me to work at the women's shelter, I won't do it. I'm his wife—for the next ten and a half months, anyway. He has a right to have a say in anything his wife does that might reflect on him."

"Megan, I promise you, this isn't a question of what's socially acceptable for the wife of Nick Ballenger," he assured her. "I just don't want you to become involved in anything that could be even slightly dangerous."

"Neither do I. But I can't just sit in this antique gallery and twiddle my thumbs until the baby is born."

"Then how about a compromise?" he suggested. "One of the local charities Ballenger Pharmaceuticals supports is the Carolina Crisis Center. It has statewide

CONNIE BENNETT 177

hot lines for everything from suicide prevention to spouse abuse to teen pregnancy. It's one-on-one, but the telephone will provide a layer of protection that you wouldn't have at the women's shelter. How's that?''

Meg felt the sudden urge to cry. She'd needed him to understand, and he'd come through for her. "I think that's perfect, Nick. Thank you."

He accepted her thanks with a nod. "And there's something else you might consider if you find yourself at loose ends."

"What's that?"

"House hunting," he replied.

Meg felt a strange ache twist in her stomach. Was he anxious to get rid of her already? "So soon?"

"It doesn't have to become a full-time occupation," he assured her, "but Charleston is a large city and choosing a home to suit your lifestyle isn't as easy as it sounds. A little casual house hunting is the best way to become acquainted with the most desirable suburbs and neighborhoods. And if you choose something that needs work, we could be looking at months of renovations."

"I'll start investigating the real-estate market, then," she said, hoping that she didn't look as hurt as she felt. Everything he said made sense, but she couldn't shake the feeling that he was looking forward to getting her out of his life.

"Good." Nick rose and slipped into the gray suit coat that had been hanging on the back of his chair. "Don't wait dinner for me, Nan. I'll have something carried in at the office." And then he was gone.

The silence that settled over the room was thick with Eleanor's displeasure. Meg nibbled at the fresh fruit on her plate, wondering if there was any point in trying to soothe the dowager's ruffled feathers. Despite Meg's best efforts for the past six weeks, she hadn't found a single soft spot anywhere in Eleanor's icy armor. Though it seemed pointless, she decided to keep trying.

"I'm sorry you don't approve of my decision," she said finally.

"What I think is irrelevant, Megan," Eleanor replied, carefully folding her napkin and placing it beside her plate.

"I disagree," Meg replied. "We're living under the same roof."

"For a few more months," she said pointedly.

Meg cocked a surprised eyebrow at her. "You don't have any plans to see your great-grandchild after I move out?"

Eleanor looked at her. "Given the terms of your pre-nuptial agreement, I don't see how that will be possible with the child in your custody for the first three years."

Meg frowned and placed a hand on the swell of her abdomen. "Eleanor, surely you know that I would never try to keep you away from this child. I want you to be a presence in his life."

Eleanor's hard, cold smile sent a chill down Meg's spine. "Oh, you can count on that, my dear. Now, if you'll excuse me…" She rose and strolled out as regal as a queen, leaving Meg alone to ponder the meaning of the assurance that had sounded almost like a threat.

ELEANOR SLIPPED into her morning room on the first floor and closed the tall pocket doors behind her. She was so angry she didn't trust herself to be civil to anyone, even the servants.

How dare Megan speak to her in such a fashion? Magnanimously offering her visitation rights when the trashy little hillbilly wasn't fit to raise a dog, let alone the Ballenger heir!

Well, the girl would sing a different tune when Eleanor finally confronted her with the wealth of information that James Hamilton had uncovered about her sordid past.

There had been a time, briefly, before the reports began coming in, that Eleanor had considered calling off her private investigator. The girl was clearly trying so hard to fit in that Eleanor had felt a twinge of guilt.

Then the first report arrived and erased all her doubts completely. Hamilton's very first piece of information exposed a bald-faced lie—Megan had told Eleanor plainly that both her parents were dead, when in fact her father was very much alive.

And there was more.

Eleanor wanted to tell Nick what she'd learned, and after this morning she might not be able to wait much longer. He had been keeping his distance from Megan, but when they were together Eleanor sensed undercurrents of a sexual tension that could never be allowed to grow. Something had happened during the couple's so-called honeymoon, something that had brought them together and then set them apart.

Eleanor had still been in Savannah when she heard that Nick and his new wife had been seen cavorting like love-struck newlyweds on the golf course at Seabrook. That's why she'd come home ahead of schedule—to see if the bond that had been so obvious to everyone at their wedding reception had deepened into something more.

Eleanor had nothing against Nick being happy, but not with Megan Linley. Considering the way he had capitulated to her at the breakfast table, it would be good for Nick to learn the truth.

Unfortunately, the time wasn't right to bring Nick into her confidence yet. Hamilton knew a great deal, but there were still important details that were proving difficult to unearth. It wouldn't do much good, for example, to tell Nick that his wife had a criminal record if Eleanor couldn't also tell him why the girl had spent a year in jail.

The records pertaining to her incarceration were sealed, but Hamilton was confident that with time and patience he could find a way to quietly unseal them.

And there were other things, some too sordid to even think about. A teenage pregnancy and a shotgun wedding to a man who was now serving his second prison term. An alcoholic father who was a convicted felon, as well. A mother who had died under strange circumstances.

Oh, yes. There was a great deal to be shared with Nick when the time was right, and it would prove once and for all that Megan Linley was not a fit person to raise the Ballenger heir. The girl had plenty of secrets to go around, and once they were all unveiled wresting custody from her would be easier than Eleanor had ever imagined it could be.

It was simply a matter of biding her time.

CHAPTER ELEVEN

NICK DIDN'T HAVE any choice but to consider the fund-raiser a personal success. He introduced Megan to his curious friends, and she charmed the collective pants off them with her unique brand of quiet dignity, wit and charm. They worked the crowd as they had at the wedding reception, with an instinctive precision, sensing each other's moves, finishing each other's sentences, improvising effortlessly when someone asked an unanticipated question about their courtship and unexpected marriage.

Through it all, Megan never faltered, and Nick knew that he was the only person in the room who could tell that she was actually very frightened. More than one of his friends commented privately to Nick on how charming his new wife was, and the women seemed to accept her as well, probably because they perceived nothing threatening about her. She wasn't the most glamorous woman in the room, or the most outgoing, or the most seductive. She was simply Megan, and everyone she met seemed to respond to her sweet, reserved smile.

In truth, the only person who had a problem with Megan that night was Nick himself. He'd thought that keeping his distance from her these last few weeks would immunize him against the attraction he felt, but he couldn't have been more wrong. Nothing in the world could have inoculated him against the way she looked in her black evening dress, with its halter top. The front had clever gathers emanating from a beaded star burst between her breasts, and he spent the evening entirely too aware of her bare shoulders and the swell of her breasts.

He still wanted her, despite the clamp he'd put on his emotions since that insane night in the conservatory. But wanting his wife was only a fraction of his problem. Mostly he missed the fun they'd had, and the good times he knew they could have together in the future. He missed the easy-as-breathing way he'd felt in her presence on their honeymoon, and he missed the music that had flowed so freely out of him for those few minutes in the conservatory.

He'd been like another person those few days, and he liked that Nick Ballenger—the one who was capable of being happy. But in order to become that Nick, he had to let down his guard with Megan, and he wasn't sure he could do that without crossing the line between friend and lover. It was probably his greatest flaw, but he was an all-or-nothing person, and he wanted *all* of Megan Linley Ballenger.

It had occurred to Nick more than once that he was a little bit in love with his wife. Maybe even more than a little bit. But whenever he allowed himself to think about it, he was overwhelmed with guilt for coveting something that had belonged to his brother—and still did. He'd killed David, and now he wanted the woman who loved him. It had a disturbing Old Testament feel to it— a man coveting his brother's wife.

Only Megan was *his* wife, damn it, not David's, and the thought of romancing her, trying to win her love, held more appeal to Nick every time he saw her. He'd never actually courted a woman before, and the challenge of it was enticing. And a little intoxicating.

But could he do it? *Should* he do it?

The desire was there, but was it the right thing to do?

"You were brilliant, as usual," he complimented her as soon as they were in the car headed for home. The ball wouldn't be over for hours, but when Megan pleaded exhaustion, Nick had been happy for an excuse to escape. She was snuggled into the passenger seat of the Mercedes, her head back, eyes closed, as though she was soaking up the pleasure of being seated for the first time in hours. The beaded sacque coat that matched her dress was wrapped around her, leaving nothing exposed to the night, or to Nick, but he was still too aware of her. He needed to erect some barriers again, but he didn't want to.

"I didn't feel brilliant," she replied. "I felt like a gate-crasher waiting for someone to realize I didn't belong there."

"Don't be silly, Megan. You can belong anywhere. Your image of high-society snobbery is at least a generation out of date."

She turned her head, and Nick could feel her looking at him in the dark. "You mean pedigrees don't count? Then why did you force me to marry you?"

Damn it. How long would it be before she stopped working the origins of their relationship into every conversation?

"All right, pedigrees do count to some of them. Maybe too many of them," he admitted reasonably, keeping his eyes on the traffic as he negotiated the freeway on-ramp that would take them across the Ashley River back into the city. "But when you get to know some of those people one-on-one, you'll find that they're no different from you. They have the same hopes and fears, the same insecurities. The same dreams for their children.''

''Oh, please. You can't be that naive, Nick.''

He glanced over at her. ''I'm not naive, but basic human needs—''

''Have nothing in common in the world where you live and the one I came from. You can't even imagine what it's like to be poor unless you've lived it. Or at least *seen* it up close. Do you know what it's like to be hungry and not know when there might be food in the house again? Did you ever do homework by candlelight because there was no money to pay the gas bill? When you were a kid, did you ever stand by your mother's side at a supermarket checkout wearing Salvation Army hand-me-downs, with the people in line behind you looking down their snooty noses because your mother was taking too long to count out her food stamps? Do you know what that's like? Is there any humiliation you suffered as a child that could possibly compare?''

Nick's childhood had been about as emotionally barren as any life could be, but no, he couldn't think of anything that would equate to the humiliation she described. ''No. I guess not.''

''Then don't tell me I want the same things as those people tonight,'' she said without any rancor, bending forward to work at the ankle-strap buckle of one of her shoes. Nick had discovered on their honeymoon that she hated wearing shoes and had a habit of coming out of them at every opportunity. The endearing little quirk made it hard for him to concentrate on her serious lecture as she went on without pause. ''Those people take their wealth for granted. They think their place in society is a birthright, and anyone who wasn't born at the top of the social ladder is an outsider. Think about it. How many times tonight did someone ask me where I'm from?''

''Quite often,'' he had to admit. ''What's wrong with that? Didn't people in Singapore ask you where you were from?''

''Of course. Politely, as a conversation icebreaker. But no one over there ever asked me what my 'people' do for a living. What your friends really wanted to know was how my father earned our family's fortune.''

''True enough,'' he admitted reluctantly. He remembered that question and the discomfort on Megan's face when she answered that she didn't have any family left in Missouri. Her parents were dead, she'd told them. To spare her more discomfort, Nick had quickly steered her away from that little cluster of social jackals.

He knew she was right about their motives. There were rumors floating around Charleston that Nick had married ''out of his class,'' but so far no one had gleaned the fact that his new wife had worked her way out of desperate poverty.

Megan slid her foot out of one shoe and went to work on the buckle of the other. ''If I had told those people the truth tonight, you'd never be able to hold your head up at a society function again—not until after the divorce, anyway.''

Damn it. There it was again. Another reminder that their marriage was only for show. ''You're wrong, Megan,'' he told her. ''*Most* of those people would admire you if they knew the truth. Half the fortunes in that room tonight are less than a generation old. A lot of them worked very hard to get where they are.''

''Whereas *I* married money,'' she said sarcastically,

slipping out of her other shoe. "Oh, yes, Nick. Very admirable."

"Oh, for heaven's sake."

She leaned back in the seat again. "You just—" A sharp grunt strangled whatever she'd been about to say, and Nick looked at her. Even in the dark he could see that her eyes were wide with panic and pain. She made another strangled cry, drawing her knees up and wrapping her arms across her midsection protectively.

"Megan! What's wrong?"

"Oh, God," she gasped out. "It hurts, Nick. It…hurts."

Panic pulsed through Nick. He stretched out a hand to her, but didn't know where to put it or what to do. "Is it the baby?"

"I don't know." She choked back another cry.

"Describe the pain," he commanded, keeping his voice firm but calm as he dug into the storage compartment between their seats for his cell phone.

"Sharp. Stabbing. But it won't…let up. Oh, God, Nick. Don't let it happen again. Please don't let it happen again."

Again? Nick heard the hysteria rising in her voice, and didn't give himself time to wonder what she meant. "Shh… Just try to stay calm, sweetheart. It'll be all right," he promised her, hitting a key on the phone.

Meg finally saw what he was doing. "My purse. Dr. Michaelson's number is in…my purse."

But Nick was already two steps ahead of her. The day that Robert Michaelson had confirmed Meg's pregnancy Nick had programmed the doctor's number into the speed dial of all his telephones. He barely had time to tell Meg that before the doctor's service picked up.

He explained the situation and told the girl in no uncertain terms that he was taking his wife to the hospital and he expected Dr. Michaelson to meet them there.

When Nick got off the phone and looked at Meg, her face was wet with tears that were equal parts pain and terror. He reached out to her. "Hang on, Meg. The hospital is just across the river. We're only five minutes away. It'll be all right," he crooned in a soothing voice. "You'll be just fine. You'll be fine."

But would the baby?

Nick couldn't make that promise, and he was just as frightened of the answer as Meg was.

WHEN NICK CARRIED Meg into the emergency room, a trauma team rushed forward, leaving him no choice but to relinquish her to their custody. Her pain had subsided, but as they laid her on the gurney, it struck again, and she grabbed Nick's hand. He moved with them as far as the swinging doors, still crooning to her without really knowing what he was saying, then one of the nurses forced him to let go. They swept her away from him and the doors made a sickening *flap-flap* as they closed in his face.

Only one time in his life had Nick ever felt as alone and helpless. When he'd learned of David's death there had been nothing for him to do, and no one he could turn to for comfort. He had swung wildly between numbness and rage, certain that if he could just get on a plane and go to Singapore he could somehow bring David back to life. But Eleanor had begged him not to go. He'd seen her fear and he'd recognized his impulse as irrational. David was dead and not even the great and powerful Nicholas Ballenger could bring him back to life. And now David's child was in danger, and Nick was equally powerless. All he could do was pace and pray. It wasn't enough.

Thirty minutes passed like an equivalent number of hours. He did the obligatory paperwork and paced some more. When he demanded to know what was happening, he learned that Dr. Michaelson had been upstairs in the delivery room when they arrived, but he was on his way down now. There was no news to report.

Finally, the nurse who'd separated him from Meg came through the swinging doors, and Nick pounced on her.

"How is my wife?"

"She's out of pain for the moment. You can come and see her if you like," Barbara Conlon, R.N., informed him with a friendly, professionally optimistic smile that had soothed a thousand frightened relatives.

"And the baby?" Nick pressed as he set a quick pace out of the waiting room.

"Doing fine," the nurse assured him. "We've got her on a fetal monitor."

Nick wasn't reassured. They went through the flapping doors past a half-dozen curtained cubicles. Nurse Conlon pulled back the last curtain on the right, and there was Meg, curled on her side, partially covered by a white sheet, surrounded by machines that beeped and bleated and made her look too tiny for words.

She was wearing a blue hospital gown now, and the relief on her face when she saw Nick erased some of that terrible emptiness inside of him. He wasn't facing this alone, and neither was she. It was a deeply stirring realization.

Meg held out her hand to him. "So far, so good," she told him as he sidled between the machines and took her hand.

"What did Dr. Michaelson say?" he asked, using his free hand to gently brush a lock of hair off her forehead.

"A lot of platitudes that aren't as much comfort as he thinks they are. He's checking on some test results. Said he'd be back soon. But look…" Her face lit up as she pointed to one of the beeping machines near the foot of the bed. "The baby's heartbeat."

Nick twisted to look and found the steady but rapid pulse that was displayed on the monitor. It was an encouraging sign, but he was afraid to be too reassured. "Did they do an ultrasound?" he asked her.

She nodded. "Michaelson said everything seems normal."

"Did you see it?" Nick asked her.

"No." The machine was at the head of the bed, well out of Meg's viewing range.

Nick glanced over his shoulder at the nurse. "Did you record the ultrasound? Could we take a look at it?"

Conlon smiled at him. "I don't see why not." She moved Nick to the opposite side of the bed and rolled the equipment cart in closer, turning it to face Megan. The nurse cued up the tape, and within seconds a fuzzy black-and-white image began pulsating on the screen. The image shifted and blurred, then steadied, and finally Nick could see the outline of the perfectly proportioned fetus.

Nick had seen ultrasounds before. For a time, he'd considered having the company develop and market medical equipment in addition to pharmaceuticals. But this was different. This was his child.

No, he reminded himself sternly. It was David's child, not his. He would raise him as his own, *love* him as his own, but the seed that was flourishing in Megan's womb was David's.

The reminder didn't diminish Nick's joy. There was something of his brother left in the world. That ultimate realization made the fuzzy little baby on the monitor all the more precious.

Nick didn't realize that he had placed one hand protectively on Megan's abdomen until he felt her hand cover his. He looked at her, startled, and started to pull away, but her attention was on the monitor and she had already woven her fingers with his. He left his hand where it was, and they watched the playback on the monitor.

"Well, I see you're enjoying the in-flight movie," Bob Michaelson said cheerily as he came through the curtains with Meg's chart folded against his robust midsection. "What do you think of Baby Ballenger?"

"That he gave us quite a scare," Nick said, straightening to look at the doctor on the other side of the ultrasound monitor. "Hello, Bob."

"Nick. Good to see you again."

Nick frowned, suspicious of Michaelson's good mood. "Even under these conditions?"

"Absolutely! I was between deliveries upstairs, and I hate waiting around with nothing to do."

"Then Megan and the baby are both all right?"

"Right as rain," the doctor said as the nurse stepped out of the way so that he could take her place at the ultrasound cart. "Did you catch this? Look." He studied the tape a second, then backed it up to a clearer patch. When he found what he wanted, he froze the tape. "See? If I read this right—and I'm actually pretty good—she's sucking her thumb."

"Oh my God," Meg said with a little laugh.

"She is!" Nick said, his voice filled with wonder.

Then he realized what they'd said—even the nurse, earlier—and he looked at the doctor. "Is it really a girl?"

"Weeelll..." Michaelson rocked from side to side. "Ultrasound is never a hundred percent accurate, and I wouldn't want to make an official guess for another two or three weeks, but if someone used the rack and thumbscrews on me, I'd say it's a girl."

Nick smiled and looked down at his hand and Megan's resting on her stomach. "Hi there, Princess. I guess we'll have to stop referring to you as he."

Meg looked up at Nick, searching for any sign of disappointment on his face and couldn't find a trace. There was just wonder and happiness, and they looked to be in about the same measure as Meg's.

"Well, if everything is so hunky-dory, Dr. Michaelson, why was I in so much pain tonight?" she asked.

"What were you doing right before it started?" the doctor asked, opening his chart again.

"Just sitting in the car."

"No, she was bending over, taking off her shoes," Nick corrected. "She straightened up and the pain hit her."

Michaelson hummed thoughtfully. "Have you been doing those exercises we talked about at your last appointment?"

Meg nodded. "Yesterday I moved up to twice a day."

Nick was frowning again. "What exercises?"

"An isometric abdominal series," the doctor answered. "They're very passive, but over the course of a pregnancy they strengthen and tone the abdominal muscles considerably. Helps with the birth and makes an enormous difference in how quickly mothers are able to get their figures back."

"And you think the exercises caused the pain?" Meg asked.

"Yep. Probably worked a new muscle group that you're not accustomed to using." He flipped a page on the chart. "And your blood test shows a slight electrolyte imbalance, which could make you more prone to muscle cramps."

"You mean I had a charley horse in my stomach?" Meg asked incredulously.

Michaelson nodded. "That's about the size of it."

"Not a miscarriage?" Nick asked.

"Nope. Everything seems to be perfectly fine." He outlined a course of action that included hot packs if the muscle spasms returned that night and regular blood tests for the next few weeks, then he stood over her while she swallowed a moderately vile-tasting sports drink to replenish the electrolytes.

Just as he was telling Meg she could get dressed and go home, his beeper went off.

"Aha! Mrs. Jermanksi is fully dilated," he announced after a quick glance at his beeper. "I gotta run. Take good care of our girls, Nick. I'll look forward to seeing the both of you back here sometime around Christmas. Happy holidays!"

CHAPTER TWELVE

LIGHTS WERE ON at Ballenger Hall when Nick pulled through the gate and parked just short of the carriage house. He had called ahead as they left the hospital, and Fetridge was waiting with the door open, ready to receive them.

Over Meg's protests, Nick came around the car and scooped her into his arms to carry her into the house.

"It's about time," the butler murmured in his distinctive Irish brogue as he stepped back to allow them to pass.

"I beg your pardon?" Nick said, turning to look back at him.

"That you carried Mrs. Ballenger across the threshold. Sir." His expression was solemn, but there was a merry twinkle in his eyes.

Meg's face flamed. "You can set me down now, Nick."

He grinned at her. "Why would I want to do that?" He moved on down the wide entry hall. "Fetridge, does Effie have everything ready upstairs?"

"Yes, sir," the butler answered, trailing along behind them.

"Has my grandmother returned yet?" Eleanor had attended the charity ball with her sometime companion, Giles Brisbane, and, as was often the case at events of that nature, Nick hadn't seen much of her during the evening.

"No, sir. She's not returned," Fetridge informed him.

"Well, don't alarm her when she comes home," Nick instructed as he started up the stairs. "I'll speak to her before she turns in."

"Of course. If I may ask, sir, how is Mrs. Ballenger?"

Meg craned her neck over Nick's shoulder to inform the butler, "Mrs. Ballenger is fine, Fetridge. A little embarrassed that she overreacted to a common muscle cramp, but otherwise healthy. *Mr.* Ballenger is just being overly protective."

"Dr. Michaelson advised you to move carefully and slowly until you got that cramp worked out," Nick reminded her.

"Yes, but he didn't suggest that I become an invalid."

Nick ignored her dig and performed his long-standing ritual with the butler. "Were there any calls while we were out, Fetridge?"

"Only for Missus Eleanor. A gentleman from the Charleston Art League."

"All right. Thank you," he said as he emerged onto the second-floor landing.

Mrs. Fetridge, who looked like the bookend companion of her lean, russet-haired husband, was waiting to lead their little procession into Meg's bedroom. "I have everything ready just as you asked, Mr. Nick. There's tea on the cart, a hot pad waiting, Missus Megan's bed is turned back, and I took the liberty of laying out the Missus' nightgown."

Nick froze just inside the door. Everything was exactly as Effie described it, including the nightgown lying across the foot of the bed—the diaphanous cloud of white that Meg had worn that night in the conservatory.

He felt Meg tense in his arms and knew that she was thinking the same thing. But was she remembering their kiss or the warning that came after about the dangers of wearing sexy lingerie?

"You can put me down now, Nick," she said softly.

"That's right, sir. I'll help the Missus get ready for bed," Effie offered, stepping forward as Nick reluctantly set his wife on her feet.

"That won't be necessary, Effie," Meg assured her. "The best way everyone can help me is to stop making a fuss. I'll be fine. Really." She started for her dressing room. "Thank you for everything."

"But Missus Megan—your nightgown," Effie said, scooping it up off the bed with both arms.

Meg darted a self-conscious glance at Nick as she accepted the gown. "Thank you," she murmured, then disappeared into the dressing room.

Nick thanked the housekeeper again and sent her off to prepare for Eleanor's return. She closed the door on her way out, and Nick slipped through the parlor into his own room to get rid of his tux coat, tie, cummerbund and diamond shirt studs. He dropped his silver monogrammed cuff links into the box on his bureau, and then hurried back to Meg's room when he heard the door to her dressing room.

He'd left both parlor doors open, but he rapped once on hers before he poked his head in. "May I come in?"

There was a short pause before he heard a hesitant, "Sure."

He stepped in, expecting to see a vision in white. Instead, he found a blob of gray. Meg was standing by the tea cart wearing a long-sleeved, calf-length jersey sleep shirt that was at least three sizes too big and hung on her like a potato sack. Emblazoned on the front was a caricature of a grumpy cat and the legend, I Don't Do Mornings.

Nick couldn't hold back a laugh. "If that's for my benefit, it's not working. My libido also responds to cute as a bug's ear."

Meg's face flamed. "Darn. Then I guess it wouldn't do any good to put on my fuzzy-bunny slippers."

"Not a bit," he said, still chuckling. He moved toward her. "Do you want some tea?"

"I can pour it," she assured him, but she didn't fight him for the privilege. As he approached, she sidled out of the way like a skittish kitten.

Nick fought back a sigh of exasperation. After what had happened in the conservatory, he deserved her mistrust, but he didn't have to like it. "Don't worry, Megan. I'm not going to pounce."

"Hey, you're the one who warned me not to flaunt myself in front of you," she reminded him without any rancor. "I'm not sure exactly how you define flaunt."

Nick did sigh this time as he straightened from the tea cart and looked at her. "Megan, I'm sorry for what I said to you that night. And I'm sorry for what I did. You have to know that it wasn't your fault."

She looked at him. "Really? If you kiss me and five seconds later I tell you to stop, it's your fault, Nick. If you kiss me and I don't tell you to stop for five *minutes*, we're both to blame."

"Good point."

"I'm just sorry that it spoiled the friendship we were forging. I...miss it," she admitted hesitantly.

"Me, too."

She raised her eyebrows hopefully. "Does that mean we don't have to go back to being enemies tomorrow?"

"No. No, we won't go back there," he promised her.

"I don't like that Nick any more than you do. Why don't you hop into bed and I'll bring your tea."

She shook her head. "I have to get my hair down first," she said, but when she reached up for the pins that held her chignon the muscle in her abdomen began to contract painfully and she brought her arm back down quickly. "Damn. That's what happened a few minutes ago." She rubbed the muscle and it eased from a sharp pain to a dull soreness.

"Why don't you let me do that?" Nick suggested. "Come sit at the vanity and I'll take your hair down."

She looked decidedly uncomfortable with the suggestion. "No, Nick. That's all right. I can do it."

"When? Between muscle spasms?" He moved toward her dressing room, but when he glanced over his shoulder he found that she was still standing near the tea cart. He stopped and studied her gravely.

Meg frowned. "What's wrong?"

"Is this pride, stubbornness, or are you still afraid that I might attack you?"

"It's embarrassment," she told him, giving up the fight and moving past him into the huge dressing room that had a walk-in closet on one wall and a jarringly modern mirrored vanity on the other. "Everyone is making such a fuss over nothing—me, most especially. I'm a nurse. I should have known this was just a surface muscle cramp."

"You were scared," Nick said, stepping behind the chair as she sat. "And even if you had told me what it was, I wouldn't have taken the chance that you might be wrong. I'd have rushed you to the hospital anyway."

"I'm just sorry—"

"Don't be sorry," he said as he began searching her

hair for pins. "I wouldn't have traded seeing that ultrasound for anything in the world."

There was a long pause punctuated only by the tinny clatter of the hairpins Nick tossed onto the vanity.

"Nick…"

He found her gaze in the mirror and saw her hesitancy. "What?"

"Are you going to be disappointed if Dr. Michaelson is right? If the baby is a girl, I mean. We've both been referring to it as a boy."

"Well, I wouldn't mind having a son to carry on the Ballenger name and all that." He grinned. "But being wrapped around my daughter's little finger has a certain appeal as well."

Meg looked down at the vanity and began gathering up the pins Nick had tossed there.

Nick regarded her soberly, understanding the source of her silence and wishing it didn't hurt him. "You don't like me referring to the baby as mine, do you?"

She collected the pins, carefully turning them all in the same direction without ever glancing up. "I think that was really the first time. I'll get used to it," she admitted cautiously. "There are certainly times when I have no difficulty imagining you as an integral part of this child's life. Like tonight. It was easy to see how much you care."

"But it's David's baby and you'd rather I didn't lose sight of that fact," he said, drawing the conclusion for her.

She still didn't look up, and it was a long moment before she responded, "I signed the contract, Nick. I agreed to your terms."

"But you don't like it," he pressed.

"No," she admitted. "I don't like the idea of leaving

David's name off the birth certificate. For me, it's like telling the world that he never existed. That he had no part in my life, when the real truth is, he was the best part of it.''

Nick ran his fingers through Meg's hair and let it fall onto her shoulders. The bright lights that rimmed the mirror made the unshed tears in Meg's eyes sparkle, and she still hadn't raised her gaze to his. If she did, the tears would spill over, and Nick didn't think she was going to let that happen. She was still grieving, which was no surprise, but if David had been the best part of her life, what had been the worst? He was pretty sure she'd given him a clue tonight.

"Megan, what did you mean earlier when you said, 'Don't let it happen again'?"

A startled, guilty gaze flew up to his. The tears spilled and she quickly brushed them away, then used reaching for a tissue as an excuse not to look at him again. "When did I say that?"

"In the car. Right before I called the doctor. What did you mean?"

Watching Meg, Nick was reminded of a doe he'd once caught in the headlights of his car while on a camping trip. The animal froze, shuddering, not knowing whether to go left or right. But Meg settled herself quickly, shoulders erect, like a condemned woman who'd made the decision to face her firing squad bravely.

"I meant exactly what you would assume from that statement," she replied finally.

"This isn't your first pregnancy?"

Her eyes darted up to his, then down again. "No. It's not."

"Did you lose the baby in a miscarriage?"

Meg folded her hands in her lap. "Yes."

Nick wondered what it would take to get more than single syllables from her. "Why? What happened?"

"I was in my seventh month. I fell down some stairs. It was winter.... There was ice." Like the doe who'd finally made the decision to flee, Meg rose and moved into her bedroom.

Nick followed. "I'm sorry, Megan."

"So was I," she replied, turning to face him when she had the safety of half the room between them. She was lying to protect herself, to protect her baby, but what she wanted more than anything was to admit the truth. But she couldn't give Nick the facts, only the substance of what losing that child had done to her. "It was a long time ago, and I was probably too young to raise a child, but I still remember the pain of seeing my son in an incubator, fighting to live. He was just too tiny."

Nick knew better than to try to take her into his arms, but wanted to very badly. "Were you—"

She raised a hand, palm out, trembling a little. "Nick, I don't want to think about this. I got scared tonight when I thought I was having a miscarriage—I've been scared about that since the day I discovered I was pregnant. Don't make me relive it."

He nodded slowly. "I'm sorry. I just want to understand you."

"Please don't be offended, but really...it's none of your business."

Nick wasn't offended, but her pronouncement stung. He very much wanted everything about Meg to be his business. "Sorry," he said again. "But can you blame me for being curious?"

"Yes, I can. Have I asked you about your life? Your ex-wife? Your marriage? You told me that first day in the boardroom that you had no children and never expected to have any. Have I asked you why that is?"

Nick stiffened. Well, she'd very handily put the shoe on the other foot, hadn't she? Should he duck the issue or answer the question she hadn't really asked? If he wanted Meg's trust, maybe he needed to start earning it.

"My marriage dissolved because Camille and I couldn't have children," he told her. "So in a sense, I can understand how painful it would be to lose a child."

He saw Meg's face soften. "You didn't consider adoption?"

Nick shook his head. "Camille wanted her own. She deserved that, and...well, I couldn't make it happen."

She wanted to ask why. Nick could see her mouth almost forming the words, the curiosity in her eyes. She was making the natural assumption and her face held a tinge of pity that he really didn't want to see. It was a blow that struck at the heart of his manhood.

"There were no other options? In vitro? Artificial insemination?" she asked him.

"The problem was a...low sperm count," he admitted reluctantly. "There was a possibility of conception if we had taken fertility drugs, but Camille was afraid of the multiple births that sometimes result."

Something that might have been relief flashed across Megan's face. "In other words, you could have children of your own."

Nick shrugged. "Only if I find the right woman."

"One who isn't afraid of twins or triplets?"

"That, and someone I can love in the way I *didn't* love my first wife."

"If you want to fall in love, Nick, you have to be open to it. Willing to take risks with your heart." Meg's voice was as gentle as a caress.

"I'm finding that out, Megan," he said softly, his eyes fixed firmly on hers.

Her look of surprise as she digested his remark—and the emotion behind it—was almost comical. Nick didn't regret what he'd said, but he certainly didn't want to give her a chance to comment. He'd been forced to deliver the painful "unrequited love" speech once or twice in his life, and he didn't want to be on the receiving end tonight. Not with Megan.

"Come on," he said briskly, changing the mood before she could gather her thoughts. "Get into bed. I'll bring you a cup of tea and tuck you in. I think we've had about all the personal revelations we can handle for one night."

"I'll say," she murmured as she sat on the bed, leaning back against the propped-up pillows before gingerly sliding her legs under the covers.

Nick went around the bed and poured her tea, keenly aware that she never took her eyes off him. He brought the cup back, but when Meg shook her head at him, he set it on the nightstand beside the bed.

"Nick, what you just said, were you insinuating that—"

"Let's drop it, Megan, shall we?" he suggested, sitting on the bed facing her. "It's been an emotional night for both of us."

"But—"

There was a crisp rap on the door. Meg almost cursed, and Nick said a silent "Thank God."

"Come in," he called out, and Eleanor stepped into the room, still wearing her conservative black sheath evening gown and carrying her black beaded bag. In her other hand she held a pink slip of paper like the ones Fetridge used when he took messages for the family.

"Megan. Nicholas." She took in the sight of them on the bed together, and the expression on her face made Nick wonder if perhaps the scene looked more intimate than it was.

Of course, the scene couldn't get too much more intimate, considering that he'd all but told Megan outright that he was in love with her.

Whatever Eleanor was speculating she kept to herself, fortunately. "Are you all right, my dear? Mrs. Fetridge said there was some difficulty."

"It's nothing, really," Meg told her. "I just overreacted to a muscle spasm."

Nick related a shorthand version of their hospital visit and Dr. Michaelson's assurances that there was nothing to worry about. "I was just helping Megan get ready for bed," he concluded.

"Of course." Eleanor nodded and came a bit closer, looking at Meg as she approached. "It's such a relief to know that the baby is healthy, my dear, but it does concern me that you're overextending yourself." She looked at Nick and suggested, "Perhaps it's time for us to hire Megan a personal maid. We have more than enough room in the staff quarters for another live-in."

Nick knew exactly what his grandmother was getting at. If it would keep him from tucking Megan into bed at night, Eleanor would happily pay for an expensive live-in servant out of her own pocket.

But Meg was quick to protest. "That won't be necessary, Eleanor. I don't need a maid."

"Are you sure, my dear? You are starting your volunteer work next week, which can only add to the strain you're under. Perhaps you should postpone—"

"Megan is not going to delay her work at the crisis

center,'' Nick interjected before Meg had the chance.
''She's made a commitment to work three days a week,
and she intends to keep it. What happened tonight has
nothing to do with her schedule.''

''Of course,'' Eleanor said with a formal nod of her
head. ''Well, I'll leave you to get your rest, dear. I'm
sure Nicholas will do the same very shortly.'' She fixed
her gaze on her grandson. ''May I count on a word with
you before you turn in?''

Nick nodded brusquely, certain that he knew exactly
what was in store. Eleanor had been perfectly content to
remain mute about his relationship with Megan as long
as he'd been keeping his distance. But he wasn't at arm's
length anymore, and he didn't intend to be again. He
was in love with his wife, and he decided in that instant
that he was going to do everything in his power to win
her love in return.

He didn't care if it took a month or a year or a decade,
he would make it happen and there was nothing Eleanor
could do or say to stop him.

''You think if I found a president or a *Mayflower* passenger on my family tree, I could get her to like me?''
Meg asked as soon as Eleanor was gone.

Nick smiled and gently reached out to brush a lock
of hair off her cheek. ''Better look for kings or princes.''

She raised one eyebrow. ''Sorry. My Grandma Boyd
used to claim a distant kinship to Hopalong Cassidy, but
that's the best I can do.''

''Don't worry about Eleanor,'' he urged her. ''She'll
get used to the fact that you're a part of this family and
you're here to stay.''

''For another ten months,'' Meg reminded him.

Nick stood and gave her a cryptic little smile. ''We'll

see about that,'' he murmured as he bent to brush his lips to her cheek. ''Sleep well.''

And then he was gone before Meg could fashion an answer, a protest or anything else.

WHEN NICK ENTERED his grandmother's private sitting room she was sitting in her chair very much as he'd found her the night he proposed to Megan, just as still and equally as disapproving. Instinct told him she had an agenda, and Nick made up his mind to proceed carefully.

''You wanted to see me, Nan?''

She nodded. ''Help yourself to a drink, Nicholas. You may need it.''

''Why is that?'' he asked, moving deeper into the room, but staying away from the spirits. ''If you're concerned about the baby, you needn't be. There really is nothing wrong.''

''I believe you.''

''Then what did you want to see me about?''

Eleanor looked up at him, but her pale, regal face gave away nothing. ''You and Megan made quite a hit tonight at the ball.''

The way she said it didn't sound like a compliment. ''Did that surprise you?'' Nick asked. ''Megan's a very charming young woman. She has a remarkable chameleon-like talent for fitting into any situation.'' He took a seat in the companion chair angled near Eleanor's. ''I suppose it's her counseling experience, but she knows how to put people at ease.''

''You, most especially, it would seem,'' Eleanor said pointedly. ''I can't tell you how many people commented to me on how remarkably happy you were. And how much you obviously love her.''

Ah. There it was. Nick put a warning edge in his voice when he replied, "You say that as though it's a bad thing."

"If that perception were the result of a fine performance, I would applaud you, Nicholas, but what I saw tonight at the ball and what I witnessed just now in Megan's room led me to believe that my prediction has come true. You think you're in love with her, don't you?"

Though he'd hated the idea of discussing his feelings for Megan with his grandmother, he knew better than to try to put her off. If he really planned to court his wife, he was going to have to enlist Eleanor's cooperation eventually. And though he doubted he could count on her support, at the very least he needed an assurance that she wouldn't interfere.

"I don't just think it, Nan. I know it," he said firmly.

Eleanor shook her head, not in disagreement, but in feigned disbelief. "Nicholas, how can you possibly love a woman about whom you know so little?"

"I know all I need to know."

"Really?" She rose, moving across the room, and Nick realized that he had given her exactly the answer she'd wanted. Eleanor was making a power play. He recognized the symptoms only too well. But what was the game, and what were the rules? And why did he feel as though he was already several moves behind?

Eleanor opened the top drawer of her writing desk. "I had hoped to wait a while longer, until the information was more complete, but now I see what a mistake that would be."

"Waiting for what?" he asked, coming to his feet.

She extracted a thick portfolio from the drawer, then turned, but made no attempt to hand it to him.

"What is that?" he asked.

Her chin lifted with a touch of defiance. "I dare say, you will be upset with me, Nicholas. At first. But your decision to forgo a hard look at Megan's background was ill considered. I have rectified that error in judgment."

Nick's jaw stiffened in anger. "You didn't."

"Of course, I did. And when you read this file, you'll thank me. Mr. Hamilton assures me that there is more to come—he is on his way to Missouri, even as we speak—but this will give you a realistic picture of your wife even though it is somewhat incomplete."

"Jim Hamilton of Hamilton Security?"

"Yes."

Nick glared at her. "How could you do this, Eleanor? I told you specifically that we wouldn't investi—"

"You were wrong."

Nick fought the urge to strangle his grandmother. "Damn you! Megan's past doesn't matter to anyone, Eleanor—except you, apparently. Can't you see what a decent, loving person she is and accept her for that?"

"What I see is a charming, clever liar with the morals of an alley cat."

Nick advanced an angry step. "Now just a damn—"

"What has Megan told you about her parents?" she asked, cutting him off coolly.

"That they're dead," he said tersely.

"She lied. Her father is very much alive. He's a drunk and a convicted felon," Eleanor announced with infuriating efficiency.

Nick scowled at her, trying to assimilate the revelation. Just this evening he'd heard Megan state plainly, and not for the first time, that both her parents were dead. She had lied, obviously.

But was it so hard to see why? In the car as they left the ball she'd told him that he would never be able to hold his head up in society if she told his friends the truth about herself. Was she also afraid of what *he* would think if he knew the truth? Certainly she had good reason to fear what Eleanor would think of it.

"There is much more," Eleanor said, taking advantage of the hesitancy she obviously sensed in her grandson. "Megan apparently has a habit of getting pregnant out of wedlock and trapping her paramours into marriage. She dropped out of school when she was only fourteen years old to marry the father of her first child— an upstanding citizen of high moral fiber who is currently serving his second term in prison. This time for armed robbery, and the first time, for multiple counts of auto theft. And you should also know, Nicholas, that Megan herself has a criminal record, though we have yet to be able to determine the nature of her crime. I believe that is why Mr. Hamilton has returned to Pine Ridge this weekend, to—"

"That's enough, Eleanor! Enough!"

Nick couldn't bear to hear any more. If there were things he needed to know about Megan, he wanted facts that were untainted by his grandmother's warped interpretation. He crossed the room and snatched the portfolio out of her hand.

"Nicholas, I know you're angry now."

"Angry? *Angry?*" He advanced another step, towering over her with a fury that would have sent anyone with good sense fleeing for her life. "You have no idea just how angry I am, Eleanor. What you have done is unforgivable!"

"I did it for your sake, Nicholas," she replied with calm dignity. "And my great-grandchild's."

"No, Eleanor, you did it because you're a narrow-minded prig!"

Her outrage was muted but palpable. "Manners and good breeding are not priggish, Nicholas."

"Really? Well, I'll stack Megan's sense of honor and decency up against yours any day of the week. If she's lied, it's only because she sees a need to protect herself and her child from judgmental ol—" Nick stopped before he went too far. Eleanor deserved to be called a judgmental old biddy, but his ingrained respect for her wouldn't let him say the words.

He backed off two steps, then a third. "I'm going to read this," he said in a voice as hard as a diamond glass cutter. "And then I'm going to talk to Jim Hamilton and tell him he's fired. You said he's on his way to Missouri. How do I reach him?"

Eleanor hesitated a moment. "His cellular number is just inside the folder," she admitted reluctantly. "But I beg you, Nicholas, don't dismiss Mr. Hamilton until he's completed his mission. We've worked very hard to obtain trial transcripts—" She stopped abruptly, silenced by the molten glare he leveled at her.

As soon as she was silent, Nick flipped open the folder and found the pink message slip that he'd seen her carrying earlier. It had the current date and a message from a Phillip Henderson of the Charleston Art League. Nick felt sick at his stomach. "How long have you and *Mr. Henderson* been snooping into Megan's life?"

"When you refused to do it, I hired him shortly after you signed the marriage contract."

"Well, it's finished, Grandmother. Hamilton is off the case. You're to have no further contact with him or any other private investigator. Do you understand me?"

"Of course. Once you've read the sordid facts, I'm

certain there will be no need for any further intervention on my part. And you will also realize that I was only doing—''

"I don't want to hear your reasons, or your excuses," he said harshly. "What you did was wrong, and Megan is not to know about this under any circumstances. Do you understand me?"

"Of course. Using the information now would be pointless."

"Damn you, Eleanor! You still don't get it, do you? I don't care what's in this file, no one is going to use Megan's past against her!" In two angry paces he was towering over her again, his voice dangerously low. "And make no mistake about this, *Grandmother*. If you do or say anything, *anything at all*, to hurt Megan or interfere in my relationship with her, you will regret it until the day you die. You've already lost one grandson this year—you don't want to go two for two. Maybe this would be a good time for you to spend a month or so on the Continent."

He turned on his heel, slammed out of her room and went straight downstairs to his office.

Still struggling to conquer his anger, he placed the file on his desk and poured a stiff drink. When he returned to the desk, he stood for a long moment, staring at the black portfolio cover and sipping his bourbon.

Oddly, he wasn't afraid of the contents of the file. Megan obviously had a past, but he knew that nothing he might find in there would change the respect and admiration he felt for his wife. It didn't matter how low she'd fallen—or had been flung; the only issue of importance was how magnificently she'd risen above the tragedies of her life.

When he finally sat and began to read, his only feeling was that of regret for the fact that Megan hadn't trusted him enough to tell him any of the details herself.

CHAPTER THIRTEEN

As ELEANOR HAD SAID, the details—even unvarnished—
were sordid in the extreme. Megan's father was a drunk
who'd served time for assault in 1993. That was bad
enough, but Nick was sickened to find that the charges
had been brought against him by Megan herself after her
father brutally attacked her in the parking lot of the
Holmby Clinic as she was leaving an evening counseling
session.

And the assault on Megan wasn't Linley's first crime
against his family. Seventeen years ago, at about the
same time Nick had been taking hold of the reins of
Ballenger Pharmaceuticals, George W. "Dub" Linley
had beaten his wife, Loreen, and thrown her out into the
snow wearing nothing but a flimsy cotton robe and a
pair of house slippers. When thirteen-year-old Megan
had tried to let her back in, Dub had knocked her across
the room. It wasn't until he collapsed in a drunken stupor
that Megan had been able to get her mother back into
the house, but the damage was already done.

An asthmatic who suffered from perpetual lung infec-
tions, Loreen Linley didn't have the strength to fight off
the pneumonia that had resulted from her exposure. She
died two days after her husband's assault.

Though the police had taken a report at the insistence
of Loreen's doctor, Lewellyn Holmby, no charges had
been brought against Dub. Holmby had also reported

Linley for child abuse, but the social worker who investigated hadn't seen any need to remove Megan from her father's custody.

Nick couldn't begin to imagine what it had been like for Megan after that, living in the same house with the drunken animal who had murdered her mother. Was it any wonder that the next year, only a few weeks before her fifteenth birthday, she quit school to marry Russell Corday, the eighteen-year-old high-school dropout who'd gotten her pregnant.

It didn't take much reading between the lines for Nick to realize that she had jumped out of the frying pan and into the fire. Four months after her wedding she had a miscarriage as a result of a fall down a flight of steps— just as Megan had described to him except for one crucial detail. The "accident" had happened in August. The only way she could have slipped on ice was if her own personal hell had frozen over, and Nick didn't think that was the case. Repeated domestic-disturbance complaints showed that Russell Corday liked beating up on his wife; if Megan had lost her baby as a result of a fall down a flight of stairs, it was because she'd been pushed.

As he read the cold facts of Megan's life, Nick formed a chilling image of a lawyer in a courtroom presenting the same facts to a judge. Even a mediocre shyster could make Megan sound unfit to raise a child.

It wasn't true, of course, but a lawyer could make a judge believe it. Megan had known that, and feared it. Feared *Nick*. She had married him because he'd threatened to investigate her and take her child away.

"You'll be lucky to have one court-supervised visit a year," he'd flung at her.

Was it any wonder that she had hated him? It was

nothing less than miraculous that they had come as far toward friendship as they had.

Considering what he was learning, he had to wonder how much further they could go—how much further Megan would *allow* it to go? Could she ever let herself fall in love with a man she was so afraid of?

David had known all of her secrets, of course. Megan would have confessed them to him long ago as they were falling in love. She would have handed him the truth as a symbol of trust.

Will she ever love me that much?

The question battered at him as he read and reread Hamilton's report. He knew he would never be satisfied with less. The all-or-nothing quirk in his personality was like a little demon pestering him with questions it was much too soon to ask.

If he could earn Megan's love, could he also earn her trust? Would there ever come a time when she truly believed there was no danger in giving him her secrets?

Nick had to know. There were a dozen ways he could rationalize his decision not to tell Megan about Eleanor's investigation, but only one really mattered.

If there was any hope for them to have a future together, Megan had to trust Nick enough to tell him the truth herself.

That day was a long way off, of course. In the meantime, there were more immediate issues that Nick needed to make peace with. So many wrongs had been done to her in the little town of Pine Ridge. Though Nick knew there was nothing he could do to set them right, he couldn't escape the desperate need to go there.

Megan had told him that he'd never be able to understand what her life had been like unless he saw it for himself. Well, she was right. He needed to see the people and places that had shaped her childhood. Mostly, he needed to see Dub Linley—even if it was only from a distance—to make peace with the horrible urge he had to beat the bastard to a bloody pulp.

It was a little after 2:00 a.m. when Nick made a terse phone call to the number Jim Hamilton had left. A second call took care of the necessary flight arrangements. He left a note for Megan, stating that he'd been called away to handle a labor dispute at the company's distribution warehouse in Ohio and probably wouldn't be back until late Sunday night or Monday. By 3:00 a.m. he was in the air. By six-thirty he was in his rental car leaving the Springfield, Missouri, airport headed for Pine Ridge, a hundred and thirty-two miles away. By nine o'clock he and James Hamilton were settling in at a table in the coffee shop of the Ridge Runner Inn.

The restaurant wasn't too crowded; mostly local farmers, a few travelers and a handful of truckers whose big rigs were lined up outside like contestants in a road rally.

"It'll clear out in a few minutes and won't get busy again until the church crowd starts showing up at eleven," Hamilton told Nick as he reached for one of the plastic laminated menus tucked between the aluminum napkin holder and the salt and pepper shakers in the center of the table. A jukebox on the far wall was cranking out Sawyer Brown's "Six Days on the Road," and one of the truckers was singing along.

"I can highly recommend the biscuits and sausage gravy. Great coffee, too," Hamilton said, waggling the menu at a waitress who had bleached blond hair with two inches of dark roots.

She popped over and poured coffee for both of them. "Mornin', gents. What can I git for ya?"

"Just coffee for me, thank you," Nick said.

"I'll have the Number Three. Eggs over easy," Hamilton said, putting away the menu.

She scribbled in her pad. "Okeydokey. My name's Wendy. If you need anythin' else, just holler."

She jabbed a pen behind one ear and disappeared behind the counter to the left of their table.

Nick sipped his coffee and found that Hamilton was right. It was good. "You must have spent a lot of my grandmother's money here if you know the traffic and the menu so well," Nick said curtly, wishing he didn't feel so much antagonism for the man on the other side of the cracked Formica tabletop.

He knew the silver-haired P.I. by reputation only, as a discreet investigator who always got results. It wasn't Hamilton's fault that Eleanor had stuck her nose in where it didn't belong.

The detective didn't seem to take any offense with Nick's brusqueness. "This is only my second trip, but it doesn't take long to get the feel of a place like Pine Ridge."

"How long were you here before?"

"Five days."

"And that's when you dug up all this garbage?" Nick asked, pushing Megan's file into the middle of the table.

"No. Some of the medical records and court transcripts took a lot longer to come by."

"What exactly is it you're here for this time? And if you tell me that you've found a way to get your hands on Megan's juvenile records, I'll have your license revoked. According to this—" he tapped the file "—she was barely sixteen when she was incarcerated for a year in a juvenile reformatory. They seal records like that for a reason, Hamilton. Besides, it's pretty obvious why she was arrested."

According to the file, Megan's incarceration coincided with her husband's arrest as a member of a large, well-organized interstate auto-theft ring. It didn't take a genius to figure out that Megan had somehow gotten caught in the net that snagged her husband.

"Relax, Mr. Ballenger. I'm not here for her juvenile records," Hamilton assured him. "Your grandmother wanted them, but I didn't think they were worth going to jail for."

Nick's respect for the P.I. went up a notch. "Then why are you here?"

"I had a meeting last night with Luke Vincent, the retired highway patrolman who made the case against Russell Corday and the rest of his auto-theft ring. He confirmed that Megan was arrested with her husband at an automobile dealership in St. Louis delivering a car they'd stolen in Oklahoma City and 'refurbished' at a chop shop in Pine Ridge."

"What do you mean, 'they'?" Nick said, scowling. "If Megan was involved it was because her no-account husband—"

Hamilton held up both hands. "Whoa, Mr. Ballenger. I'm on your side."

"No, you're on my grandmother's payroll, which means that you're nowhere *near* my side of this!!" Nick snapped back. "And after we finish here today, you won't be on anyone's payroll. Your investigation is at an end."

"I have no problem with that, Mr. Ballenger," Hamilton said equitably. "But I do think you'll want to know what the highway patrolman told me."

Nick cocked his head. "All right. Spill it."

Hamilton leaned closer. "Vincent said—"

Wendy appeared just then with his order, and the P.I.

leaned back. She replenished their coffee, and when she left them to wipe down the surrounding tables, Hamilton began again.

"Vincent said the reason he was able to make such a good case against the entire gang was that he had an anonymous informant. A woman who fed him names, transport dates, copies of invoices, records of stolen parts... Virtually everything needed to close the ring down entirely."

"Was Megan the informant?" Nick asked, though his heart already knew the answer.

"Well, that's the kicker," Hamilton said on a sigh as he dug into his breakfast. "Vincent is positive she was, but he never met his benefactress. When Megan was arrested, she denied being the informant, even though she could have walked away scot-free, never done a minute in jail." He shrugged. "But she wouldn't cop to it. She did a year in juvie rather than admit she was a hero. Vincent still doesn't understand it."

Nick did. A frightened but resourceful young girl had concocted the perfect way to divest herself of the brutish husband who caused her to lose the child she'd wanted so much. Nick remembered only too well the haunting sadness on Meg's face when she'd described the pain of watching her baby die in a hospital incubator. In one fell swoop she'd taken her revenge, earned her freedom, and at the same time found a way to live that didn't include going back to her father's custody.

"If you don't mind me asking, Mr. Ballenger..."

Hamilton paused while Nick brought himself into the present, then continued. "What precisely are you doing here, sir? If you want to call off the investigation, why didn't you just tell me so on the phone last night or wait until I returned to Charleston? Why go to all this trouble?''

"Because I want to see where Megan grew up, and you can give me the guided tour. I want images to go with the facts." He tapped the file again. "The woman you've profiled in here is just an abstract to you. But she's much more than that to me. Megan is my wife, and there are things I need to see to understand.''

"Really?" Hamilton asked, then leaned forward and lowered his voice to barely more than a whisper. "Or are you just hoping to find an opportunity to beat the hell out of Dub Linley?"

Nick didn't bother to dispute him. "Do you know where he lives?"

The P.I. nodded. "He's shacked up with a girl named Rhonda Mabry. She's a barmaid at the Cupie Doll Lounge down on Front Street. Normally when the bar's not open, he can be found at her trailer down in Old Town.''

"Normally?" Nick questioned, picking up on Hamilton's phrasing.

"He got drunk Friday night and picked a fight in the bar. The police showed up just as the bouncer went to throw him out, and Linley got into it with a city deputy. Luke Vincent figures he'll get at least three months in the county jail for it," Hamilton informed him. "If you want to take a poke at him, you're going to have to wait till long about Thanksgiving."

Nick sighed heavily. "I just wanted to see him, but given the way I feel about him, this is probably for the best. I'll have to content myself with a tour around town. I'm particularly interested in seeing where Megan grew up. The house out on Sugar Creek Road."

"That's doable," Hamilton told him, scooting his

chair back. "Just let me pay a quick visit to the men's room, and we'll get out of here."

The P.I. rose, and Nick looked around for their waitress. He found her polishing the counter to their left. "Could I have the check, please, Wendy?"

"What? Oh. Sure thang." She quick-stepped over and pulled out her pad. "You here on business, or just passin' through?" she asked as she found their ticket.

"Just passing through," Nick replied, reaching into his back pocket for his wallet.

Wendy laid the check facedown on the table, but didn't move on. "I was just wonderin', 'cause your friend, he looked kinda familiar."

"He's been here before," Nick told her. "On business."

"Oh." She looked as though she wanted to say something, but had forgotten how words were formed.

Nick pulled a bill from his wallet. "Do I pay you or the cashier?"

"Oh, you pay Cathy up front."

"Thanks." Nick smiled politely at the woman, and reached for the check.

WENDY WATCHED as the black-haired hunk stood, dropped a tip onto the table and moved on up to the cash register by the door. A minute later his silver-haired friend emerged from the restroom, and together they went outside and climbed into a big black Lincoln.

Somebody in that car had money, Wendy decided, and she was pretty sure it was the hunk who'd taken the wheel. And not just because he'd left her a five-dollar tip on a $4.89 breakfast ticket.

"The crowd's thinned out, Howie. I'm takin' my break," Wendy announced to the short-order cook behind the counter. She already had a pack of cigarettes in her hand as she moved into the alcove where the pay phone was located. With the skill of a practiced smoker, she managed to dig a coin from her apron pocket, dial the number she wanted and light up without missing a beat.

The phone rang three times on the other end, and a slurry female voice came on the line.

"Aunt Rhonda? It's Wendy."

"Huh? What? Are you crazy? What time is it?" Rhonda Mabry groused between hacking coughs as she tried to get awake. Her forty-six-year-old voice had a distinctive two-pack-a-day scratch in it.

"Pretty near ten o'clock," Wendy answered.

"Damn it. You know what time I got to bed last night? The bar don't close till 2:00 a.m., Wendy."

"I know, I know, but this is important," the waitress told her, taking a quick but efficient drag on her cigarette.

"All right, all right. Hang on. I gotta find my smokes."

Wendy waited, leaning against the wall, tapping her cigarette occasionally, heedless of the ashes, until her aunt returned. The rustling and hacking on the other end of the line finally settled down.

"Okay. What's so all-fired important, honey?"

"You remember hearin' the name Ballenger before?" Wendy asked.

"Mmm...yeah, sure," Rhonda said, mumbling around the cigarette she was lighting. "Idd'n that the name of the big drug company Dub's girl, Meggie, went to work for over in China?"

"That's what I was thinkin'," Wendy replied. "I remembered it 'cause it was all over the news a few months back. Her boss got killed in a plane crash, or somethin'."

"That's right. Dub thought maybe the company would go belly up, and Meggie would have to take her snooty nose out of the air and come crawlin' home so she could take care of him like a good daughter should, but he ain't heard from her. Then a'course he heard about that guy who was askin' questions around town a while back 'cause she applied for some big job or other."

Wendy was making a yak, yak, yak motion with her thumb and fingers as she waited for her aunt to wind down, then finally jumped in with, "That's what I'm trying to tell ya. That investigator guy is back, and he's got this good-lookin' dude with him that he called Mr. Ballenger, real respectful-like. You know, the way you kiss up to somebody who's got money?"

"Yeah? So what?"

"I'm gettin' to it! They were talkin' low so I couldn't hear too much, but I did hear him say one thing real clear, and you're not gonna believe it..."

Rhonda waited, but when Wendy didn't continue, she dutifully prompted, "What? What?"

"Our little Meggie Linley, who I personally went to school with, is this Ballenger guy's wife!"

"What! You're kiddin' me!"

"I am not. I was wipin' tables close by 'cause I recognized his name, and when the Ballenger dude said he was wantin' to see where *Megan* grew up, I snuck in a little closer. I heard him say she was his wife, plain as day, and that he needed to understand somethin'."

"What'd he say next?"

"I don't know," Wendy replied, taking her irritation out on her nearly extinct cigarette by dropping it and crushing it into the tile floor. "That investigator guy started whisperin', and I figured I'd better back off a little so they wouldn't suspect I was eavesdroppin'. I didn't hear nothin' after that."

"Hot damn," Rhonda said. "Dub's gonna love this. You reckon this Ballenger guy is as rich as the one who got killed? I mean, he's gotta be somebody important in that drug company, don't he? His name bein' on the company, and all."

Wendy shook her head. Her aunt wasn't exactly the brightest bulb in Pine Ridge. "Oh, for cryin' out loud. Of course he is! He's probably the president, or something. And unless I miss my guess, he's richer than God. Seein's how Dub don't ever seem to have two nickels to rub together when it's time for you to pay the rent, I thought maybe he'd wanna check it out."

"Yeah, right. Where do you think Dub's gonna get the money to go to China?"

"What's that got to do with it? I heard 'em talkin' about Charleston. I'll betcha Meggie's back."

"Well, I'll be damned. This is sure a helluva time for Dub to be in jail." Rhonda lowered her voice confidentially. "Just between you an' me, Wendy, I was kinda glad he popped Junior Voit 'cause it was gonna git him out of my hair for a couple of months. But now there's no tellin' how long it'll be before we can cash in on this."

"Well, considerin' what all you put up with from that old coot, you oughta cash in big, Aunt Rhonda. If Meggie's got money now, she can just fork some of it over and take care of her family like she shoulda been doin' all along."

"You're damn right. Dub's her daddy, and there ain't a snowball's chance in hell that he's gonna let her forget

it. We just gotta figure out one thing." Rhonda paused
as she lit another cigarette.

"What's that?" Wendy prompted.

"Where the hell's Charleston?"

CHAPTER FOURTEEN

WITH HAMILTON as a tour guide, Nick drove through Megan's hometown, seeing the places he'd read about in her file…Dr. Holmby's old clinic, the cemetery where her mother was buried. The school where she had learned to love the piano from a hiding place in the shadows. He strolled on the campus of the community college where she'd gotten her nursing degree, but left when he realized that he was sticking out like a sore thumb.

The final stop was the house out in the country, down a twisting two-lane blacktop, turning onto a dusty gravel road serviced by the county. They went up and down nearly vertical hills, around blind curves, then made one more turn.

"This is it. Sugar Creek Road."

"This is a road?" Nick said as he pulled slowly onto the almost nonexistent dirt lane. "I should have rented an all-terrain vehicle at the airport in Springfield."

"It's about a mile and a half, but it doesn't get much worse than this," Hamilton assured him. "Just take it slow and you'll be fine. That was her bus stop, where we turned off, by the way."

"She walked this every day?" Nick asked incredulously.

"Hard to imagine, isn't it?"

To say the least. "Did they have any neighbors?"

"Yeah. About three miles down the road."

"My God…" They fell silent as Nick considered their desolate surroundings, trying to imagine Megan as a little girl walking down this long road. Had her mother come with her, holding her hand and reassuring her that there was nothing to fear? Or had Megan made the trip alone?

Somehow, he suspected the latter.

The house itself was nothing more than a two-room saltbox shack covered in peeling brown shingles with patches of black tar paper showing here and there.

On one side of the shack sat an old cylindrical natural-gas tank that had once been painted silver and was now rusted beyond reclamation. In its day, it had powered the gas furnace and fueled the generator that provided electric lights and ran the motor of the well on the other side of the house.

The boards of a decrepit outhouse were crumbled like matchsticks, and the rusted-out tank of an ancient cistern was lying in a maze of weeds, reminding Nick of the parched bones of an animal that had gone extinct before the dawn of man. It was a fitting analogy for a place that was no longer fit for man nor beast and probably hadn't been much better in its prime.

Nick tried to imagine Megan in the house and couldn't. He visualized the house blanketed with snow and thought of Megan's mother huddled on the porch with no place to go, too afraid of her drunken husband to come inside. He tried again to imagine Megan in the house, but his mind rebelled and he finally realized what a mistake it had been to come here.

He stood for a long time looking at the broken-down porch, his hands clenched into fists that rested on his hips, wishing he had a sledgehammer, or better yet, a bulldozer, so that he could tear down the place and make it as though it had never existed. Then he would gather the little girl who had lived here into his arms and protect her. Never let anything cruel or ugly touch her life again.

"What would you say, Hamilton, if I told you that last night the woman who grew up in this place charmed the pants off a roomful of Charleston aristocrats with her sweet smile, kind words and gentle laugh?" Nick asked the detective who was behind him, leaning against the hood of the car.

"I'd say that makes your wife a remarkable lady," the P.I. replied.

"It does indeed," he said, his voice choked with emotion. "So why can't my grandmother see that?"

Not waiting for an answer, he turned abruptly, and moved toward the car. "All right, Hamilton, let's get the hell out of here. I've had enough."

MEG DID A LOT of pacing on Sunday. She rationalized it by claiming that she was exercising to work out her pesky muscle cramp, but mostly she was just worried. The house was in chaos because Eleanor was packing to leave for the family's villa in Italy. Meg knew that she typically spent quite a bit of time there, using it as her headquarters when she traveled in Europe, but the trip came as a complete surprise to everyone.

As did Nick's sudden departure. He'd said last week that he was concerned about a possible strike at the Ohio warehouse, but Meg had to wonder if this was really an emergency or he was just using it as an excuse. Something had happened between Nick and Eleanor last night, and it made the shoot at the O.K. Corral pale by comparison.

As usual, Eleanor was glacial when she bade Meg farewell with a simple "Now that you're settled in so nicely, I see no reason to delay my trip to Tuscany any longer."

She was gone by early afternoon, and her departure brought Meg a guilty flush of relief. Ballenger Hall still felt like a museum, but it wasn't quite as oppressive without its stern, forbidding curator. It felt strange when Effie came to her later to ask for instructions on what to do about supper, and there was the little matter of the menus for the week that Eleanor usually prepared on Sunday.

Meg took stock of the other responsibilities that would fall on her in Eleanor's absence, and by the end of the afternoon she felt like the second Mrs. deWinter come to Manderlay. Only she wasn't going to let the house defeat her. She wasn't a mousy young girl intimidated by a ghost.

Still worried about Nick, she settled into the visiting room downstairs to answer some of the correspondence she'd made a fuss about last week, but the house was just too quiet. She brought down the CD player she'd added to her bedroom weeks ago, and before long, the house resonated with music.

Fetridge poked his head in almost immediately, ostensibly to see if there was anything she needed, but the look on his face suggested that he was just trying to determine whether he was hallucinating. Effie, too, looked ill at ease as she served supper for one in the dining room, and Meg had to wonder if anyone had ever played recorded music in the house before. If so, it couldn't have been recently, given the fact that there wasn't even an old-fashioned stereo to be found anywhere downstairs.

Meg didn't let the notion that she was breaking a Bal-
lenger-family tradition deter her from enjoying the CDs
she'd brought down. She'd been at the Hall almost two
months, but couldn't recall even one evening that she
had spent downstairs. Typically she and Eleanor went to
their respective quarters after dinner. Nick had been
spending most of his evenings at the office, or maybe
with friends; Meg had never asked and he had never
explained.

Would that change now that Eleanor was gone? Meg
wondered.

Probably not, she decided. Eleanor wasn't the reason
he'd been spending so little time at Ballenger Hall. And
as for his cryptic response to her advice about taking
risks with his heart... Meg still didn't know what to
make of that.

When she finally heard the front door a little after
nine, she shoved aside the lap desk and practically ran
into the hall. ''Nick?'' She caught sight of him and
stopped short, a little afraid to let him know how glad
she was to see him. They stood there with a dozen feet
of hall between them. ''You're back. How are things in
Akron?''

He looked tired and rumpled, as though the only sleep
he'd had for the last thirty-six hours was on the plane.
His face lit up when he saw Meg, but he held her gaze
for only a second. ''Not much improved, I'm afraid.''

''Is the plant going to strike?'' she asked.

''Not yet.'' Nick shifted uncomfortably. He felt like
a first-class cad for lying to Megan, but he'd made his
decision not to tell her about his trip to Pine Ridge even
before he'd made the trip itself. He had a plausible excuse ready, and it wasn't a complete lie—there *was* a
labor dispute and he *had* conferred several times with

the vice president he'd sent to Akron last week. "We've hammered out a temporary settlement that gives us three more months to negotiate. Hopefully we'll have reached a long-term agreement by then. Now, how are you feeling? Any more muscle cramps?"

Meg shook her head. "No. I'm just a little sore."

"That's good. I hated leaving, knowing you weren't feeling well."

"I was fine," she assured him. "But there is something—"

"Mr. Nick! Welcome home," Fetridge said as he hurried down the hall.

"Thank you, Fetridge." Nick handed him the hastily packed overnight bag that he hadn't used. "Just take that upstairs if you would, please, and I'll unpack it myself."

"If you wish, sir. Missus Megan instructed Effie to leave a plate in the warming oven in the hope that you might make it home this evening. Would you like it served upstairs or could I bring it to you in the visiting room where Missus Megan is spending the evening?"

"Neither, Fetridge. I had a bite on the jet. Why don't you and Effie turn in for the evening."

"As you wish, sir. Good night."

"Good night," Meg responded.

Nick approached the visiting room door where Meg stood. He cocked his head toward the music that had pleasantly surprised him when he opened the front door. "What is that?" he asked as he moved past her into the room.

Meg turned to follow him. "It's a CD player. I just couldn't stand the silence," she explained. "Don't worry. It's portable. It won't decrease the property value."

Nick chuckled. "No. I meant the music."

"Oh. It's the sound track from the movie *The Piano*."

"It's magnificent," Nick said, stepping closer to listen as an intricate piano solo played through. "It sounds complex, but it's deceptively simple."

He cocked his head to one side, concentrating, and in a few minutes his hands were moving over an imaginary keyboard.

Meg doubted that he was even aware of the gesture. Why on earth didn't a man who loved music as much as Nick live in a house filled with stereo equipment and fine recordings? Why was someone with his talent letting it atrophy?

"You know, Nick, there's a real piano just down the hall," she reminded him when the music ended.

He looked at her. "Yes. I remember." His gaze shifted to her lips and Meg found it hard to breathe.

She stepped away, pretending she didn't have a sudden ache that would have gladly responded to Nick's immediate and personal attention. Going the long way around him, she circled the sofa in order to reach the side table where the CD player was located. She touched the power button and the music faded away.

"There's something we have to talk about, Nick. Eleanor's gone," she said soberly.

"Oh?"

He didn't look terribly surprised and not at all disappointed. In fact, Meg couldn't read much of anything on his face. "She left for Tuscany this afternoon."

"Did she say why?"

"Nothing that explains the suddenness of her departure," she answered, coming back around the sofa. She moved her lap desk onto the oval occasional table and sat.

Nick joined her. "Eleanor loves to travel," he told

Meg. "When I was a boy, she spent more time in Italy and the south of France than she did in the United States. If it hadn't been for David's death, she would have left for the villa at least a month ago."

"I don't doubt that, but it still doesn't explain why she left so suddenly," Meg replied. "Did you and Eleanor quarrel last night after the ball?"

"Yes."

"About me?"

He nodded. "Eleanor thinks I've lost sight of our original agreement."

Meg studied him closely. "Have you?"

"Would you be more comfortable if I said no?"

"Nick—" she began uncertainly.

"You're carrying David's child," he said for her. "And part of you is still in love with my brother."

"Part of me always will be," she said quietly.

"What about the rest of you, Megan? Is there the slightest chance that part of you could care for me, too? We are pretty spectacular together, you know. We read each other's moods, we make each other laugh. And you can put me in my place quicker than anyone I've ever known. Most important of all, though—" he reached out to splay his fingers across Meg's abdomen, and her breath hitched in her throat "—we're going to share the nurturing of this child. For her sake, can you at least give us a chance to be more than just partners in a business proposition?"

"We are, Nick. We're friends," she said, but there was nothing platonic about the melting sensation going on inside her beneath Nick's hand.

"But can we ever be more?" he asked softly.

Meg swallowed hard. What he was asking should have sounded impossible, but it wasn't. She had unde-

niable feelings for him. She liked the Nick who was
learning how to laugh. Her heart was warmed by the
sweet Nick who brought her ginger tea and was already
calling the daughter they would raise "Princess." She
even had a grudging respect for the tough-businessman
Nick.

But this Nick, the one who looked at her with uncon-
cealed adoration in his midnight-blue eyes...this Nick
made her feel like a woman on the verge of falling in
love.

She didn't know whether to embrace the feeling or
run like hell. She'd had enough pain to last a lifetime,
and so much of it was still fresh.

It flitted through her mind to wonder what David
would want her to do, but she pushed the thought away.
David was dead, and as much as she loved and missed
him, he couldn't make her loneliness or her fears about
losing her child go away.

If Nick cared for her, if he could love her and they
could somehow build a life together, Meg knew she
would be a fool to turn away. Last night she'd counseled
Nick on being willing to take risks with his heart. It
should have been too soon for her to take her own advice, but somehow it wasn't.

"What, exactly, do you have in mind, Nick?" she
finally asked him.

The half smile that played across his lips went well
with the relief and hope that mingled in his eyes. "That
we pick up where we were before our honeymoon got
sidetracked. Getting to know each other, becoming
friends."

"And sex?" she ventured boldly, tackling the subject
that she knew wasn't far from his mind, either.

Nick shook his head. "I don't want to have sex with

you, Megan. I want us to make love. Someday. When you're ready to take that step."

She smiled ruefully, a little surprised that she wasn't embarrassed about discussing the topic so openly. It was the first time her counseling experience had spilled over into this particular area of her personal life. "You say that now, Nick, but in another month or so you may change your mind about making love with a blimp."

He didn't smile. "I can't imagine not wanting you, Megan."

Her heart skipped a beat and she had to be honest with him. "I want you, too, Nick. That's been pretty obvious since that night in the conservatory. But I'm not ready yet."

"I know," he said easily. "I can wait."

She tilted her head to one side. "And in the meantime?"

He grinned. "We have fun."

Meg grinned, too. "I think I can handle that." She reached out to gently caress his cheek. "I think I could handle a kiss, too."

He obliged her most willingly.

THAT WASN'T the only kiss they shared during the next few weeks. Nick began staying for breakfast every morning and was home by six most nights. Meg worked an eight hour shift at the Carolina Crisis Center Tuesdays through Thursdays, which left them with long weekends that they often spent at the cottage.

They began accepting a few social invitations, mostly small gatherings with a select circle of his friends and business associates. Meg found two women in particular, both wives of Ballenger executives, who she seemed to have a lot in common with, and finally began making friends her own age.

Her pregnancy became obvious almost immediately, which also made obvious the reason for their hasty marriage, but no one questioned the validity of their union. How could they, when everyone who knew Nick universally agreed that they had never seen him so happy.

Nick accompanied Meg to all of her doctor appointments, of course, and sometimes he coddled her a little too much, but the thing that Meg treasured most in those ensuing weeks were the evenings they spent alone at the Hall with Nick at the piano and Meg curled in a chair, arguing over baby names between piano solos. Meg had joked more than once that she was glad Dr. Michaelson had confirmed that the baby was a girl, otherwise the child would be stuck with the name Ludwig or Johann Sebastian. Nick always laughed, no matter how often she made the joke.

"Do you believe in reincarnation?" she had asked one afternoon on the *Rhapsody*.

"I don't really know," Nick had replied, wondering if she was thinking about David, but that wasn't what was on her mind this time. When he asked "Why?" she explained, "I think I do believe. It's the only thing that makes sense."

"Of what?"

"Us," she replied. "Of why it's so easy for us to be together."

Nick had hoped for a moment then that she might open up and share her secrets, but that didn't happen, and he tried not to let it bother him. Once or twice he tried to give her an opening to talk about her past, but she never walked through the door. He had to believe, though, that someday she would.

In the meantime, there were other, more pleasant diversions.

"What would you think about us doing some house hunting together?" he'd asked her one Sunday afternoon between the eleventh and twelfth holes at Wild Dunes. They played a lot of golf during those weeks, and the number of games Meg lost increased in direct proportion to the growth of her stomach.

"If we're lucky, we might find something and be ready to move in by the time the baby is born," he had said as though their separation-after-six-months contract didn't exist.

Meg agreed to his suggestion and a week later he appeared at the counseling center at lunchtime to take her to see a magnificent old mansion down on Rainbow Row, the strip of colorful late-Victorian houses on the Battery that everyone thought of when they visualized the city of Charleston.

There was an unobstructed view of the bay from the second-floor balcony of the Gothic Revival mansion, and the breeze smelled of the sea. The house was much newer than Ballenger Hall, of course, but it was still a hundred years old.

"What do you think?" Nick asked as they wove in and out of an interconnecting warren of second-floor rooms.

"It's beautiful," she replied, peeking into an enormous bathroom with a huge claw-foot tub. "Absolutely magnificent."

Nick was coming to know her too well, though. "You don't like it," he adjudged.

"Of course I do! What's not to like?" She looked at him and found him waiting for her to tell the truth. She shifted uncomfortably. "Nick, it's lovely. Really. It's a beautiful slice of nineteenth-century elegance."

Nick frowned. "I thought you'd like something historic."

"Why would you think that?"

"Because Dav—" Nick ground to a halt. David wasn't a taboo subject by any means, but this didn't seem like the time to invoke his memory.

But Meg knew what he meant. "Nick, you think that because David was so enamored of history, I am, too?"

"Aren't you?"

She shook her head. "I'm my own person. It took me a long time to find myself, but I was *me* even when I was with David. Granted, when I first came to Charleston I was a little obsessed with history because it was a way to stay close to him…"

"But?" Nick prompted.

She shrugged. "No offense, but three months in Ballenger Hall has convinced me that I don't want to live the rest of my life in a museum. In fact, one *night* was enough for me."

Nick grinned. "Thank God! Come on. Let's get out of here," he said, taking her hand to lead her out of the maze.

"You're not upset that I don't like the house?" Meg asked as they went.

"On the contrary. I couldn't be more relieved. When I married Camille, I wanted us to live elsewhere, but she wanted all the trimmings that went with the Ballenger name—including the Hall. By the time we were divorced, I didn't have a life so it didn't make much difference where I lived it."

"What kind of a house do you want, Nick?" she asked as they reached the stairs and started a slow descent, one hand sliding along the banister, the other held snugly in Nick's. She was reaching the stage where moving with any semblance of grace was becoming nothing more than a fond memory.

"I want something big, bright and contemporary that doesn't have tourists peeking through the wisteria vines. What about you? What do you want?"

Meg would have been perfectly content with a small, clean apartment in a safe neighborhood, but she wasn't foolish enough to think that a man of Nick's wealth and social position would settle for something so modest. She wouldn't even consider asking him to.

But maybe there was a happy middle ground. "I think bright and contemporary sounds wonderful, so long as it doesn't require a houseful of servants to run it."

"Then consider it done," he announced, and a week later, he delivered on the promise.

The five-year-old house, called Pepper Tree for reasons the Realtor hadn't been able to explain, had been built carefully around the existing live oaks so that there were luxurious patches of shade everywhere, even on the stone-tile patio where Nick and Meg ended their tour. The house was wonderful, with large, airy rooms that flowed from one to the other, from indoors to out. Best of all, there was nothing ostentatious about it. Even without furniture the house had a warmth that made Meg feel comfortable in every room.

"Well? Do you like it?" Nick asked hopefully.

"It's perfect," Meg said, looking down the sloping lawn.

Nick stepped close behind her in the fashion that had become a welcome habit for both of them. One arm under her breasts snuggled her close against him; the other hand rested on her stomach, which was growing daily.

He loved holding her like this and he suspected that their daughter did, too, because whenever he touched his wife he could always feel the baby moving beneath his hand. He'd never told Meg, but he liked to believe that the little girl sensed his nearness and was trying to snuggle closer to him.

He'd never told Meg, either, that he couldn't wait to hold his daughter, but he was pretty sure she already knew that.

Meg was six months pregnant now, and despite the nineteen pounds she'd gained around her midsection she was still the most beautiful woman Nick had ever seen.

"So, what do you think? Should I make an offer?" he asked her. "Do you think we could be happy here?"

She turned in his arms, sliding her own arms around his waist as she looked up at him. "That depends on us, Nick. Not the house."

All Nick needed to see was the soft, sweet, loving, maternal light in her eyes. "Then we'll be very happy," he decreed, and leaned down to seal the promise with a kiss.

CHAPTER FIFTEEN

MEG KNEW the exact moment she fell in love with Nick. It was a September afternoon about ten days after the old owners of Pepper Tree accepted his offer on the property and the long process of transferring ownership began. Nick was coming home early so that they could attend their first childbirth class tonight, and Meg was on the stairs headed down to the kitchen to check on supper.

Barely halfway down, she stopped dead in her tracks when Nick came through the front door wrestling the biggest stuffed teddy bear Meg had ever seen—a furry white monstrosity almost as tall as Nick and twice as broad. He had the toy in a choke hold, its feet dragging the ground, the pink paisley bow that should have been tied around its neck twisting between Nick's legs, threatening to trip him as he maneuvered the bear through the door and tried to close it behind him.

He barely managed, but as he turned, the bear got the better of him. Nick stepped on the ribbon and went stumbling, catching himself before he fell, but dropping his briefcase in the process.

Meg was frozen on the stairs, blissfully unobserved, trying desperately not to laugh, and she could practically see the wheels turning in his head.

Do I put the bear down to pick up the briefcase and risk not being able to pick this monster up again, or try to bend over with the bear in tow? he was asking himself.

He finally did the latter, and the sight of him trying to retrieve the briefcase was even more comical than the sight of him dropping it. Her imagination created another even funnier image of him wrestling the toy into his car and driving through the streets of Charleston with a fuzzy white bear in the passenger seat. Had he remembered to buckle up? she wondered, and couldn't hold back her laughter any longer.

Realizing he was being watched, Nick froze like a cat burglar caught with the crown jewels in his pocket. He looked up the stairs at her, and that's when Meg fell in love.

How could she not when the look on his face was too adorable to resist—a combination of little-boy see-what-I-brought-home pride and grown-man humiliation that his prize had gotten the best of him. Meg's heart swelled to twice its normal size as she continued down the stairs.

"Go ahead. Say it. This is too corny for words, right?"

Meg let him stew as she walked deliberately down the hall and circled him slowly. "I've got news for you, Nick," she said finally, then gestured at the bear. "Corn doesn't grow this tall."

"I gave into impulse. I saw it and knew that Baby B. couldn't live without it," he said defensively, using the nickname they had agreed upon until they could decide on the real thing.

"Saw it where? Did the lab run out of test mice? Someone left it on a shelf in Toxicology? What?" she asked, taking delight in giving him a hard time.

"Noooo," he said, dragging the word out. "I had—"

Down the hall, Fetridge popped through the service

door, already greeting the master of the house as he hurried out. "Good afternoon, Mr. Nick. I was just helping..." He stopped as he caught sight of Nick and Meg and the bear.

"Oh my, sir."

"Run for your life, Fetridge," Meg advised him.

"Oh, no, I couldn't do that," he answered as though she'd been serious. He finally jumped forward to assist. "May I help you with that, sir?"

It was everything Meg could do to keep from laughing as she stepped between the butler and his boss. "No you don't, Fetridge. This is Mr. Nick's bright idea. Let's let him wrestle with it."

Nick quirked one eyebrow at her. "Gee, thanks. You're a real pal." He looked at the butler. "If you'd get my briefcase and put it in the study, I'd appreciate it, Fetridge."

"Yes, sir."

Nick started toward the stairs, the giant bear in tow, and Meg joined him. "You were telling me how you came into possession of Harvey, here, if I recall," she reminded him.

"It's no big mystery. I had a meeting downtown at the Finance Center, and as I was walking back to the car, I just happened to pass a toy store."

Meg wasn't familiar enough with the business district to determine whether it was a plausible story, but she wouldn't have been surprised to learn that it had taken a several-block detour to "just happen by" a toy store.

"Uh-huh. And what else did you get?" They started up the stairs and she dropped behind because there wasn't room for the three of them side by side.

He glanced over his shoulder, guilt written on his face.

"What makes you think I got something else? Isn't this enough? Don't you think I have any self-control?"

"This is ten times more than enough," Meg said. "But I know you. If you're going to get carried away, you get carried *all* the way. So fess up. What else did you get? Are they in the car or being delivered?"

"Being delivered," he admitted sheepishly. "There's a musical mobile with butterflies and ladybugs for her crib, and a floppy-eared bunny with a ticking clock inside it that's supposed to remind her of you."

"Gee, thanks. You think my ears are floppy?"

"Not your ears, your heartbeat," he replied.

He had finally manhandled the bear to the top of the stairs and Meg looked at him expectantly. "Now what?" she asked. "It's not going into my room, and the nursery is a shambles."

"All right." He made a left turn then a right and finally found a cozy resting place for the bear on one of the guest-room beds. Along the way, he rattled off a list of the other toys he'd splurged on.

"My God, Nick. She's not even out of the womb and already you're spoiling her," she chided him, though her heart was so overflowing with love that she could hardly contain it.

"I'm not spoiling her," he said, gathering Meg into his arms. "I'm spoiling *myself*. I can't hold her yet but I've got to do something to make myself useful."

"You are useful, Nick," she assured him as she snuggled against him. Baby B. responded predictably by kicking Megan in the ribs.

"Ouch," Nick said for her.

Meg chuckled. "You're going to be lots of fun when I go into labor. Maybe you should practice panting tonight and I'll coach."

"Whatever will make you happy."

She was happy, she realized. So much so that it was a little frightening. The last month had been like a fairy tale. She was Snow White, Nick was Prince Charming, and they were acting out roles in a fantasy that was too perfect to be true.

Meg had never experienced perfection before, not even with David. Their happiness had been marred by his displeasure with life in Singapore and her frustration over his inability to take control of his life.

But she had perfection with Nick, and though part of her was screaming for her to be cautious, she didn't want to listen. Her feelings were real. She believed that Nick's were, too. If there was something missing from this Eden, she didn't want to know what it was.

She would have told Nick right that moment that she was in love with him, but she heard footsteps in the hall and held her tongue. A second later Effie came bustling in to see the bear and satisfy herself that her husband hadn't been nipping the cooking sherry.

The feeling that she was bursting with love didn't leave Meg during supper that night, nor during the two-hour childbirth class. It was wonderful, sitting on the mat, leaning back against Nick, supported by him physically and emotionally, his hands on her belly, and their very active daughter responding as she always did to Nick's touch or his voice.

They watched a film and listened to a lecture, then Nick coached her through her first breathing lesson. The whole time, she could hardly wait for the evening to be over so that she could be alone with him. She had to tell him how she felt. Mostly, though, she wanted to show him.

Unfortunately, it wasn't until they were on their way

home that Nick mentioned the briefcase full of reports he had to read before tomorrow.

With a soft kiss good-night and a "see you in the morning," Nick disappeared into his study. Meg went upstairs, sat on the edge of her bed and tried to decide if she was making a huge mistake.

She wanted to make love with Nick. She'd wanted it for a very long time, but something in her heart was waiting for the time to be right, and this was it. She was sure of it. And she had to factor in that she was twenty-five weeks pregnant. She was fit and healthy, but if the experiences of other women held true for Meg, it wouldn't be long before she'd be too miserable to entertain the notion of making love.

She wanted Nick now, though. She ached for him, but there was the important consideration of whether or not Nick still wanted her.

She went into her dressing room to prepare for a shower, but before she slipped into her robe she paused and looked in the full-length mirror, trying to see herself objectively, to see if there was anything here that Nick would want.

Her breasts were swollen. She suspected Nick would respond to that, and the thought of him touching her, his dark head bent to suckle at her breast, sent a flush of heat through her.

He loved caressing her swollen belly through her clothes. Would he love touching her like this, as well?

Meg couldn't be certain. Some men were repulsed by their pregnant wives, others were turned on. She could only guess which category Nick would fall into, but if the sight of her wasn't enough to make him want her, there were other ways....

Meg knew what men liked. Her first education had

been at the rough hands of Russell Corday, who had taught her how to please him in the front seat of his pickup truck. Meg had learned because she'd been willing to do anything to escape from her father.

Russell had taught Meg about sex the hard way, and it had taken her years to realize that there was more to it than just a man's selfish pleasure. She'd learned from books and novels, psychology courses and gossip among the other nurses where she worked. She'd even learned from a moderately skilled lover she'd taken while attending school in St. Louis.

But it was David who had let her experience the true joy that went with making love. He'd shown her how sweet and how gentle the act could be when two people were in love.

Meg wanted to believe it would be that good with Nick, too. That he would sweep her along on the same gentle currents of passion.

She climbed into the shower and afterward dabbed just a touch of perfume on all her pulse points, then deliberately chose the white nightgown and peignoir that she hadn't worn since that night in the conservatory. The bust was tighter now, and her breasts strained at the confinement, but the diaphanous gathers were more than enough to accommodate her stomach. She put her hair up with a clip because she knew Nick would enjoy taking it down. She opened the door to her side of the parlor between their rooms, turned out all the lights except the one by the bed and waited.

She'd dallied so long with her preparations that it was only a few minutes before she heard a soft footfall in the hall. She heard Nick's door open, saw the light come on under his parlor door. The door to the hall closed. She imagined him moving into his dressing room as he unbuttoned his shirt, unbuckled his belt, removed his trousers.

He preferred to shower in the mornings, so it wouldn't take him long to get ready for bed. The light under the door blinked out, then a much softer light replaced it. His bedside light, she guessed.

That's when she moved from her room through the parlor and knocked on his door.

"Megan?" She could hear surprise and concern in his voice.

"Yes, Nick."

"Are you all right?" She heard movement and guessed that he was putting on a bathrobe.

"I'm fine," she said just as the door opened. She gave him a second to absorb her appearance. A fire ignited in his eyes and Meg knew she wasn't making a mistake. "But I'm very lonely."

"Um, uh...Meg..." It was obvious she'd shocked him, but she was going to shock him even more.

"Let's discuss this analytically, shall we?" she asked, slipping past him into the masculine inner sanctum that she'd breached only a few times in the last weeks, and never late into the night.

"Dis—" Nick cleared his throat and lowered his voice an octave. "Discuss what?"

"The mechanics of making love with a six-month-pregnant woman."

"Making...? Meg..."

"You don't want me?" she asked with an impish grin because she knew perfectly well now that he did. He wouldn't be stammering like a schoolboy otherwise. "If you're going to turn down this offer, you'd better think twice, because I'm rapidly reaching the point of no return. Even now, I think the missionary position is pretty much out of the question, but there are certainly alternatives.''

She crossed the room and crawled onto his bed.

"Am I dreaming?" Nick asked as he approached the end of the bed. "Because if I am, I'm going to be in a world of hurt if I wake up too soon."

"I don't want to hurt you, Nick," Meg said, coming to her knees and gathering her gown so that she could inch her way over to him. "I don't want to make you miserable. I want to make you happy. I want to make you feel as loved as you make me feel."

"Oh, Megan," he whispered, cupping her face in his hands and bringing his lips to hers.

She opened to him instantly, accepting his kiss, drinking it in, mating her tongue to his with an urgency that they'd been very careful to exclude from their other kisses. She finally dragged her mouth away from his, gasping for air, and her head fell back, offering him her throat. He accepted the invitation eagerly, his mouth blazing a trail down her throat until he reached the swell of her breasts. He unfastened the ribbon of her robe and slid it off her shoulders, then gathered up her gown and pulled it over her head, leaving her naked.

He kissed her again, hard, and Meg wove her hands into his hair, urging him on with soft whimpers. She brushed at the lapels of his robe, running her hands across his chest to send it off his shoulders, then leaned into him, pressing her breasts against his chest. It put her off balance, but Nick supported her weight as he knelt on the bed and lowered her gently to the sheets. His mouth left hers so that he could taste her breasts with delicious, exacting precision, then pressed loving kisses against her belly while one hand slid into the curls at the junction of her thighs and turned the ache there into an inferno that stole her breath.

It seemed to go on forever. The touching, the kisses, the eager writhing against his hand… Sanity abandoned her and before she was even aware that it was near, an explosion of pleasure rocked her. She cried out Nick's name, but he swallowed it with his mouth on hers until the star burst of pleasure was just a glorious glow.

And that was only the beginning.

CHAPTER SIXTEEN

NORMALLY WHEN Eleanor traveled she returned to Charleston no later than mid-September. This year, she didn't live up to that schedule, and it had nothing to do with the lateness of her arrival in Tuscany. In a moment of rage, Nick had suggested she leave, and she had complied because she hoped that her absence would soften him more quickly than her presence ever could. Besides, she could not have stayed without coming to resent Megan for the rift between her and Nick, and such antagonism would only have worsened her relationship with her grandson.

So September came and went, as did all of her friends who returned to the States at the end of the summer season, leaving Eleanor alone and lonely, feeling older than she had ever imagined possible.

She wasn't completely cut off, though. She had heard from correspondents in Charleston that Nick and Megan were highly visible socially, and were to all appearances very happy. He called her Meg now, and they were openly demonstrative in public. It was said that Nick was like a different man, and there were rumors that he had bought Megan a modest home out on the old Ashley River plantation road.

If that was true, Eleanor would miss him at the Hall, certainly. But how much she would miss him in her life was entirely up to her, and whether or not she could accept the woman with whom her grandson was so obviously in love.

To Megan's credit, Eleanor had received two very pleasant letters from her, and one had contained a postscript in Nick's distinctive handwriting. She could almost imagine Megan urging Nick to add it to her missive. Unfortunately, it was nothing more than a coolly worded hope that she was well and enjoying herself that could just as easily have been a message from a passing acquaintance.

The only other communiqué from Nick came early in November in the form of James Hamilton's final report on Megan's background. A hand-written note had accompanied the document:

Dear Eleanor,
   You initiated this and I have finished it. Please read it carefully and if you can, imagine yourself in Meg's place. See where she came from, what her choices were and why she made them. Don't judge, and don't fault her for her poverty or the sins of her parents. Look at her life for the triumph over adversity that it has truly been.

   Meg knows nothing of this document, nor will she until I am confident that I have all of her trust. We are together now, Meg and I. Husband and wife in every sense of the word. I see it as the greatest joy of my life, and it would mean more to me than you can know if you would embrace our relationship and return home. I have loved you as long as I can remember, and I am not ready to imagine a life without you.

   I suspect you feel the same.

Meg and I will hope to see you in time for the holidays.

Nick

Eleanor knew the letter by heart, and as Nick had asked, she tried to read the narrative account of the life of Megan Linley Ballenger with an open mind. Though she could see Nick's hand in some of the conclusions the report drew, she had to admit it was a remarkable story.

A rise from impoverished waif to productive citizen was undeniably impressive, but for all that, Eleanor still had difficulty getting past the lies. The fact that Nick had not told Megan about Hamilton's investigation only confirmed Eleanor's suspicions that the girl was still guarding her secrets closely, and that made it very difficult to place the same trust in her that Nick apparently did.

But despite that, Eleanor knew when she was defeated. She had taken the risk of defying Nick, certain that she could control his response and deal with his anger. She had miscalculated, and it was costing her dearly. With this letter, Nick had opened his arms to welcome her back home, and she could let pride separate her from her family for only so long.

She would return home and do nothing to impede the relationship between Nick and his wife. If there was a hard lesson for her grandson to learn, he would have to do it without Eleanor's help.

She hoped she was wrong, but only time would tell.

Dub Linley was going stir-crazy. He'd served nine weeks of his three-month sentence for busting Deputy Junior Voit's nose, and the remaining days were going by slower than molasses in January. He had dried out, and most of the time he was over the shakes, but there was nothing to do in the county jail except look at his institutional gray walls and the tantalizing pictures of his daughter, Meggie.

She was married now, and Dub had the pictures to prove it. With the help of Mildred Wallace at the public library, Rhonda had found all kinds of information about the company Meggie had worked for and the man who'd showed up in Pine Ridge claiming to be her husband. He was, all right, and just as Rhonda's niece, Wendy, had guessed, he was rich.

One magazine, for instance, said that Nicholas Ballenger was one of the wealthiest men in the United States. Granted, he was pretty low on the list, but in a country as big as this, being in the top five hundred had to mean the guy was pretty well off, didn't it?

There were other articles about the company, and there were pictures from Charleston, South Carolina, of Meggie's wedding back in June, and one picture taken just last week of her and her husband dancing at a fancy party.

It was obvious from the last photo that his daughter was pregnant—at least seven months along—and even Dub could do the math from June to November. She'd gotten knocked up again, but this time he said ''more power to you, girl,'' because she'd landed in clover.

Mildred had helped Rhonda find the address of his son-in-law's company, and his girlfriend was saving her tips and putting away Dub's disability check to pay for their trip to Charleston. If Meggie came through for him, he might not need money to get back home. He and Rhonda might stay right there in Charleston where Meggie could take care of him in style.

He deserved that after what she'd done to him back

in '93. He'd done hard prison time because of her, and he would have made her pay for that a long time ago if she hadn't snuck off to live halfway around the world.

But she was back now, and she was rich. He'd gladly accept his compensation in cash, and if she didn't co-operate, he'd take it out of her hide, just like the old days.

Dub checked off the days on the wall calendar in his cell and figured that with a few extra days for good behavior he'd be out of jail and on his way to Charleston by Thanksgiving.

WHEN NICK RECEIVED the letter from Eleanor telling him she'd be home in time for Thanksgiving, he was almost afraid to tell Meg. Escrow had closed on their house and Meg was working feverishly to get their new home ready to move into by Christmas. She refused to cut back her hours at the crisis center but fortunately, her two new friends, Kathleen Desmond and Abby Wyeth, were lending a hand, and Nick was happy to help, too. For the first time in his life, Nick had the makings of a *real* family, and he was genuinely happy.

Would Eleanor's homecoming upset all that? he had to wonder. He couldn't imagine her actively opposing him again, but he had no illusions that his grandmother would return ready to embrace Meg as a true member of the family.

Dreading the effect it would have on his wife, Nick saved the news of Eleanor's impending return until after supper. As was her habit, Meg asked Nick to play the piano for her, but he declined and they retired to the visiting room where Fetridge had a cheery fire waiting for them. Gigantic floor pillows were waiting for them, too, and Nick helped Meg get down to the floor.

He stretched out behind her, reclining on his elbow so that she could lie back on him, their bodies forming a comfortable T in front of the fire.

"Why do I have the feeling that I'm being softened up for something?" Meg asked when Fetridge left after serving them glasses of sparkling cider.

"Because you are," Nick replied, rubbing her back and shoulders. He felt her tense under his hand.

"What is it?"

He heaved a heavy sigh. "Eleanor will be home in time to spend Thanksgiving with us."

"Oh." Meg tried to decide how she felt about the news. On one hand, she felt terribly guilty that she had been the cause of conflict between Nick and his grandmother. On the other, she and Nick were blissfully happy without Eleanor around to interfere.

But their own home would be ready in a month or so, and she wouldn't have to contend with the dowager's disapproval on a daily basis. Surely what she and Nick had together was strong enough to survive Hurricane Eleanor. He hadn't said that he loved her, but Meg didn't care. He made her *feel* loved, and actions were more important than words. Nick showed her every day in a hundred ways how much he cared for her, and Meg felt truly secure for the first time in her life.

"Are you okay?" Nick asked her.

Meg nodded. "It was bound to happen sooner or later. Having her here for the holiday means a lot to you."

"It does. In fact…I wrote to her," he confessed. "I told her we were together now and that we hoped she could accept our relationship."

"Did you tell her about Pepper Tree?"

"No, but I'm certain she already knows. Eleanor's

friends will have kept her apprised of everything that's gone on back here. Do you mind? That I asked her to come home?''

''Of course not, Nick. You're the most important thing in the world to Eleanor.''

He shook his head ruefully. ''No, I'm not. The Ballenger family is what she loves—not so much the people, but the *idea* of a dynasty that will outlive her.''

''I think you're wrong, Nick. She loves you, too. She just doesn't know how to express it. No one ever taught her by word or deed that there is a difference between nurturing and manipulation.''

''Maybe you're right.''

Meg bit her lower lip thoughtfully. ''This hadn't occurred to me before, but I guess we ought to talk about what we're going to do.''

''For what?'' Nick asked, pleased that she was taking it so well. He hadn't really expected anything less, but he knew she had to be worried. He certainly was.

''For the holiday,'' she replied, turning just a little to face him. ''What are your Thanksgiving traditions?''

''For the last few years? I go to the office in the morning, Eleanor pays social calls in the afternoon. We meet back here at night for a quiet dinner of roast duck or pheasant.'' He grinned. ''Does any of that appeal to you?''

Meg gave a mock shudder. ''You call that Thanksgiving? What about turkey and pumpkin pie? The Macy's parade? Stuffing yourself with stuffing and falling asleep with a football game blaring on TV?''

Nick chuckled at the image. ''I didn't know you liked football.''

''I don't, but those are real traditions. Manly

traditions. Not social calls and pheasant," she teased him.

"Was that what your Thanksgivings were like growing up?" Nick asked her casually. "Turkey, parades and football games?"

Meg made a huff of disgust and looked into the fire. "Hardly. My father didn't fall asleep, Nick. He passed out. And we didn't have turkey because he'd take the one that the church ladies brought by every year and sell it or trade it for a bottle of whiskey. Thanksgiving comes late in the month, as you recall, and Dub's government check was all gone by then."

Nick felt something that was half joy and half pain twist in his stomach; joy for the fact that she trusted him enough to give him a piece of her past, and pain that she'd had to endure such a nightmare. This was the first thing Meg had said about her childhood since that night in the car, and he knew he had to proceed very carefully.

"Your father was an alcoholic?" he asked because he wasn't supposed to know that.

"Yes."

"Was your mother?"

Meg shook her head. "No, she was just the classic codependent. No self-esteem, and no one in her life to give her any hope that things could change."

Meg's hair was long and silky now, and Nick brushed it back over her shoulder. "How did you survive that, Meg? How did you come out of that situation so...whole? So loving? So centered and sure of yourself?"

She looked at him, astonished. "Sure of myself? Nick, that's the last thing I am. And as for being whole...well...there is a complete person in here," she admitted, tapping her chest. "But she's a work in progress with a long way to go."

Nick took Meg's hand and brought it to his lips. "Well, I'm very glad she's taking me along for the ride." He rubbed his thumb over the back of her hand. "Meg, how did your parents die?"

She tensed against him, shifting her gaze back to the fire, and Nick could sense her conflict. She wanted to tell him. He could feel it. But he could also feel her fear.

Please, Meg, please, his heart begged. *Trust me.* He felt guilty as hell for deceiving her this way, for not telling her that he already knew the answers to his questions, but he needed the truth to come from her. He needed her to give him the secrets she'd shared with David. He had no trouble accepting that a part of his wife would always love his brother, but Nick had to know that she loved him just as much. It wasn't a competition and he didn't begrudge David Meg's love, but he didn't know how much longer he could live without his wife's trust.

"Meg?" he prompted gently when she didn't answer him for what seemed like hours instead of mere seconds.

"My mother was never a healthy woman. She died of pneumonia when I was thirteen, and my father..." She hesitated. "My father died from cirrhosis of the liver shortly before I went to Singapore."

She wouldn't look at him, and it was just as well. If she looked in his eyes now, Nick knew she'd see his disappointment. She'd probably even see the stab of pain that he tried quickly to cover up.

It didn't surprise him when Meg began to shift as though she was having trouble getting comfortable.

"I'm sorry, Nick. I hate to break up our depressing little tête-à-tête, but nature is calling. Do you mind?"

"Of course not."

She started struggling to rise, and Nick helped her to her feet. "Are you going to turn in for the night?" he asked.

"I think so. Are you coming up?" They had been sleeping in Nick's room since the first night they'd made love, even though sex was no longer on the menu. Every night it seemed to get harder for her to sleep, but they were doing fine in his king-size bed. For the sake of convenience, though, they did maintain separate dressing and bathrooms.

"Not just yet," he told her. "I have to make a call to Singapore before I turn in. Fletch is meeting with Minister Chau tomorrow about renegotiating one of the leases. I'll be up shortly."

"Send Fletch and Mei Ling my love."

"I will." He kissed her good-night, and she waddled off.

Feeling sick at heart, Nick removed the screen from the hearth and banked the fire. He crouched there for a long time, staring into the dwindling flames.

Meg had lied. She loved him—or thought she did—and was committed to building a life with him. But deep in her heart she still remembered his threats to search out her secrets and use them to take her child away. Part of her was afraid of him, and Nick didn't understand how she could know him so well and still not know him at all.

But he could wait. No matter how painful it was, the joy of loving her far outweighed the pain. For now, anyway. He had to be patient. He had to make her happy. He had to keep proving that she could trust him until one day she finally would.

* * *

MEG MANAGED to hold back her tears until she reached her room, but as soon as the door closed behind her, they spilled over, hot and anguished, and so very, very guilty.

She had lied to Nick! How could she have done that if she really loved him? Why hadn't she told him the truth? It had been on the tip of her tongue so many times, but she'd justified her silence with the excuse that she didn't want to soil their lives with the ugliness of her past.

But was that the reason? Or was she really afraid, as she had been with David, that Nick would reject her. That he would be disgusted and wash his hands of her?

That he would take her secrets and use them as a weapon against her?

Meg had never trusted anyone in her life. Back in Singapore she had convinced herself that she trusted David, but that had never been put to the test. If the plane hadn't crashed, if Nick hadn't ordered David to go back to the office that night, would she have told him the truth as she'd planned? Or would she have balked when it came time for the words to be spoken? Would she really have been able to lay it all on the line and risk losing the first good, decent man she'd ever loved? Who'd ever loved her?

Looking back, she wasn't sure.

But the past wasn't the test she had to pass or fail now. It was the present she had to worry about. It was Nick who deserved her honesty, but how could she look him in the face and tell him she'd lied, confess her sins of omission? How could she bear it if he was disappointed or disgusted? How would she survive if he decided that the truth made her unfit to raise Baby B.?

That precious, warm sense of security Meg had felt these last two months slipped away from her like a ghost dissolving into the mist. She had no idea what it would take to bring the feeling back, but deep into the night, long after Nick had slipped into bed with her, moving quietly and gently because he thought she was asleep, she examined her fears from every angle.

Finally, when it was very, very late and she was certain Nick was deeply asleep, she rose and went back to her own room, closing both the parlor doors before she turned on the light. She took pen and paper from the desk and began to write.

My beloved Nick...

CHAPTER SEVENTEEN

WHEN NICK WENT down to breakfast the next morning, Meg was already at the table, but instead of a plate in front of her, she had a pencil and pad of paper.

"Good morning, beautiful. What are you up to?" he asked as he slipped behind her chair and bent to kiss her cheek. She turned her face up to his and got a kiss on her smiling lips instead.

"I'm making a list," she replied. "But before I proceed any further, we have to talk."

"Okay," Nick said cautiously, pouring a cup of coffee before he sat at the head of the table. "Shoot."

"Would your family show up if we had a big Thanksgiving feast here in honor of Eleanor's homecoming?"

Nick's face registered his total surprise, but it was only a moment until he grinned. "Do vultures pluck at the flesh of dying animals?"

Meg laughed and grimaced at the same time. "Gee, what a lovely image of your relatives."

"I'm joking." He reconsidered. "No, actually, I'm not. They'll come, of course. But are you up to something like that? Thanksgiving is barely four weeks before your due date, you're still working nearly thirty hours a week at the crisis center, and there's the house..."

Meg searched his face. "You don't like the idea of a family Thanksgiving?"

"No, I love it. I think." He shrugged. "It's certainly worth a shot, anyway."

"Well, I think I can pull it off. With Effie's help, of course." She reached out and covered Nick's hand with her own. He turned his palm up, and when they linked fingers tears welled up in Meg's eyes, surprising them both.

"Hey," he said, using his free hand to brush the tears off her cheek. "What's wrong?"

"I'm a pregnant, sentimental idiot," she told him. "I've always wanted a family, Nick. I've dreamed about cozy holidays, kids underfoot, spices smelling up the house." She laughed shortly. "If I told you my fantasy of the perfect Christmas, you'd lock me up and throw away the key. I know the real thing can never be as flawless as my dreams, but it would mean the world to me if we could start making our own holiday traditions."

Nick had to clear a knot of emotion from his throat before he could promise her, "Then we will."

She grinned, and another tear spilled down her cheek. "We'll use Thanksgiving as a test case, and if it's a disaster, we'll correct the flaws at Christmas. We'll have our own family by then, and if your vulture relatives don't behave, we won't invite them."

"That sounds like a plan," he said, slipping out of his chair to kneel beside Meg's and take her into his arms.

It was a plan indeed. And a good one, she hoped. Meg had started a letter last night, the hardest she had ever written. It might take weeks to finish it, but when it was done, it would be Meg's Christmas gift to Nick, and she wouldn't back out.

She had already given him her heart. His name was written on her soul. On Christmas Day, she would give him her secrets, and trust that no matter how he felt about the lies she had told or sins she had committed, he would realize that she was giving him the most precious gift she possessed.

She would let him into the dark places that no one else had ever touched and pray that he could forgive.

ELEANOR RETURNED home the day before Thanksgiving, cool but cordial. The Hall became formal again, a place where CD players and pillows in front of the fireplace were unthinkable effronteries to the dignity of the historic manse. Meg didn't let it bother her because Pepper Tree was almost ready for its new family.

On Wednesday night after dinner, Nick told Eleanor about the move they had planned, and she accepted the news with her usual calm. Meg expressed her hope that Eleanor would visit often, and their conversation quickly moved on to the Thanksgiving celebration that had been planned for the next day. Tomorrow evening fifteen members of the Ballenger and Tate families would sit down to a Thanksgiving feast.

Eleanor seemed genuinely surprised and not altogether displeased.

"It was Meg's idea," Nick told her, quickly outlining the guest list, which included every relative who hadn't had plans or had been able to change them.

"You've been away so long, I thought you might enjoy seeing the family all together," Meg explained.

"That's very kind of you, Megan."

Nick caught his grandmother's gaze, silently asking if she really believed that, but as usual her face betrayed nothing.

"Is there anything I could do to assist you with your preparations for tomorrow?" Eleanor asked her.

"Not that I'm aware of, but thank you," Meg replied. "I turned to Effie for advice on how you would have planned the day had you been here, and she's been absolutely wonderful." She hesitated a second. "It would be a great favor to me, though, if I could count on you to help me make all the right decisions tomorrow."

That seemed to surprise Eleanor, too. "Of course."

Nick was amazed at Meg's handling of his grandmother. Not only was she graciously turning the reins of the household back over to Eleanor, she'd bravely invited the etiquette-obsessed dowager to criticize her at will.

Blessedly, it was an invitation Eleanor didn't abuse. She was content to sit back and be the guest of honor, observing Meg in her hostess duties and making quiet suggestions only rarely and never critically.

Nick caught her watching him as well, and wondered what she was seeing.

Had she really changed her opinion of Meg? he wondered. When he'd sent her the file he'd helped Hamilton complete, he hadn't expected it to do much good. Maybe he hadn't given Eleanor enough credit, though. He could always tell when she was up to something—if he hadn't been so preoccupied with sorting out his tangled feelings for Meg, he'd have seen the signs back in June when she was conspiring with Hamilton.

She wasn't being devious now. Her behavior didn't have an edge of deception or the feel of a manipulation. She was being genuinely supportive of Meg—as supportive as Eleanor knew how to be, anyway.

Nick didn't think the day was exactly the Norman Rockwell holiday that Meg had been hoping for, but it went flawlessly. The cocktail hour before dinner was a great success. The Thanksgiving feast, even more so. Meg asked Eleanor to preside as hostess at the foot of the table, which seemed to please the matriarch enormously and freed Meg to sit next to Nick at the head of the table.

The meal progressed smoothly from course to course and conversations ebbed and flowed. Nick and Meg fielded the inevitable questions about Pepper Tree, and there was a ceaseless string of inquiries about the baby— especially the names being considered. Everyone laughed when they learned that the current favorite— Beatrice—had been arrived at because they'd gotten used to the nickname Baby B. They hadn't decided, though, if she would be called Bea or Bebe.

One thing particularly pleased Nick that afternoon. There were no sly looks askance or innuendo about the pregnancy and their hasty nuptials. Meg had seen all of the relatives outside of the Hall in a variety of social settings as her pregnancy progressed, and Nick finally came to realize that what had impressed Eleanor today was Meg's gracious ease with both the Tates and the Ballengers. In her absence, Eleanor's family had accepted Meg as one of them.

That would put a considerable pressure on her to accept Meg as well, and Nick finally allowed himself to hope that things might turn out right after all.

"Splendid feast, Eleanor. Simply splendid!" Wayne Currant said boisterously as two waiters began clearing the table under Fetridge's watchful eye. Wayne was Great-Aunt Ophelia's only son, making him Nick's first cousin once removed.

"I'm afraid I can't claim any of the credit, though I would be very happy to," Eleanor demurred. "Mrs. Fetridge was the engineer of our feast, and Megan was its architect and dessert chef. Your compliments should go to her.''

"Consider yourself complimented, Megan," Wayne said with a friendly wink. "It's been too long since we got together like this, but you've managed it twice in one year—your wedding and now this." He raised his glass. "To Nick's lovely wife, and the happiness she has brought into this house.''

"Hear, hear," Nick seconded.

Meg blushed. "Thank you. But don't throw bouquets at me just yet. There's still more to come. I have a surprise for all of you—if Nick will indulge me," she added, throwing him a flirty glance.

"Indulge you how?" he asked suspiciously. He was familiar with that look. It was the one Meg knew he couldn't resist.

"I've had Fetridge set coffee and dessert in the conservatory. Will you make this holiday perfect and play for us? Please?''

Meg had thought the room was already rather quiet, but suddenly it grew as still as a tomb. The only sound was the tinkle of the chandelier overhead as the room's air currents brushed the ropes of Baccarat crystals against each other. Animation was suspended like something from a bad sci-fi movie where evil aliens stopped time, freezing everyone like statues.

What on earth was wrong with these people? Meg wondered. You'd think she'd asked Nick to cut off a limb.

Meg ignored the peculiar reaction, even when nervous coughs began to replace the silence. "Well, Nick?"

Like Meg, Nick was keenly aware of his startled relatives, but unlike Meg, he knew the reason. He had banished music from the house years ago because he hadn't been able to bear reminders. In those early years before he conquered his bitterness, he could recall any number of unpleasant scenes he'd childishly created when one hapless relative or another asked him to play.

But he wasn't that bitter, angry young man anymore. He smiled at his wife. "Couldn't you at least have given me some warning?"

"Why? So you could practice? What's the point. You're already brilliant. What do you say?"

"Megan, please," Eleanor interjected, her face almost ashen.

"It's all right, Nan," Nick assured her. He glanced around the table. "It would seem we're bound for the conservatory. Any requests?"

MEG WAS INVITED to choose the music and she elected to make use of the new sound system and one of the *sans* piano orchestral recordings Nick had recently purchased.

Everyone settled in the conservatory, uncomfortably, at first, as though they were afraid to believe what was happening. But as Gershwin's *Rhapsody in Blue* filled the Hall, pouring out of Nick's soul, the air grew hushed with astonishment, then admiration.

Those who knew music and still remembered Nick's concerts were amazed by the maturity of his playing. Those who had only heard the family whispers about Nick's youthful desire to be a concert musician were flabbergasted to discover the talent that had been buried in their remote and unapproachable relative.

But Eleanor, who'd deliberately chosen a seat behind the others, watched her grandson embrace the music that she had taken away from him. She saw the joy in his

playing, heard it in every note, and she finally realized
what was so different about him. She'd thought at first
that it was only a manifestation of his infatuation with
Megan, but that wasn't it. Nick was whole now.

She had taken his music away from him, and in so
doing had wrung all the joy out of him. He'd become a
cold, hard businessman like his father and grandfather,
and because it was good for the family, Eleanor had
convinced herself that it was also best for Nick.

Something had freed Nick from that emotionless
prison she'd trapped him in, and he was soaring.

When the piece ended and the Hall resonated with
applause, Eleanor saw that it was Megan who clapped
the loudest. And it was Megan to whom Nick turned,
smiling as though he was returning the gift she'd given
him.

Eleanor had taken his music from him. Megan had
given it back.

No wonder Eleanor's control over Nick had changed
so drastically. Megan had usurped Eleanor's role as the
most influential woman in her grandson's life.

That was the natural order of things, of course, but it
was going to be very hard for Eleanor to accept.

"THIS IS the busiest shopping day of the year, Meg. How
can you possibly want to face those crowds? You should
stay home and rest," Nick told his wife.

"And you should stop fussing like an old mother
hen," she replied, but didn't make any attempt to dis-
engage her hand from his supportive arm as they moved
down the cantilever staircase.

"But just yesterday you were entertaining a houseful
of relatives."

"Nick, please... We have a plan," she reminded him.

"We agreed on it. All three of us. I ride to work with you, then drive over to the Galleria to do my shopping. I come back and pick you up at noon and we go to Biehlman's showroom so you can help me make the final decision on the living-room and master-bedroom furniture, then we pick up Eleanor and take her out to show her Pepper Tree. It's a plan. It's efficient. It works. We're not changing it," she decreed.

"All right, all right," Nick said. "I'll shut up and enjoy a ride to work with my wife."

"That's the spirit."

They ate breakfast with Eleanor, who'd been remarkably subdued last night after Nick's performance. She'd said very little, but after an encore of Chopin's "Heroic" polonaise she had taken his hands in hers and kissed his cheek.

Later, in bed, he'd told Meg that he couldn't recall his grandmother ever having kissed him before.

Eleanor had also surprised him by asking if she might be permitted to see Pepper Tree today, and he chose to see that as a good sign. They'd been living under the same roof for years, and though their lives seldom intersected except for their morning breakfasts together, he knew Eleanor would miss his presence in the house. He felt sorry for her, and was astonished to learn that his wife did, too.

Meg was looking forward to showing Eleanor their new home, but she was also nervous about it. Their relationship seemed to be on better footing now that Eleanor had returned with an improved, less imperious attitude, but Meg wasn't ready to trust Nick's grandmother. She'd do everything she could, though, to facilitate harmony between them.

As planned, she rode to work with Nick, then got

behind the wheel and adjusted the electronic seat to accommodate her legs and her baby. She'd gained only twenty-seven pounds so far, but it felt like fifty, and on her small frame looked like a hundred. She expected Nick to start calling her Blimpie any day now, but so far he'd been unbelievably supportive and indulgent.

The multilevel Galleria was mobbed. Nick had warned her, but while Meg had been to the spacious shopping mall several times, her image of "busy" didn't match the shoulder-to-shoulder reality. This was the first Friday-after-Thanksgiving Meg had spent in America in seven years, and there hadn't been any malls in Pine Ridge while she was growing up.

Still, she was here, and she was an intrepid soul. She was anxious to get what she needed so that the new house was ready before the baby was born. Surviving the busiest shopping day of the year was simply a matter of practicing a little self-protection. She was using an enormous beach bag as a purse which came in handy as a shield, too. Meg shifted it frequently from one shoulder to the other, keeping it between her stomach and the flow of heedless shoppers who couldn't have cared less if they bumped and jostled a pregnant woman.

The bed and bath shop on the second floor of the Galleria was having a fabulous holiday sale, and Meg made it safely up the escalator. Four hours later, she was satisfied that she had successfully chosen all the linens she would need for Pepper Tree's kitchen, bedrooms, baths and pool house.

She made arrangements for the delivery of her purchases, but couldn't resist taking a crib blanket and bath set with her that matched the hot air balloon theme of Baby Bea's room.

It was a load she didn't really need to be carrying, but

she reasoned that she could use the packages as a second shield to protect both sides of her once she got up the nerve to fight the crowd on the concourse again.

Dreading the shuffle, Meg stood in the gigantic archway where the jazzy rendition of "Jingle Bells" that was being piped into the concourse clashed jarringly with the orchestral majesty of "God Rest Ye Merry Gentlemen" playing inside the store.

"Are you all right, Mrs. Ballenger?"

Meg glanced at the friendly young salesclerk who'd helped her earlier. "I'm fine, Monica," Meg assured her. "I'm just trying to visualize myself plowing through that daunting sea of humanity."

The clerk grinned at her. "Are you sure you wouldn't like to sit down again? Rest a few more minutes before you go?"

It was tempting, but Meg was due to pick up Nick in less than half an hour. If she was one minute late, he'd call out the National Guard to come looking for her.

"No, I'll be fine," she reassured the girl. "Thanks again for all your help, though."

"You're welcome," Monica replied, then called after her, "Have courage!" as Meg plunged into the current and let it sweep her along to the nearest escalator.

Unfortunately, she didn't know the mall as well as she'd thought, because she'd ended up at the granite stairway, not the Down escalator.

"Nope, don't think so," she murmured, moving out of the flow of traffic. The stairway was only moderately congested, but even under the best of conditions with Nick at her side to steady her, she avoided stairs whenever possible.

She looked around to get her bearings and finally

caught sight of the elevator on the opposite side of the concourse.

Turning back to retrace her footsteps, she found herself in the wrong traffic flow, swimming upstream like a hapless salmon, doing her best to protect Baby Bea from protruding elbows. She murmured "Excuse me" when she merged headlong into a human brick wall more than half a foot taller and nearly twice as broad as she was.

Meg stepped to one side, registering the fact that the man's ratty camouflage jacket did nothing to cover a generous beer belly. But when Meg moved left, the big man moved with her, blocking her way. Traffic separated to go around them, temporarily shielding Meg from its ebb, and that's when she recognized the man in her path.

Oddly, it was his smell that clued her in. Even before his cruel, bloated face registered, she recognized the unmistakable scent of family, and her stomach turned sickeningly. Revulsion hit her next. And hatred. Then panic.

"Hello, Meggie. Been a while," he said with the malicious grin that had haunted her nightmares even after she escaped to Singapore.

"Dub?" she said stupidly.

"No! Daddy!" he insisted, reaching out and leaning closer as though to kiss her.

Meg gave him a hard shove and turned her face away from the stench of beer and cheap whiskey. "Don't touch me, you son of a bitch. What are you doing here? How did you find me?"

"Wudd'n too hard," he drawled, seemingly unoffended by her rejection of his fatherly show of affection. "Once I heard the good news, I just had to come look you up."

Oh, God. "What news?"

"About you gettin' married and all. To the president of the Ballenger drug company."

Meg's panic mounted. If Dub knew about Nick, he was here for money, and giving him a few dollars now wouldn't make him go away. She'd tried that before, when she was first out on her own and waiting tables to put herself through nursing school, and later when she was finally earning a decent living at Dr. Holmby's. No matter how much she gave him, he always came back for more. When she'd tried to stop, to correct her "enabling" behavior, he'd nearly killed her.

But that wouldn't happen again if she got hold of herself and controlled her fear. She wasn't a child anymore and she wasn't alone with Dub in a dark parking lot. There were hundreds of people on the concourse, and there were surely security guards among them. Dub couldn't hurt her here.

The danger was more insidious than a slap in the face to stun her, a hard jab to knock her down and brutal rib-crunching kicks. Dub only had one good arm, but years of drunken bar brawling had taught him how to minimize his disability. Unless he was drunker than he appeared, he wasn't stupid enough to attack her here.

"...somebody I want you to meet—she's around here somewhere," Dub was saying, and Meg forced herself to listen. "My woman, Rhonda, come with me, but we lost you in the crowd so we split up to look. You remember Rhonda, don't you? Rhonda Mabry?"

Meg didn't remember, and didn't give a damn about meeting any of Dub's friends. She pulled herself together and tried to take hold of the situation. "You and your girlfriend heard I got married, so you thought you'd cash in, Dub? Is that it?"

"Damn right." He leaned in again, and Meg forced

herself not to flinch. "You owe me, Meggie, girl. I done two years at Maynard because of you."

"You spent two years in prison because you tried to kill me!"

"And I had a damned good reason!" he exclaimed. "You wudd'n treatin' your daddy like a good daughter ought."

"Only good fathers deserve good daughters, Dub. You don't qualify," she said, her voice laced with disgust.

"Like hell I don't. The Bible says honor thy mother and father, girl," Dub said, reaching out to grab her arm, but Meg jerked away, jabbing a passerby in the shoulder and earning a dirty look from him and others because they were impeding the flow of traffic.

Meg didn't care. The more people around her, the better.

"Touch me again, and I'll scream for security and have you arrested, Dub. What you're doing is extortion, and if you think I wouldn't love to put you back in prison, you've got another think coming."

"Extortion?" He looked stupid and confused, but still dangerous.

"Blackmail, Dub. You're dead wrong if you think I'll give you money to keep my husband from finding out my father is a mean, drunken, miserable excuse for a human being."

"Now, just a damn—"

"You can't threaten to expose me because Nick already knows everything. About you, Mama, Russell— even me bein' in juvie for a year." She flung the lie at him in self-defense and with a clear conscience. She'd finished her letter to Nick. It was hidden in the lingerie drawer in her dressing room, already in an envelope with

Nick's name written on it in the fancy calligraphy lettering she'd learned from an artist in Singapore. She couldn't afford to wait until Christmas to give it to him, of course. He'd have to know the truth before the day was out, but telling him herself was a million times better than having the truth come from her disgusting father.

Dub's stupid frown deepened. "What kind of an idiot do you think I am, Meggie? 'Course your husband knows about me." A lightbulb went on in his head, and a sly grin replaced his frown. "But I got me a feelin' he didn't find out the truth from you, did he, girl? Otherwise, he wouldn't have needed to hire him no investigator to come to Pine Ridge and ask all sorts-a questions about you, now, would he?"

"What are you talking about? You're insane!" she all but shouted at him over the din of a hundred conversations on the concourse. "Nick didn't hire anyone. He doesn't even know—"

She stopped herself, but it was too late.

"Dudd'n know what, Meggie? Dudd'n know what a little slut you usta be? And still are, by the looks of you?" Dub laughed in the gravelly cackle that turned Meg's stomach. "You was bluffin', wudd'n you? You played all sweet and innocent to get yourself knocked up by a rich man, and you thought you had him buffaloed. Well, you're wrong, Meggie, girl. Dead wrong."

He took a step, closing the gap between them, forcing Meg to give ground as he continued, "How do you think I found out that you got married? And to who? Your rich husband and his hired man paid a visit to Pine Ridge a coupla months back. They found out all about you, Meggie. You ain't got no secrets from him, girl, but since he didn't tell you that, I reckon he's got some secrets of his own. Like maybe what he's gonna do to you in court after that baby there pops out.''

''Shut up!'' Meg screamed, backing away from Dub, and the truth. ''You're lying! You're a lying, murdering son of a bitch and you always have been! Nick wasn't in Pine Ridge! He didn't hire anyone to investigate me! He wouldn't do that! He loves me!'' She was screaming, drawing attention even as the passersby gave her a wider berth as they continued on their way.

Meg didn't care. She could barely breathe, and the people moving past were suddenly going too fast. Everything was a blur except her father and his lies. But he couldn't be lying, for how else could he have known about her marriage to Nick? If he was telling the truth, though, it meant that Nick had never loved her, that he'd been playing a vicious game to lull her into a sense of false security. It meant that he had made good his threat to investigate her because he planned to take Bea away from her.

''Oh, my God,'' she cried out, tears cascading onto her cheeks as the truth washed over her, threatening to crush the life out of her. She had to escape, to get somewhere so that she could think what to do, how to protect herself and her baby, but the pain in her heart was crippling her. She whirled away from Dub, but her father had other plans.

He grabbed her and Meg yanked her arm away again, nearly stumbling in her haste and fear. ''Touch me again and I'll have you arrested!''

''Don't you threaten me, girl!'' Dub yelled back. He grabbed for her again, but got sidetracked when someone yelled, ''Dub! Dub-honey! Did ya find her?''

He looked around and waved. ''Over here, Rhonda. Come on!''

The distraction gave Meg the second she needed to slip into the crowd, letting the momentum carry her along.

Behind her, she heard Dub shout, "Hey! Meggie, girl!" and he sounded closer than she'd hoped, but she didn't look back, not even when she heard a commotion that could only have been Dub shoving people aside in his haste to catch her.

Meg hurried on, realizing on some abstract level that she was headed for the stairs, but she was too sick and too scared to care.

She reached the stairs and broke to her left, jostling the shopping bags of a woman who groused, "Hey, watch it."

Meg kept going, grabbing the handrail and starting down one clumsy step at a time. She heard the woman yell, "Hey!" again, and then felt Dub's rough hand grab hold of her shoulder. He spun her toward him, and she lost hold of the rail. Her feet got tangled just as her heavy bag fell off her shoulder, stealing her balance completely, and there was nothing she could do.

Her eyes widened in terror as she started to fall backward, and she flailed her arms wildly, reaching for something, anything to stop the inevitable, but all her hand came up with was the lapel of Dub's jacket, and it wasn't nearly enough.

Caught off guard, the big man's balance was no better than Meg's and he wasn't near enough to a railing to grab hold. He began to topple headlong, plowing into Meg like a two-ton pickup, knocking the wind out of her even before she hit the stairs. He fell on her heavily, kneeing her hard on the stomach as he tumbled over. People scrambled out of the way and watched in horror as they plunged down the stairs.

When Dub finally came to rest, his head was angled oddly against one of the metal posts that supported the stair railing. His open but sightless eyes were aimed back at Meg who'd come to rest several steps above him, dazed, in pain and afraid to even move.

Somehow, she managed to curl into a ball, but it was too late to protect Baby Bea. She knew she was losing her even before someone yelled, "Call an ambulance!" and someone else stooped to help her and said, "Oh, Lord, she's bleeding."

"*Noooooo!*" Meg's cry of anguish and pain resonated through the concourse above the din of Christmas carols and holiday shoppers.

In the distance, as her consciousness began to fade, she heard a woman scream, "Oh, my God, he's dead! She killed him! She killed him!"

"Good," Meg murmured as the light and the crowd slipped away. "Good...good..."

CHAPTER EIGHTEEN

NICK WAS FLYING down the hospital corridor when Bob Michaelson stepped out of the room at the end of the hall. The doctor caught sight of him and moved to intercept.

"Slow down, Nick. Meg is going to be fine," he said, holding up his hands like a school crossing guard.

Nick didn't stop. "Is that her room?"

"Yes, but I don't think you should see her right now." Michaelson tried to block his path, but Nick darted around him and the doctor had to grab his arm. "Nick. Stop! You need to listen to me."

"I've *been* listening for an hour, Bob! To you, to the nurses, to the police, to that crazy woman who's accusing Meg of murdering her father. I have to see her."

Michaelson nodded sympathetically. "I understand, Nick, but Meg isn't handling this well. I'm sorry to say it, but she seems to be blaming you."

"That's because it's my fault," Nick retorted. He'd spent what seemed like an eternity down in the emergency room feeling helpless and frightened, then the police had come in to ask some questions, and added guilt to the emotions that were roiling inside Nick. He had a pretty good picture of what had happened at the mall, and he was terrified that Meg would never forgive him for the role he had played in what had happened. "But she doesn't know the whole story, Bob. She has to be thinking things that aren't true, and if I can just talk to her, explain..."

"She's sedated right now. It wouldn't do you any good."

Nick scowled at him. "When I saw you downstairs, you said she and the baby were all right—that the fall had forced you to take the baby early, but Bea's lungs were strong enough for her to breathe on her own."

"That's right. I suspect that Meg and I misjudged Bea's due date by at least a week, maybe two. She's tiny—only five and a half pounds—but she's fully developed. You should be able to take her home in four or five days."

"Then what's the problem?"

"It's Meg. She's suffered both physical and emotional trauma here, Nick. Not just the contusions on her face and the cracked ribs," Bob explained. "I'm sure you know that she had a lot of fears about having a miscarriage. Women who have already lost one child often do, and Meg has transferred the emotions of that previous incident onto this one."

"What? In English, please, Bob," Nick said tersely.

"Meg doesn't believe me when I tell her that the baby is going to be all right."

"But if she sees for herself... Can't you bring Bea to her?"

Bob shook his head. "Meg has seen her, Nick. But I've put the baby in an incubator. I want to keep her on monitors and control her oxygen for a day or two. When I told Meg that, she got hysterical and had to be sedated."

Nick felt as though a huge weight was crushing his chest. "Her first baby died in an incubator, Bob. She has that image in her head..."

"And she's transferred it to Bea. I don't think she's going to let go of it until she can see the baby outside of the incubator—hold her, smell her, feed her. And that's not going to happen until tomorrow, at least." Bob clasped Nick's shoulder. "Go see your daughter, Nick. Satisfy yourself that she's all right, then come back tomorrow."

Nick looked uncertainly at Meg's door.

Bob read his mind. "She's sleeping, Nick. She couldn't hear you anyway."

He looked at the doctor. "What terrifies me, Bob, is that she won't hear me even when she's awake."

NICK SPENT the night at the hospital. As Bob advised, he went to Neonatal CCU where they put him in a paper gown and plastic gloves and led him to a rectangular plastic bubble that was labeled Baby Ballenger in white surgical tape.

He got his first sight of her and something that felt like a fist squeezed his heart until he couldn't breathe.

"It looks worse than it is," the nurse tried to reassure him. "It's just an IV for fluids and electrodes to monitor her heartbeat and circulation."

Nick glanced around and found another bubble with a baby half the size of Beatrice and twice as many machines, including a respirator. Bea was breathing on her own. She was pink and perfect, with a shock of silky blond hair like her mother's and a beautiful little bow of a mouth that she was puckering in her sleep.

They let him put his arms in the bubble so that he could touch her, and he leaned in as close as he could get. "Oh, David," he whispered. "Are you watching? Can you see this?"

When he felt the heat of tears on his cheeks, he tried

to check them but couldn't. He hadn't cried when they told him David was dead. Now, in a sense, David was reborn, and Nick's tears were as much joy as sorrow.

He stayed with Bea as long as they would let him, and came back as often as they would allow him to return. Deep in the middle of the night shift, one of the nurses approached him with a clipboard to ask if he'd like to fill out the form for the birth certificate, and without really thinking about it, he filled in the name Meg had told him was her final choice—Beatrice Nicolette Ballenger.

He completed the rest of the form, but stopped short of affixing his signature when he realized that he was presuming too much. He gave the document back to the nurse and told her that he would prefer to have his wife verify the information before either of them signed it. Considering what he'd done, he couldn't be certain that Meg would still want any part of his name attached to the baby's. In reality, his only claim on Bea was the hold she already had on his heart.

When he wasn't with Bea, Nick paced the halls, and once he even managed to doze off in the waiting room outside the nursery around the corner from NCCU. He'd tried to slip into Meg's room at one point in the middle of the night, just to see her sleeping and satisfy himself that she was all right, but nurses had stopped him. He was *persona non grata* until Dr. Michaelson or Mrs. Ballenger told them otherwise.

He didn't see Bob again until the next morning when the doctor stopped by NCCU on his morning rounds. Michaelson hadn't seen Meg yet, and couldn't do anything more than urge Nick to be patient.

Several hours later, Bob came back to NCCU while Nick was enjoying one of his all-too-brief visits with

Bea. Michaelson accepted the baby's chart from a nurse and announced that she was doing even better than he'd hoped.

"Her blood gases are excellent, she's suffering no respiratory distress... This is one healthy little girl," he said with a smile as he handed the chart back to the nurse.

"Who knows her daddy's voice," the nurse added. "She coos like a dove every time Mr. Ballenger comes in."

"Well, we'll let you hold her later this afternoon, Nick," Bob promised. "But right now we're bringing Meg in to feed Bea. I think it will do Meg a world of good to hold her."

To say the least. "How is she today?" Nick asked. "I went up an hour ago, but the nurses still wouldn't let me in. I'm going crazy here, Bob."

Michaelson shrugged helplessly and pulled Nick to one side, lowering his voice as he replied, "What can I say, Nick? Meg is still upset. I don't pretend to understand exactly what's going on between you two, but she's got it into her head that she can't trust you. That you've somehow betrayed her and may even be conspiring to take the baby away if the child survives. I've seen this sort of paranoia in postpartum depression before, and I've learned that it's not wise to challenge a patient's delusions head-on. I've already called for a psychiatric consult, and there are a number of very good antidepressants that work wonders on postpartum—but you know that, of course, since Ballenger Pharmaceuticals makes more than one of them."

Nick just nodded because he didn't know how to tell Michaelson that Meg wasn't delusional. From her perspective she had every reason to believe that he had betrayed her.

And he supposed, in a sense, he had. Now, if he could only make her understand why.

"I want to be here when Meg comes in, Bob."

Michaelson shook his head. "I'm sorry, Nick. I can't let you stay. When I told Meg you were here, encouraged her to see you, she made it very clear she didn't want you anywhere near her. Or the baby," he added reluctantly. "You're just going to have to give it time."

"Time won't help, Bob! You don't understand. She believes things that aren't true—and it's got nothing to do with postpartum delusions. If she'll just let me explain—"

"All right, all right. I'll see what I can do," the doctor promised. "But in the meantime, the best thing for Meg is that she see for herself how healthy her baby is. Let me put Bea in your wife's arms, and maybe the other problems will be easier to deal with. Okay?"

How could he refuse? "Okay. I'll go," he said, but first he returned to Bea's bubble. She was awake and crying, but when Nick reached one hand in to gently stroke her cheek she stopped wailing and turned her mouth into Nick's hand, rooting for his finger in the hope of finding a more tangible nourishment than love.

"Sorry, Princess. Not this time. Mommy's coming, though. And Daddy will be back later. I promise."

Drawing back hurt more than he could have made anyone understand, but he did it anyway, stripping out of his gloves and throwing them at the waste bin by the door as he punched out of the doors and vacated the area.

ELEANOR RODE the elevator up to the maternity ward on the fourth floor carrying the overnight bag she'd taken upon herself to pack for Megan.

Since his arrival at the hospital, Nick had called her
several times with reports. While he hadn't been exactly
curt with her, Eleanor could tell that he held her responsible for what had happened. The police had questioned
her because it was her investigation that had led George
W. Linley to Charleston and ultimately to his death.
Eleanor could summon no remorse for that aspect of the
tragedy, since Linley's girlfriend had admitted under
close questioning that their purpose in coming here was
to extort money from Megan and Nick.

The woman was holding to her story that Megan was
responsible for her father's death, but fortunately, witnesses at the mall swore that Megan was blameless. Linley was pursuing her, and it was his manhandling of her
on the stairs that had precipitated their fall. Eleanor had
contacted Judge Nathaniel Warren and he had used his
contacts on the police force to learn that there was no
question of bringing any charges against Megan.

Linley's death had already been ruled accidental, but
that didn't absolve Eleanor of her part in the premature
birth of David and Megan's baby. If anything happened
to the baby because of her, Eleanor wasn't sure she
could forgive herself, and she knew her grandson never
would.

There was a waiting room outside the nursery, and
that's where Eleanor found Nick, standing at the glass
wall looking at the cribs that held a dozen or more
healthy, squalling babies. He looked worn, exhausted,
dispirited, as though all the life had been drained from
him, and Eleanor paused just inside the door, mentally
comparing this Nick with the one she had seen yesterday—the man who had rediscovered his music.

The vast, sad difference was enough to break her
heart.

"Nicholas?"

He turned in surprise. "Eleanor? What are you doing here? I told you there was no reason to come. Everything is fine."

She held out the bag to him. "I had Mrs. Fetridge pack some things for Megan. Toiletries, a nightgown... Given the nature of her injuries, it seems likely that she might be here for a few more days."

Nick nodded and escorted his grandmother to the bank of chairs nearby. "I'm going to make sure that they let her stay until Bea is ready to come home. Wherever that may be," he added quietly.

"Have you spoken with Megan yet?"

"No. She won't see me." He rubbed his hands wearily over his unshaven face and leaned forward with his elbows on his knees. "She thinks I hired Hamilton myself, Eleanor. She's convinced that I'm going to use what I know to take Bea away from her the way I threatened to months ago. She's never going to trust me again, Nan. Never."

Eleanor reached out tentatively and brushed her fingers across his hair, so lightly that he didn't even feel it. She withdrew her hand and cleared her throat delicately.

"I doubt that is the case, Nicholas. Once the trauma of this incident has passed, I'm sure—"

"You'll find some other way to come between us," he said harshly. He stabbed an angry glare at her, then brought it quickly under control. "I'm sorry. That was uncalled for."

She didn't comment, except to say, "You really should come back to the Hall with me and get some sleep."

He straightened. "I can't. Meg is feeding Beatrice

now, and I'll get to hold the baby later.'' He rose rest-
lessly and moved to the window again. ''I heard one of
the nurses say they might bring her in here as early as
this evening.''

''Really? If that happens, please let me know. I'd like
very much to see her.''

''All right.''

Eleanor moved to him and touched his arm. ''Nicholas, I had Fetridge put together a few things for you.
They're in the bag as well. I'm sure there is someplace
where you could shower and shave. You would feel so
much better if you did.''

''I suppose you're right. Bob said earlier that I could
use the doctors' locker room if I wanted,'' he told her.
''I guess I'll do that now. Are you going back to the
Hall?''

''Yes.''

''Then I'll call you if there's anything to report. Thank
you for coming.''

He could have been thanking a total stranger instead
of his grandmother, and the distinction wasn't lost on
Eleanor. He turned to leave, but when she didn't join
him, he stopped and looked at her curiously. ''Aren't
you coming?''

''If it's all right, I'd like to stay here for a few moments.'' She stepped to the windows and looked at the
babies. ''There's something reassuring about being here,
even though Beatrice isn't in there. I'm sure you understand.''

He looked surprised by her sentiment, but didn't dispute it. ''Yes. Well... Thank you for coming.'' He
turned and was gone.

Eleanor didn't waste any time outside the glass window. Though she thoroughly expected to love Beatrice

Ballenger, she wasn't particularly sentimental about babies in general. She had another reason for staying behind.

As soon as Nick was out of sight, she marched down the hall and to the nurses' station to request the number of Megan's room. Since Eleanor's name wasn't on the Do Not Admit list, they told her and even invited her to go on in and wait for Mrs. Ballenger to return from NCCU.

Eleanor accepted the invitation. It was time she and her granddaughter had a long talk.

"IT LOOKS WORSE than it really is, Mrs. Ballenger," Janet Kennedy said as she wheeled Meg into the neonatal unit. "Once we take her off the IV, there shouldn't be any reason for her to be in here at all."

Meg heard the nurse's words, but they didn't mean anything to her. In her wheelchair she was eye level to the incubator beds, and her gaze was riveted on a pitiful little infant on a respirator with tubes and wires and a nurse hovering over the monitors surrounding the bed. It was the embodiment of all her fears, and even though she knew it wasn't her child, because Dr. Michaelson had told her Bea wasn't on life support, Meg couldn't drag her gaze away from the critically ill infant.

But then Janet wheeled the chair sharply to the right, saying, "Here we go, Mrs. Ballenger," and there was Baby Bea, crying boisterously and flailing her arms in the air as though she was searching for something.

Meg's throat tightened and tears welled in her eyes. "Let me hold her. Please. Now," she begged, reaching out to touch the plastic bubble that encased her daughter. "*Please.*"

One nurse handed her a bottle as another removed the

monitor leads from Bea's torso and legs. It was everything Meg could do to sit still as they freed the baby, wrapped her in a blanket and finally placed her in Meg's arms.

She gave Bea the bottle, and the crying stopped as the baby nestled in to feed. It was the sweetest homecoming Meg could have imagined. She'd waited more than a few months to hold her baby like this—she'd waited years.

It didn't seem real at first, but her joy solidified as she counted Bea's tiny pink fingers and toes, kissed her forehead and drank in her sweet baby smell. She laughed when Bea began to hiccup after she'd finished her bottle, and then she cried when the nurses took her out of Meg's arms. The incubator had a slightly richer oxygen content, and they couldn't leave Bea out for too long.

Even after Bea went back into her bubble, Meg sat watching her sleep, studying every twitch, every sigh. She shut out everything except the sight of her baby. The terror she'd felt for the last twenty-four hours had finally receded, but not the pain of Nick's betrayal. It was still fresh and raw, and the only thing that made it bearable was this new and precious knowledge that her baby wasn't going to die.

But there was more than one way to lose a child, and that's what Meg had to fear now.

At the nurses' insistence, Meg finally agreed to let Janet wheel her back to her room, but only after they promised that she would be returned later for Bea's next feeding.

All the aches and pains that she hadn't felt while she was holding Bea settled back in as she got farther away from her baby. Her surgical incision wasn't nearly as painful as her two cracked ribs, and none of the injuries were as excruciating as the game Nick had played with her heart.

When they rolled through the door of her private room, Meg's first thought was that her eyes were playing tricks on her. Eleanor was seated primly in a chair by the window, as motionless as a portrait of the queen. But then Nick's grandmother turned her head, leveling her regal gaze at the door, and Meg knew this was another reality she'd have to deal with.

She let Janet help her into bed before she gave the slightest acknowledgment of the other woman's presence. "Eleanor," she said as soon as the nurse was gone.

"Megan." The frosty dowager rose and approached the bed. "I dare say you have no desire to see me now, but it would be in your best interest to hear me out."

Meg couldn't help but be reminded of their first meeting in Nick's study. "Is that a threat, Eleanor?"

The old woman clucked her tongue. "No, Megan. It is not. But since you have refused to see Nicholas and hear him out, it appears that it is up to me to sort out this sordid mess."

Meg's eyes glittered dangerously as the anger that had been hidden behind her fear began to bubble up. "Nick made this mess, Eleanor. Not me."

"No, Megan, he did not," Eleanor retorted crisply. "I did. If you would like to lay blame for that horrifying incident with your father yesterday, lay it at my door. It was I who hired a private investigator to dig into your past despite Nick's orders to the contrary. When I told him what I had done, he was so angry that he suggested I spend a few months abroad. I doubt, frankly, that my relationship with him will ever the be same."

Meg didn't trust what she was hearing. There was nothing accusatory in Eleanor's stance, and nothing defensive, either. She was simply stating what she apparently wanted Meg to believe were the facts. But why on earth would Eleanor want to mediate a relationship she'd tried so hard to break up? "And you don't blame me for the rift between you and Nick?" Meg asked suspiciously.

"How can I when it was I who created it? He negotiated your marriage contract in good faith. He was quite enamored of you, even then, and I grossly underestimated the bond that the two of you formed."

"Are you saying you regret what happened, Eleanor?"

One of her perfectly sculpted eyebrows went up. "Yes. I suppose I am."

"And does Nick regret it, too?" she asked harshly. "When you told him what your P.I. had discovered, did he come to me and ask if it was true? Did he offer me a chance to explain? No! He went to Pine Ridge, didn't he? That's how my father found me—because of Nick! That's why my baby is in an incubator instead of here in my arms!"

"I don't know why he felt compelled to go to Pine Ridge, Megan," Eleanor replied calmly. "Nick has a powerful instinct to make things right. Perhaps he felt that he could somehow make things right for you if he went back to the place where you endured so much."

"That still doesn't explain why he didn't tell me."

Eleanor thought it over for a moment. "Perhaps he was waiting for you to tell him. Trust is an important thing to a man like Nicholas. I suspect that he wanted yours."

"So he betrayed my trust to earn my trust?" Meg scoffed. "That makes a lot of sense."

"Yes, it does," Eleanor agreed, ignoring the sarcasm.

"He loves you, Megan. More than I ever realized Nicholas could love. But you are not a charming young woman that he met on the golf course or at a cocktail party. You came into his life as the woman who was in love with his brother. Is it so hard to imagine that he needed some significant gesture that would prove your love for him?"

"He should have known that," Meg retorted defensively. Eleanor was finally scoring some direct hits that Meg wasn't prepared to hear. "He should have trusted me."

"The way you trusted him with the secrets of your past?" the dowager asked shrewdly.

"Please go, Eleanor," Meg ordered. "I don't want you here."

"No, Megan, what you don't want is to hear the truth. You're angry and you're hurt. Understandably so. You have feared for your baby's life, and you are terrified that you misjudged Nicholas, that he has some hidden agenda that includes a plan to steal your child from you." She took a step closer. "But that is not true. The agenda was mine, and it was an error in judgment I shall regret for many years to come. It would be a terrible thing if you allowed my mistake to spoil the happiness you found with my grandson."

She backed away from the bed. "I'll leave you now to rest and consider what I've said."

She turned and started toward the door, leaving Meg in a puddle of confusion.

"Eleanor, wait."

The dowager turned at the door. "Yes?"

"Why are you doing this? Given the way you feel about me—the things you obviously know about me...

Why would you want me within a million miles of Nick?''

Even from across the room Meg could see the emotion in Eleanor's eyes. Her head went up and her shoulders squared proudly. "You gave him back his music," she said as though it should be perfectly obvious.

Meg frowned. "What?"

"The piano. His career," Eleanor replied. "I took it away from him."

"Career?"

Eleanor looked more surprised than Meg. "He didn't tell you?"

"Tell me what?"

"Before his father's death, Nicholas was one of the most gifted concert pianists in the world. He won dozens of competitions—surely he showed you the medals. Those slender velvet boxes in the music library. Those are his awards."

"Why did he give it up?" Meg asked incredulously.

"Because someone had to step forward and take the reins of Ballenger Pharmaceuticals," she explained. "You see, my son and grandson had fought for years over Nicholas's devotion to the piano, but finally, my son accepted the inevitable. He decided that he would groom David to take over the company, but his death when David was only thirteen scotched that completely. I used my elder grandson's sense of honor and family to force him to do what his father had never been able to do."

"Nick gave up his career..." Meg said the words to make them real, and to make them fit into the empty spaces in the Nick puzzle she'd been working on for months.

"Not just his career, Megan. He gave up music altogether. But somehow, you gave it back to him. I didn't know what an incredible gift that was until I heard him play last night for the first time in nearly two decades. Such beauty... Such joy... And I'm afraid..." Eleanor paused and cleared a knot of emotion from her throat. "I'm afraid that if he loses you and Beatrice he'll lose himself all over again. Please don't let that happen because of me. Now...you should rest, my dear. You're very pale." She turned to go.

"Eleanor..."

She looked back, her face a carefully composed mask that could crumble at any moment. "Yes?"

"Thank you."

"You're welcome." And then she was gone.

Meg let her head fall back onto the pillow and considered what Eleanor had told her. Gradually, the final piece of the puzzle fell into place, but it wasn't the Nick puzzle. It was the mystery of David's devotion to his brother, why he'd done everything Nick had asked, and even things that Nick *hadn't* asked—like going into the family business in the first place.

Nick had given up everything he'd ever dreamed of for the sake of the company. For the family. How could David, who had no strong goals or desires, have done less? Helping Nick run the company was the only way David had known to honor his brother's sacrifice.

Meg wondered if Nick knew that. She suspected he didn't, and she wasn't sure she should tell him.

Besides, there were other more pressing matters between them. Like the secrets they'd each been keeping, and what those secrets had almost done to their lives.

Meg reached for her call button and a few moments later Janet came breezing in. "Yes, Mrs. Ballenger? What can I get for you?"

"My husband," Meg replied.

The nurse smiled broadly. "As a matter of fact, I know exactly where he can be found. He went into NCCU not five minutes ago."

Meg threw back her covers and nodded at the wheel-chair. "My carriage, if you please, Janet."

The nurse obliged, wheeling her down the halls, and Meg felt herself grow stronger the closer she got to her baby. To Nick.

She pushed the swinging doors aside as Janet rolled her into NCCU, and there they were, in a rocking chair that had been brought up beside Bea's empty plastic bubble. Father and daughter... He was looking down at her, and the wonder on his face...the love... It was more than Meg could bear.

She waved Janet away, and rolled the last few feet until her chair was even with his. Nick didn't even no-tice. He was cooing to Bea and she was cooing back.

"She knows her daddy's voice, doesn't she?" Meg said softly.

Nick looked up, startled. "Meg..." He reached out without thinking and brushed the tears off his wife's cheek. She leaned her face into his hand, and more tears fell.

"I love you," she murmured.

The fist around Nick's heart let go, and a laugh of sheer joy started inside him and worked its way out. "Did you hear that, Bea? Your mommy loves your daddy. And he loves you both very, very much." He looked at his wife. "Meg, what—"

She shook her head at him. "Eleanor explained ev-erything. We'll sort it out later. You can tell me you're sorry, and I'll show you the letter that I was going to give you for Christmas. Right now I just want to be here with you and Bea.''

''Nothing could be better than that.'' Nick took her hand and brought their linked fingers to the baby in his arms.

''Well, this is a nice family picture,'' Bob Michaelson said jovially as he breezed into the NCCU. ''Does this mean you two are okay now?''

Meg nodded and smiled at him. ''We're very okay.''

''Glad to hear it. Then maybe you wouldn't mind finishing a little paperwork so we can make this little girl official,'' he said, pulling a paper out of the baby's chart and scanning it. ''Personally, I'm awfully fond of the name Roberta for a girl, but I see here that you've already chosen Beatrice Nicolette. Guess I'm out of luck.''

When Meg frowned in confusion, and Nick told her, ''I filled it out last night, but I was waiting for you to sign it. I wasn't sure you were certain about the name.''

Meg took the form from the obstetrician, and looked it over. ''This is fine, Nick. It's what we agreed. Do we both have to sign it, or—''

Meg stopped.

''Meg, if you don't want to call her Nicolette—''

She looked at him with tears welling in her eyes again. In the blank where she'd expected the father's name to read, Nicholas Tate Ballenger, it read, instead, David Livingston Ballenger. She hadn't thought she could love Nick more, but she discovered in that instant that she was wrong.

''Oh, Nick... Are you sure?'' she whispered. ''Are you very, very sure?''

He nodded. ''We've had enough secrets to last a lifetime, Meg. Bea has two fathers. That's what this form says, and that's what she deserves to know someday.''

''She will, Nick. She will,'' Meg murmured, her voice thick with emotion. ''Thank you.''

''No. Thank you. For giving me a life that's worth living.'' Nick leaned closer to press a kiss to Meg's lips and then very gently placed their daughter in his wife's arms. He held them both until long after Bea drifted into contented sleep, and he knew, somehow, that David was watching. And smiling.

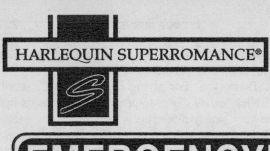

HARLEQUIN SUPERROMANCE®

EMERGENCY!

If you love medical drama and romance on the wards,
then our new medical series by bestselling author
Bobby Hutchinson will bring you to fever pitch....

July 1998—
FALLING FOR THE DOCTOR (#797)
by Bobby Hutchinson

Dr. Greg Brulotte has it all. He's a successful ER surgeon living
the good life. He loves his job, his death-defying hobbies, and
he loves women. But when the doctor becomes a patient after
a near-fatal skiing accident, he learns about the other side
of life—and about the other side of nurse Lily Sullivan,
who by saving his life may have harmed him in ways she
never intended!

Available July 1998 wherever Harlequin books are sold.

HARLEQUIN®
Makes any time special ™

Heat up your summer this July with

Summer Lovers

This July, bestselling authors Barbara Delinsky,
Elizabeth Lowell and Anne Stuart present three
couples with pasts that threaten their future happiness.
Can they play with fire without being burned?

FIRST, BEST AND ONLY
by Barbara Delinsky

GRANITE MAN
by Elizabeth Lowell

CHAIN OF LOVE
by Anne Stuart

Available wherever Harlequin and Silhouette books
are sold.

HARLEQUIN SUPERROMANCE®

HOME ON THE RANCH

Come West with us!

In July, watch for
COTTONWOOD CREEK (#794)
by Margot Dalton

Someone has been skimming profits from Clay Alderson's ranching operation, and now the government is sending an auditor to check the books. As if Clay didn't have enough to worry about—a crook on the premises and a threat of flooding—now he's baby-sitting some big-city number cruncher who knows nothing about ranching. Well, the man is just going to have to get along without Clay's help.

Except that the man—J. D. McKenna—is actually *Jenny* McKenna. And suddenly Clay is more than eager to help in the investigation.

Available July 1998 wherever Harlequin books are sold.

HARLEQUIN®

Makes any time special ™

Presents Extravaganza

25 YEARS!

It's our birthday
and we're celebrating....

Twenty-five years of romance fiction
featuring men of the world and captivating women—
Seduction and passion guaranteed!

Not only are we promising you three months of terrific
books, authors and romance, but as an added **bonus**
with the retail purchase of two Presents® titles,
you can receive a special one-of-a-kind keepsake.
It's our gift to you!

Look in the back pages of any Harlequin Presents® title,
from May to July 1998, for more details.

Available wherever Harlequin books are sold.

HARLEQUIN®

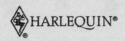

Not The Same Old Story!

Exciting, glamorous romance stories that take readers around the world.

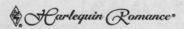

Sparkling, fresh and tender love stories that bring you pure romance.

Bold and adventurous— Temptation is strong women, bad boys, great sex!

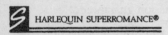

Provocative and realistic stories that celebrate life and love.

Contemporary fairy tales—where anything is possible and where dreams come true.

Heart-stopping, suspenseful adventures that combine the best of romance and mystery.

Humorous and romantic stories that capture the lighter side of love.

Look us up on-line at: http://www.romance.net   HGENERIC

COMING NEXT MONTH

#798 THE ENDS OF THE EARTH • Kay David
Guaranteed Page-Turner
To protect her nephew, Eva Solis has run to a tiny village in
the remotest part of Argentina, where she thinks no one can
possibly find them. Then a tall stranger arrives. He seems to
be watching her every move. *And* he knows where she lives.
Now Eva realizes that the problem with running to the ends
of the earth is there's nowhere else to go.

#799 HONEYMOON • Ellen James
Toni and Kyle have been assigned to find the perfect
honeymoon for Toni's sister and Kyle's best friend. But how
do two strangers go about selecting the ideal honeymoon
resort? By trial and error, of course. And if along the way,
the possibility of their *own* honeymoon pops up, the
research has already been done. Only the *wedding* needs to
be planned....

#800 HAVING IT ALL • Roz Denny Fox
Family Man
Like everybody else, Garrett Lock wants it all—love, family
and satisfying work. So does Sherry Campbell. Then Garrett
gets the job Sherry wanted—and becomes her boss. The
workplace situation is difficult enough, but their relationship
is further complicated by Garrett's eight-year-old son and by
the incredible attraction between Garrett and Sherry. Things
go from bad to worse...to great! A very contemporary story
that's warm and funny, romantic *and* exciting!

#801 IT TAKES A BABY • Dee Holmes
Count on a Cop
Kathleen Hanes is running from the law. From police
officials who want to put her in jail for a crime she didn't
commit—the murder of her husband, a deputy in a small
Wyoming town. She almost feels safe in New England, but
then she meets another cop—and this one comes with a
baby! There's nothing Kathleen likes better than a
baby...unless it's the baby's father!